Hot Cash
Cold Bodies©

By Elliot M. Rubin

Acknowledgements

I would like to thank my father, Herman S. Rubin z"l for his inspiration and encouragement to write.

He wrote essays, prayers, and poetry his whole life and his writings are treasured by those who have read them.

Also, I would like to thank my beloved grandmother, Bessie Greenberg, for giving me the gift of creativity and imagination. Her lunchtime stories of Moishe Kapoya when I was a child stirred my creative mind to picture the story, and think.

And finally I want to thank my dear wife Laura who is an avid reader, and whose encouragement to write is most appreciated.

Copyright January 10, 2016
United States Library of Congress
Registration #TXu 1-989-777

ISBN # 978-0-9913060-8-4

Hot Cash
Cold Bodies©

By Elliot M. Rubin

Chapter 1 -

Khara had met him at a local bar and now found herself embracing a total stranger.

They are standing next to his bed, in a very small efficiency apartment, on the Upper West Side of Manhattan. Before she went out for the evening Khara put on a coconut body wash when she was in the shower late in the afternoon. As he leaned in his tongue started to lick the soft ebony skin on the side of her neck. The saliva loaded touch of his tongue on her clean skin repulsed her. Then the odor of his unwashed body overtook the sweet coconut aroma, and she is incensed. Her total disgust flashed to the surface, and with a sharp thrust to his throat, she fractured his larynx. He fell to his knees holding his neck as she dashed behind him. Placing her left hand on his chin, and her right hand on his forehead, she gave a swift twist and snapped his neck. Too late she showed him it is not easy trying to date a good-looking psychopath; especially when she is also a New York City Police detective.

Khara turned around and walked over to the chair in the corner of the room. Reaching down into her pocketbook she moved her keys to the side of her purse and took out a pair of latex gloves. At all times she kept a pair or two with her. After putting them on she reached down to the motionless body and removed his wallet. Curious and wanting to find out who he is she flipped his wallet open and searched through it for his identification. The name on his driver's license is not the same one he used when he met her at the bar, and struck up a conversation after both of them were drinking for a while.

"Son of a bitch, this asshole was going to screw me, and who knows what else he was going to do. I'm glad the bastard stunk to hell."

To her way of thinking it is justification enough for killing him. No remorse is ever felt by her.

Carefully, she tore up his license, cupped the pieces in her palm, and walked into the bathroom to flush them down the toilet. Watching them swirl around in the bowl, she noticed they didn't all go down the drain; because the water pressure is weak and not flushing properly. The top of the water tank is lifted from the toilet, and she observed the water is more than halfway filled with bags of white powder. The three years of experience in the department's narcotics division instantly told her what they contained. The bags were left in the tank, as she replaced the cover as if nothing was touched. She went back into the bedroom and threw his credit cards into her open pocketbook.

The lights in the room are off as the old faded window shades are translucent. There is enough bright light though coming from the street lamps illuminating the room for her to see a Saks Fifth Avenue shopping bag sitting in the opened bedroom closet. As an experienced narcotics detective, her sixth sense told her something is out of place. "Why would a low life like him rent an efficiency apartment yet shop at Saks Fifth Avenue," she thought to herself?

Carefully she opened the top of the bag and noticed two brown toned shoe boxes as she peered inside. Anxiously she removed the first box, placed it on the floor, and removed the top. Bundles of dollar bills packed tight, in neat piles, and bound together are staring her in the face. She took out one stack and inspected the money. All the bills are hundreds, nothing smaller.

With care, she lifted out the second box, which she noticed is much heavier. Opening the lid she spotted a few more bundled hundred dollar bills and a Glock G30 pistol with extra clips filled with .45 caliber bullets. In a flash, Khara realized the man she killed must be a runner for a drug gang. From experience, she knew they would be coming back to meet with him. They would want to pick up their money and drugs. It is now too dangerous for her to be alone in the apartment any longer.

Khara is lucky his apartment is located in her precinct. The odds are good, she figured, if she walked into work just after the call is received at the office she would be put on the case with her partner.

Without wasting a moment she gathered her things and left the apartment. Not making a sound she closed the front door so as not to wake anyone on his floor. Gingerly she took the back stairwell to the ground floor, and in a calm manner walked out the rear service entrance into a litter-strewn alley which led to the street. It would be too dangerous for her to call in the murder at the moment, or to be seen at the building.

***

The next morning she took the train to work. Khara found the New York City subways repulsive. Some cars reeked of urine, and when the subway cars are packed full of people the smell of some of them turned her stomach. Often times she rode between the cars, which is dangerous, to escape the pungent odors.

The train stopped in midtown Manhattan, Khara stepped off the subway, and entered The Manhattan

Mall in the old Gimbels department store; only a few stations from her precinct. From past experience, she knew there is a public pay phone next to their restrooms on the fourth floor of what used to be the women's department, and no video cameras. Punching in the numbers she dialed her office voicemail. When the machine answered in her cubicle she played the voice recorder on her smartphone to call in the murder in a masculine intonation.

Certain the recording is saved and recorded; she hung up and walked out of the mall. Showing no excitement she went back down into the subway to catch the next train.

When Khara reached her station she exited and walked upstairs to the street level. Down the block from the subway stop is her precinct. Walking in a nonchalant manner into the lobby she took the stairs up to the detective's office area. Sitting in her cubicle she pushed the voicemail button and played the recording very loud. Her lieutenant passed by and overheard the message. Grabbing her by the arm, and with her partner Matt alongside her they all drove to the murder scene.

They are going to meet a few uniformed officers at the crime scene who were dispatched there by the lieutenant. The uniformed officers were called in before they left and would be present and waiting for them.

Upon entering the building, the lieutenant found the building manager's office. He needed him to obtain the keys for apartment 34C. Unfortunately, the manager is out, but the building's janitor is sitting in the building's office drinking coffee. When they entered the room he stood and retrieved the passkey when the lieutenant asked for it. The lieutenant requested him to go with them to open the apartment's door so they could enter without breaking it down.

On the way upstairs, in the elevator, Khara asked the janitor if the video system is working. Having observed a camera in the front lobby when they all entered the building together she thought of a question to ask about it. It wasn't noticed the evening before due to her drinking too much. If the video recorded her the night before Khara knew she would have to enter the video room to erase the tape; before anyone else viewed it. If not they might see her entering the building the night of the murder.

"Hey" Khara called to the janitor as they are standing in the elevator waiting for it to reach the third floor. "Does your video camera in the lobby work?"

"No, the camera hasn't worked for over two years. Management won't spend shit to fix the damn thing. They receive a bonus on the profit of the buildings they manage. They never repair anything here. The camera needs to be replaced."

Khara is relieved to learn the security camera is inoperative. It is one less problem for her to overcome.

When they arrived at apartment 34C, the lieutenant knocked on the door, announced they are the police, and to open the door. He heard no response, so the janitor stepped forward and unlocked the front door. Khara did not wait, pushed the door open, and went in first with her gun drawn. Wanting to show the lieutenant she is assertive and confident of her abilities she didn't ask to go first, she jumped in front of everyone and entered the apartment.

The victim's feet are protruding past the foot of the bed. Seeing a body not moving, the janitor stayed in the hallway, and Khara walked into the room first with her gun drawn. Of course, she knew it is not necessary.

The lieutenant went over to the body to see if he is still alive, but the color of his lips told him what he needed to know.

Khara went in the bathroom on the pretense to see if there are any clues in the room. Her partner, Detective Mathew "Matt" McMann, moved over to the closet to look in it. Right away he glimpsed the Saks shopping bag. After putting on his latex gloves, he lifted the shopping bag and gazed inside.

Matt at once detected the boxes full of money, and the gun, as Khara did the night before.

Lifting the cover of the toilet's water tank Khara pulled out the plastic bags filled with powered white drugs. She marched back into the bedroom. "See what I found hidden in the toilet." She held them so they could see what she carried in her hands. "And he also must have also dropped his credit card. I saw it on the floor behind the sink." Only moments before she placed it there so the credit card could be found by her.

The lieutenant called the precinct and reported what is going on. He ordered two beat cops to be stationed in the apartment to relieve them until the morgue took the body away, and the crime scene is gone over by the lab unit.

***

Arriving back at her precinct, Khara sat in her cubicle and began to write her report on the murder investigation. Matt also started to type his report while she appeared to enter something into her computer. It is not too long until Matt finished, and Khara suggested it is lunch time. They started to walk to Egan's Bar and Grill which is only a short distance away.

Egan's is tucked between two graying industrial buildings on a side street just off the West Side Highway. Located at 15 Apple Street the taller buildings shielded the bar from direct sunlight and added a touch to its dark ambiance. The street is a typical dreary looking location which could qualify as being right out of the movies.

Egan's is a favorite spot for taxi drivers and cops because it is open almost twenty hours a day. Egan himself makes the fresh hot food; nothing is frozen or prepared, ever. He even bakes his own sandwich bread all day long. Not a typical local bar, but it is also not a hot spot for the in-crowd. The bar is dark and gloomy, but the food is great, the beer on tap served ice cold, and the prices are relatively cheap. Egan's worked hard to have a winning combination New York bar and grill.

The burgers are formed by him, by hand, every morning with fresh 80/20 chop meat and with a lot of freshly grated garlic added in, a few eggs, and toasted breadcrumbs. Egan uses only real mild cheddar cheese for his cheeseburgers; none of the processed stuff found in the supermarkets. He always cooks them fresh when ordered, semi-steaming the burgers on the grill by sprinkling them with a few drops of water and covering the burgers with a pot cover.

All the food is never pre-cooked or stacked like the busy luncheonettes do all over Manhattan. Once you ordered your meal from him you know it will be fresh, tasty, and you will be waiting for it to be cooked.

Always taking the booth in the back of the place so she would be able to obtain a clear view of the doorway Khara sat at her favorite table. Some people might call it a habit, or even silly, but it is to her a survival instinct. She wants to look at everyone who enters, just in case. After many years on the narcotics squad, it taught her to be acutely careful in public. Plus where they sat is in the darkest part of the bar, and it is extremely hard to see her and Matt sitting there now they are becoming more than just partners; like even family.

With dark curly hair, standing on the tall side, and trim figure Matt is a good looking young man, and with an old world Irish charisma. Due to his personality, he makes a room light up when he enters it. Married, very friendly, and in his early thirties, Matt had been promoted to detective grade only a year before. His family is full of firemen and cops for many generations. They live in Queens in the Rockaway section of the borough. The area where he lives is a predominantly white cop and fireman's enclave on a peninsula. A gated community, the ocean on one side and the bay on the other, it is a close-knit group of people due to many having intermarried over the generations.

Growing up in that kind of atmosphere, and for him to be partners with Khara Bennett, is eye-opening to his family. They kid him about her all the time, and he resents them for it, but never voices his feelings. He is developing a soft, protective spot in his heart for her. She is his partner, and he knew they must rely on each other on the job because their lives may sometimes depend on their closeness. The stereotype in his mind of minorities changed with his pairing of Khara as a partner.

At five foot nine Khara is tall, thick, solidly built, and very muscular. Almost daily she works out in a gym also training on Krav Maga; a lethal defensive form of hand to hand combat used by the Israeli Defense Forces. Having mastered it she is considering teaching the new cadets at the police academy a form of Krav Maga.

About fifteen years ago she obtained a divorce and is now in her early forties. In her mind, she has mixed feelings towards men, and they are not always positive; she does not like to date on a steady basis. She always told her psychiatrist "the dirtbags just piss me off."

Having a father who was a physically abusive drunk, and killed in a bar fight scared her mentally for life. When Khara was six years old her mother, due to depression, committed suicide by hanging herself in front of her in their kitchen at home.

New York City Social Services placed her with a few different foster families until she turned eighteen. She had been raped and beaten multiple times by foster siblings through the many years in the foster care system. Due to her upbringing, in analysis, Khara acknowledged her emotional scars and is also working on her other issues such as compulsively showering. There is no empathy or any emotions toward most people left in her. A psychiatrist has been working with Khara on her many issues.

A marriage of convenience enabled her to wangle out of the foster care network and to be financially supported. While working for a private agency as a security guard she met her husband. He is a senior executive for a large international electronics company. Her assignment was to protect him while he was in New York City. Due to her striking features, he was attracted to her, and they started to date. They were together for three weeks before he proposed marriage. Without hesitation, she agreed to marry him. Khara was broke and there was no money in her bank account or any way to better herself in life. This marriage enabled her to go to college, and earn her bachelor's degree; he paid for everything.

While in college her grades were above average, and she did well in most of her classes. There was one class she was having some trouble in, and she needed it to graduate on time, so she asked if any classmates are available to help tutor her in the subject. Only one person said they would be able to assist her, but Khara would need to come to her apartment for the tutoring. The girl, in reality, was looking to seduce her and only offered to help her on one condition. Desperate to achieve her degree Khara went along with the girl's advances. After graduating from college she applied to the New York City Police Department and was accepted.

After graduating college she always said to herself once she worked a few years in the police department, and saved enough money to be independent, she would divorce her husband. He is a luxury who would no longer be needed. That was her side of the divorce story.

***

Khara felt Matt is different than the other men she met in her life. He didn't overtly come onto her, and he smelled nice. She had a slight sexual crush on Matt, and he thought she is a good looking woman, but he never pursued her, and neither did she in return.

Although she is a little older than him it didn't seem to bother her. The knowledge Khara had of his marriage being on shaky grounds did not influence her to make a move. Matt often spoke to her about his marriage and seeking her advice. His wife broke up with a longtime boyfriend just before she met Matt. On the rebound, she married him. Whatever love she felt for him started to fade soon after the marriage began due to her ex-boyfriend looking her up online, and emailing her. Constantly Matt spoke to Khara about it. The fact is he is not sure his wife is having an affair. He did have certain feelings about it because her marital affection for him dwindled significantly after she started to get those emails from her old boyfriend every day. He complained to Khara about it often when they were alone in a police car.

Khara and Matt are sitting next to each other in the booth at Egan's. Their legs rubbed together under the table, with a light touch, but they never went further. They both knew it would be trouble if they did anything sexual. But their eyes betrayed their platonic affection for each other.

"What-cher hav'in Honey," the waitress asked as she approached their booth.

Her long straight bleached blond hair flowed down to her shoulders, framing her flawless white copy paper skin. Only her blazing red lipstick stood out on her face, and the black mascara outlining her bright blue eyes. She typically chewed gum while working and talking to customers.

Standing at the edge of the table she put her hands down flat in front of where Matt is sitting. She leaned in toward him, pushing her chest outwards, her top buttons open and exposing a lot of cleavage. "See anything you like to have today?"

Not missing a beat Khara turned her head towards the waitress.

"We'll both order cheeseburgers medium well, and a Heineken on tap. And make the fries well done, too."

The waitress lifted her hands off the table, smiled a sardonic smile at her, and said "thanks."

Not being in a rush she ambled into the kitchen to place the order. Nothing is electronic in the place. Egan's is an old-fashioned family bar and grill. It was never modernized. He never felt the need to upgrade or spend the money.

Khara excused herself and marched to the back to go to the ladies room, at least that is the story she told him. Waiting in the hallway until the waitress returned from the kitchen she blocked her path.

"Please don't pull that shit again with my partner. He's a married man, and he doesn't need any temptation. You get what I'm telling you?"

Khara looked her straight in the eyes. Her temper is ever so simmering but under control.

The waitress stood still for a moment, digesting the veiled threat. Responding with a forced smile, she said: "Okay, no problem". The unspoken message between the two women is given and understood. Khara didn't want any competition for his attention, but she would never admit to being jealous.

With the issue settled she returned to her table and sat next to Matt to finish her food when it arrived.

While they are eating Khara turned to speak to him. "Listen...I have a lead on the murder we went to today. After we finish lunch I am going to call the lieutenant, and tell him we are following up on some information I found online; a lead."

Matt had a hard time hearing her due to the background noise in the bar. The television is blasting a Yankees afternoon game, their second baseman Lawsky hit a home run, and the acoustics in the back where they are sitting is terrible. He put his food down, leaned into her, and asked "What lead are you talking about? I was with you all day. When did you come get a lead on the case?"

"When we were in the office just before lunch, I went online and searched the dead guy's name from the credit card. There are only three people with this name in the city. I thought we visit hit each one and see what we can find out after lunch."

Khara said nothing about knowing the correct address from the driver's license she tore up the night before. "We'll go to the first location I found in Brooklyn," she told him. As she had more experience on the job and is his mentor, Matt decided to go along with her.

They hurried to finish eating and went back to the precinct to sign out an unmarked car. Matt drove them downtown to the Battery in heavy stop and go traffic. He took the East River Drive to the

Williamsburg Bridge, and once in Brooklyn, they headed to Marcy Avenue.

The apartment building they are looking for had no numbers on it. Someone painted the number on the street so it could be found. The apartment house used to be a nice place to live, but the City Housing Authority started to take in welfare and homeless residents, and decay settled in over a long period of time. The deterioration began to be noticeable to everyone once gang involvement became active in the area. The bold bright brass numbers on the front of the building were ripped off years ago, and almost certainly sold as scrap metal to a dealer on Ditmas Avenue.

After parking in front of the building, they locked the car doors and walked to the main entrance of the building. Khara savored the flavor after putting a few pieces of gum in her mouth and started to chew them.

The lawn on both sides of the concrete walkway is half green grass and half brown dirt. Blotchy would best describe the front landscaping. The entry doors are unlocked, the transom cracked and a little askew as they walked into the lobby with an air of confidence.

When they walked into the lobby they are met by a housing police officer standing next to the building's mailboxes. He stood with his back to the wall for safety reasons and is looking out at the front entrance visually inspecting the people as they entered the building.

Both Khara and Matt are wearing their badges on a chain around their necks when they identified themselves to the officer, and Khara explained in an authoritative voice they are here investigating a murder. "Follow us upstairs, and wait by the elevator when we go to knock on the door."

Pointing them to a working elevator the officer knew to call in for some backup before going with them. Together they all entered the elevator. The stench of urine in the sixty-year-old claustrophobic elevator is nauseatingly strong; it disgusted Khara and put her in a foul mood.

With a clunk and a jolt, the old elevator stopped, and the interior door slid open. Before Khara pushed the outer door to exit she took out her SIG Sauer .45 pistol and held it at her side, pointing up. Matt did the same and walked out behind her with the housing officer following them.

Project hallways are not well lit and often narrow. There are massive amounts of illegible graffiti in black marker on the walls and ceiling. The uniformed housing officer closed the elevator door and followed a few footsteps behind them. He stopped, waited, and watched while they approached the apartment door twenty-five feet down the hall. He put his hand on his holstered gun and observed Khara and Matt. The elevator is about ten feet right behind him.

Taking the chewing gum from her mouth she placed it over the peephole on the door. Her forefinger pushed the doorbell. A tinny "ring, ring" sounded in the apartment. Khara and Matt stood motionless on each side of the front door with their guns at the ready.

No one spoke, there is total silence.

Khara tried to listen at the door for footsteps inside.

She strained to hear a noise of any kind. But she couldn't, no sounds are coming out of the apartment.

Frustrated she rang the doorbell again. A tinny "ring, ring" again sounded in the apartment. Pressing her ear to the door she began to hear footsteps. Someone is walking to the door.

More silence.

Khara realized the person is trying to see out the peephole.

The loud creaking door opened no more than a few inches.

Khara took notice of a short, very heavy set, a middle-aged Hispanic woman gazing from the opening in the doorway. Wearing a white tee shirt which was three sizes too small, with rolls of fat cascading down her waist she also saw her blue iridescent spandex pants which are stretched out with bulging cellulite hugging her thick legs.

"Is Bernardo here? I have a package for him."

The woman responded. "No hablo Ingles." [I do not speak English.]

"¿Es Bernardo aquí? Tengo un paquete para él " Khara told her repeating herself in Spanish.

Realizing Khara spoke Spanish the woman told her in heavily accented English he just left to go to the store for cigarettes. She knew it was a lie. Bernardo is laying on a steel slab in a freezer in the coroner's office. That is a fact because she put him there.

No one expected the elevator door to open, and nobody even noticed. Everyone was too intent on what is happening at the apartment door. Two teenage wannabe gang bangers walked out of the elevator and looked at three officers standing in the hallway. One of the punks is wearing a Biz Markie tee shirt, with jeans hanging down below his waist and wearing the colors of a local gang. The two teens froze for a moment. With no forethought, they yelled out "cops" warning the people in the apartment Khara and Matt are standing in front of. In Spanish, they began screaming "police, police". Khara figured they are in all likelihood going to the same apartment as she is to collect their drugs and money. The young thugs pulled out guns from their pant's waist and started to shoot.

With his back to the elevator the housing officer didn't hear them behind him until it was too late, nor did Khara and Matt who are concentrating on the apartment's front door as the heavy set woman closed it without saying anything else.

Their pistols screamed as the bullets left the gun barrel. The sounds of their shots echoed off the narrow cinderblock hallway walls. The noise is deafening, and the shooters flinched a little each time they pulled the trigger from the sound. Khara thought they must have just bought the guns a little while ago from a back alley dealer as they flinched when shooting.

The housing officer is right in front of them, and he took multiple shots in his back falling forwards on the building's unwashed dirty gray tiled floor.

Matt and Khara without thinking swerved, facing the shooters, and returned fire. Their .45 pistols are even louder than the punk's .38's. For only seconds chaos reigned in the narrow hallway. Khara's instinct took over, and she emptied her gun. With her thumb, she pushed the release, and as the empty magazine fell to the floor she slammed a full clip back into her Sig. 45 as Matt did the same with his.

The thug standing next to the elevator door is shot four times in the chest, blood spurting out on an oversized Notorious B.I.G. tee shirt, and he is dead before his body hit the floor. The other shooter is wounded twice in the torso above the waist, once in his groin. He dropped to the floor holding his genitals, writhing in pain.

Running to the downed officer Matt kneeled and took his pulse. It was too late. One of the shots in his back pierced through his heart and out the front of his chest staining his uniform with blood.

Rushing over to the other shooter Khara stomped on his forearm with the heel of her boot smashing the bones in his wrist. He is still gripping his gun with his right hand and did not release it. "Where did Bernardo pick up the money and drugs?"

Without hesitation, she repeated it in Spanish. "¿De dónde Bernardo recoger el dinero y las drogas? "

Lying on the floor holding his groin, she viewed him wincing in great pain. Looking up at Khara he spits at her as best as he could. His spew landed on her highly shined and polished boot. This pissed her off. Pointing her gun at his forehead she yelled at him "you fucking spit on my boots?"

Khara pulled the trigger.

His skull exploded, and blood splattered everywhere.

"Try spitting at me now you human piece of shit!"

Turning she ran over to Matt. "He tried to raise his gun, but I took care of him. He's dead."

Seeing everything that happened, he would never rat out his partner. Shaking his head affirmatively he had her back, and he knew she had his; that's what partners do.

Multiple shots from an automatic weapon now rang out from inside the apartment. The apartment's front door shook, flew wide open, then rebounded back to being almost completely closed. For a few seconds, the automatic firing stopped. Khara and Matt realized the shooter must be reloading. Without thinking, and from inexperience, Matt kicked the door back open. Khara ran in first. She intended to shoot anyone who is moving in the apartment. She is now pissed off about her boots.

The heavyset woman is sighted rushing towards the sofa in the living room and lunged at a pistol on the side table. Firing multiple times at the running woman Khara shot at her. The small room is a perfect echo chamber, and the sounds of the gun's firing are deafening. Khara's three shots knocked the heavy set woman off her feet and flipped her onto the sofa. Blood is splattering all over the walls, and onto the sofa's clear vinyl covering. There is so much blood on the sofa it caused the woman to slide off it. A pool of bright red blood is gathering on the floor. Khara ran over to her and looked down; the woman is gasping for breath and is barely breathing.

The automatic weapon which was being held by another young gang banger standing in the kitchen is empty. He is having trouble inserting a new magazine in the chamber. In the heat of the gun battle, his nerves got the better of him as he rushed to reload. As Matt ran into the kitchen he looked at the young shooter who is trying to put it in upside down; in a moment about to insert it properly.

Matt shot him twice in the upper chest. Blood began to spurt out of his mouth and chest as he fell backward hitting the stove. Beginning to fall onto the cheap looking linoleum flooring he opened his hands and dropped his weapon. His head is at a forty-five-degree angle as he sat upright leaning against the range. Matt's third and final shot placed a bullet hole on the left side of his forehead.

Sirens are wailing outside, and multiple police cars drove up to the building. They are responding to the dead Housing Officer's previous request for backup he made only minutes earlier.

The first one shot and still living is the fat woman on the floor who is bleeding out fast. Khara said to her "I can help you live. Who has the money and drugs? If you tell me I'll call the ambulance to come to save you." Repeating it in Spanish for her she said " Puedo Ayudar a vivir . ¿ Quién Tiene el dinero y las drogas ? Si me dices voy a Llamar a la ambulancia párrafo venir a salvarte . "

"Gonzalez Boxes and ...."

Her speech started to slur.

The dying woman tried to speak again. "He at ... and...."

Her eyes rolled backward. Her body took one last heave as she is gasping for air. Khara stood there motionless, emotionless, watching this woman draw her last breath with her eyes frozen wide open. Turning her head to Matt she told him "this piece of shit is dead also."

In twenty-four hours Khara killed four people, yet she had no real feelings about it or any remorse or sadness. She knew after this shooting the NYPD would require her to have counseling to talk about what happened in the housing project's apartment.

What annoys her most is the Firearms Discharge Report she and Matt would need to fill out. Not the trail of dead bodies she left behind. The paperwork pissed her off more, but she knew it is all part of the job.

The patrol supervisor arrived a few minutes later and secured both of their guns. There would be an investigation with the final determination of events by the commissioner; assuming the District Attorney did not file any charges.

Khara is aware she is the only one who obtained another lead to follow, and no one else is going to get the information she obtained. She knew there is always another day once things eventually blew over.

Chapter 2 -

Eloise knows it is extremely perilous to play with Khara, but she always felt a deep vicarious thrill palpitate in her when she is flirting with danger. To her, it is a feeling which enhances the sexuality of the moment.

The evening before, Khara called her to make the sudden counseling appointment. Considering, as a rule, Eloise needed at least two weeks to schedule someone to see her she always made an exception for her favorite client. Upon hearing from Khara that she wanted to consult with her Eloise immediately canceled her morning appointments and moved them to the late afternoon or early evening.

The morning of the appointment Eloise began to prepare so she would ready for whatever might happen when she is with her. After being her psychiatrist for almost fifteen years she understood, by heart, all Khara's emotional triggers. She knew how to be safe and avoid them.

After showering, shaving her legs and armpits, she dried off and applied a few layers of antiperspirant to her underarms. She reached up for the Chanel No.5 on her bathroom shelf and started spritzing herself from the top down. She learned from past sessions with her Khara genuinely liked Chanel No.5's scent.

First, she put some behind her ears, dabbed some on her chest between her breasts, and finished by spraying the aroma around her inner and upper thighs as a movie star once said on a television show she watched. She appreciated better than most not to take any chances with this particular patient. Now she is ready for her special morning consultation.

As Khara approached the apartment building on Fifth Avenue the doorman recognized her approaching the entrance. He greeted her with a cheery good morning and opened the door for her. She smiled back with a somewhat small forced smile.

Upon entering the lobby she inhaled the aroma from the old solid oak paneling on the walls and felt at ease smelling the fragrance of real timber. The dark staining of the wood somehow, through the years of her walking in Eloise's hallway, seemed to be some kind of an emotional security blanket for her. She approached the concierge desk that is situated in the inner lobby.

The decision to visit her personal psychiatrist first, before she spoke to the department's psychologist, is Khara's way of preparing for the interview she knew is ahead of her. After almost fifteen years of analysis with Eloise, a trust factor has been established. In the past, she often spoke to her psychiatrist openly and almost never held anything back. Her knowledge of an existing patient-doctor privilege allowed Khara to speak most of the time freely to her. There are only a handful of significant things she never volunteered to tell her.

Due to a police officer being shot to death the apartment house shootings hit the front page of the newspapers both locally and nationwide. The shooting also made all the major national and international broadcast networks. The New York governor and mayor personally gave long speeches about needing more gun control after the officer's death.

The previous day Khara's lieutenant had been called into the precinct captain's office after the shooting, and told Khara and Matt are ordered by the chief of police to promptly seek to counsel. Khara is told to go for counseling with the department's shrink within two days or so.

They are considered to be heroes by the media, and the police department security office is keenly aware of the fact. Khara and Matt would not be able to attend the funeral of the housing officer who had been killed in the hallway. Those orders came from the commissioner. Not wanting to inflame the situation any more than necessary with the Hispanic Community he did not want them to appear at the funeral. Minority community activists ignored the facts of the case as usual. They began talking about the police shooting civilians again. It is politics; plain and simple.

***

The concierge at the desk also recognized her after all those years of her coming for her appointments. He picked up his intercom and called the psychiatrist to inform her Miss Khara Bennett is waiting in the lobby. He put the phone down and nodded for her to proceed to her appointment.

The metal taps on her boot heels made a clickity-clack on the highly polished tiled floor as she walked down the hallway, and she made a left turn into a dead-end corridor. The last door in the corner is the one she wanted. Upon opening the door Khara entered into Eloise's waiting room.

Since her divorce, Khara has been seeing Eloise. The counseling sessions are built in as part of the settlement package to the divorce; Khara's husband's attorney insisted upon including them in the final judgment. The last time her wealthy husband was discharged from the hospital his lawyer demanded, for his wellbeing, he pays for her to be seeing someone even if the sessions took forever. He believed the counseling would keep her away from him, and his client out of harm's way.

This agreement was not done for altruistic reasons. The lawyer wanted to try to keep her unchecked emotions under control, and away from her ex-husband. The divorce decree insured her husband would continue paying for Khara's counseling as a defensive mechanism against his wife. Although the sex was fantastic, after his third trip to the hospital even he made the decision to listen to his lawyer, and it was now time for his safety and a divorce.

Today Khara in a calm and collected manner walked into the familiar waiting room as Eloise came out of her inner office, and smiled at her as the two lightly embraced and kissed.

Eloise is about twelve years older than Khara, in her mid-fifties, with a little extra meat on her bones. Maybe twenty or thirty pounds or so, but the years or weight did not matter to Khara. As their bodies got closer to one another Eloise started to kiss her. There was a passion to Eloise's pursed lips; it is not a simple nice to see you again kiss. Khara kissed her back, but not at the same level of excitement.

During the fifteen years of seeing each other, they have been on again off again lovers. After the long kiss, Eloise took Khara by the hand and walked into her inner office. They both sat next to one another on the thickly cushioned burgundy Chesterfield leather sofa in her office. It is placed next to a matching burgundy leather chaise lounge Eloise sometimes also used it with some of her other patients.

While holding Khara's hand Eloise said "the evening news was on last night and I saw you on the broadcast. Your face is on every television station and newspaper. Channel Four announced to its viewers the mayor is going to give you some type of medal. Are you emotionally okay with that happening?"

Facing her on the sofa Khara slid back into the corner of the Chesterfield, and seemed somewhat more secure.

"The night started with this guy I picked up in a bar. I had been drinking a little too much, and the time is getting late. I began feeling horny, and I felt an urge of needing a man to screw with all-night. So we went back to his place to fool around".

"Khara, how many times over the years have we discussed you trying to begin a normal sexual relationship with someone on a steady basis? Whether it's a man or a woman, I don't care, that's up to you. On the other hand, at least you might bring stability into your life. Part of your psychopathic condition is hypersexuality, a need for stimulation, and it can become a dangerous and self-destructive habit for you."

"I understand Eloise, and I tried hard being in relationships before. But I literally like to sport fuck instead. The variety and the edginess of fooling around with new men I happen to find exciting."

Eloise sensed an opening in Khara's speech. "You must cut back on your promiscuity. In my opinion, it's not a healthy type of relationship for you to be in, and you also shouldn't be screwing around with strangers when you are drunk. Isn't he the fourth lover you killed so far?"

"No, he's only the third asshole who pissed me off and died. You know the fourth one is my older foster brother I told you about. Although I'm not sure if I killed him; I don't think. He was the high school senior who continued to rape me when I attended junior high school in Queens. My search for him took me almost fifteen years, but I found him, and one day I followed him to his home. You remember the result."

Khara paused for a moment getting her train of thought together. Inhaling deeply into her lungs she continued her story without prodding.

"I rang the doorbell to his apartment, and when it opened he stood still, not moving a muscle, and motionless. I thought he seemed startled when he recognized who I was, and he froze in his tracks. I had a flashback at that moment, and in my mind sniffed his bad breath again although he is only standing about three feet away from me. This time he is not on top of me. I lunged at him and I began punching him relentlessly in his face. He fell to the floor begging me to spare his life as I stomped on both his hands with my boots. I didn't want his foul hands touching my body again like he used to do."

Khara's voice started to become animated and stronger. "I wanted him to experience the pain he put me through. I went into his kitchen while he lay on the floor and I stuffed a small towel in his mouth to stifle his moans. That's when I saw his fingers are now all broken and swollen. I asked the asshole how he's going to rape me now because he can't unbutton my clothes with his fucked up fingers. He began to cry, that asshole now started to cry, do you believe it? I didn't stop. I stood over him for a moment, not saying or do anything. Then with all my might, I kicked him in his groin. The bastard passed out when I stomped on his neck. Shouting at him lying there I said we are even, and left him motionless on the floor, and not moving."

Beginning to sense the tiger starting to rage in Khara's voice Eloise placed her left hand, with a soft gentle touch, over hers and at a slow pace she started to massage the top of her hand. Inching closer to her she put her right hand below Khara's ear, and with her thumb rubbed the side of her face in a light circular manner. Eloise sensed the kitten start to purr, and the tiger's rage disappears.

"I need to be schooled on what to say tomorrow when I go to speak to the department's shrink about the shooting. They want to understand how I feel about killing someone, and do I have post-traumatic stress disorder. I don't want them to put me on desk duty forever. In my heart, I know there are no feelings at all about the assholes I killed. Still, I appreciate the fact I can't tell them how I really feel about killing people."

"Plus the department placed my service gun into evidence and wants to give me paid medical leave for four weeks to unwind. When I went back to the precinct to write my report the guys looked at me differently. I think somehow, in a way they envied me, and are jealous they are not able to knock off those gangbangers themselves."

Eloise sat back and explained to Khara what to say. How to say it and what is going to happen. Many times in the past other police officers who saw her as patients were also involved in shootings. This is not a new patient experience for her.

"Tell the department's psychologist when he asks how you feel you perceive an elevated sense of energy. It is a normal reaction for most people, even if you don't. They are going to keep you off active duty until they think you are ready to return. Also, say you feel bad about killing them, but you realized from the situation you were in it is either them or you and Matt."

Khara confirmed to Eloise this is the first time she officially shot her service weapon on the job, and she didn't have firsthand knowledge of the procedures; only is cognizant about them from reading policy manuals. She told her in confidence years ago she once used her personal gun when she was in the narcotics division but didn't go into detail about the shooting. "Those previous incidents were never reported, so nobody knew any information about them except me."

Eloise picked up on the statement, and asked her "if you would like to talk to me about previously using your gun feel free to do it now." Khara thought about telling her for a second. Composing herself she sat back on the sofa, relaxed her arms by her side, and again turned to Eloise. "I am aware of what I am going to tell you will never leave this room. I used my personal .38 against my sergeant on an undercover operation years ago."

"He was my partner at the time, we bought some crack cocaine, and arrested a street-level hustler in Crown Heights Brooklyn on Troy Avenue. The perp asked if he disclosed to us where the big drug dealer in the neighborhood operated from, his supplier, could we release him. He told us this was his third arrest for dealing, and he understood from his defense lawyer on a previous bust he could be in prison for a very long time if he is caught again selling drugs. My Sarge agreed with him, and he told us his dealer is a superintendent in a building around the corner from where we collared him, on Empire Boulevard near Schenectady Avenue."

"I was new to narcotics then so I followed my partners lead. Sarge took the street dealer by the arm, and he led us to the building. It was a quick march from where we collared the perp."

"We started to walk into the lobby of the seventy-year-old apartment house and the perp told us the super always used the boiler room downstairs to deal from. So we cuffed him to the iron railing in a stairwell, and we walked down the steps to the basement."

"The boiler room is empty, and no one is in there, and no drugs either. Sarge is pissed we were lied to. As we started to go back upstairs we passed a small basement window. We both noticed someone standing outside in the backyard next to a small shipping container."

"Going back up I released the perp from the railing and took him with us to the rear courtyard. The super recognized our guy as we approached, and waved hello to us. He must have thought we would be dealing with him."

"The doors to the container are wide open, and he is stuffing old clothes into black plastic bags. I thought he might be somewhat suspicious when three people are coming to talk to him. He turned to us and asked our perp what he wanted."

"Our guy told the super he sold some crack to us, and we wanted to buy a lot more to begin selling it for him. I think the asshole was on to us. He said he's too busy packing the container with clothes and in the morning the shipping container is being picked up and shipped to Puerto Rico. He told us to come back another time; he had nothing to sell at the moment, including illegal drugs. He turned away, and ignored the three of us standing behind him."

"We left the back courtyard and returned to our precinct with our perp. After Sarge put him in a holding cell and did some paperwork we clocked out."

"We walked out of the precinct together when Sarge turned to me and asked if I would like to make some extra money on the side. I didn't know what he was thinking, but I was curious. He told me to meet him at the Flatbush Avenue Junction by the newsstand around ten tonight."

"I am standing on the curb watching the traffic pass by on Flatbush Avenue when he pulled up in a brand new black Cadillac and motioned for me to hop in. While he is driving back to Crown Heights he told me he thought the super is full of shit. His gut told him the man must have plenty of drugs and is in all likelihood hiding them in the container he is standing in when we approached him. Sarge told me he noticed the dealer is wearing a gold Rolex watch on his left wrist. He said it's an extremely expensive luxury watch to be wearing in the area of Brooklyn we are working in. He said to me you don't buy costly shit if you aren't dealing. You know what I'm saying to you Khara? You do have your gun with you, right?"

"I told him no. I didn't know I would need one so I left my Sig .45 home. I know I lied to him. My personal snub nose .38mm is strapped to my right ankle under my pants leg. Back in those days, I wore sneakers, not boots, so I strapped the gun down there in an ankle holster. He smirked, and I don't think he seemed too happy hearing me say that, but he didn't mention anything further to me about it."

"It was at that moment I realized he's going to rip off the super, and I am being set up by him to be an accomplice. He could hold this over me, and I would be forced to go along with whatever he had in mind in the future. I was getting pissed at the predicament I am going to be placed in, and there's nothing I could do about the situation at the moment. I had to wait, bide my time, and see what developed."

"At last, we pulled up to the apartment house on Empire Boulevard. There are no parking spots so he stopped, and double parked on the busy street. Sarge got out and walked into the building. I sat for a few seconds after he started to walk away, and took my snub nose .38 from my ankle holster, and put the small gun in the large side pocket of my leather jacket. I exited the Cadillac and followed after him into the basement."

"Sarge met the super coming out of the boiler room with his young daughter behind him. She looked to me to be about ten years old, with long black hair. She was a pretty little Spanish girl. I stood way back and watched. I think the dealer realized what is going to go down. He sent his kid back into the boiler room, and told her to wait for him, and not come out until he came back for her."

"Sarge walked right up to him. They are so close I thought their noses almost touched. That's when I heard Sarge ask him if he would like his daughter to see tomorrow's sunrise? The super nodded yes. The threat worked."

"We want what's in the container Sarge told him."

Eloise interrupted. "Khara do you think your sergeant would have killed the young girl?"

"Without a doubt, he would kill her. Let me finish, and you'll understand why I think he would."

"I could see the look on the super's face, the guy seemed a bit nervous. Whatever's in the steel container is in reality, not his. If there are drugs or drug money in it, they belonged to someone higher up. In about two minutes I would find out."

"The three of us walked back to the courtyard, to the locked trailer. The super unlocked the container's doors, opened them, and hooked the doors open to the sides of the shipping container. He walked about two feet into the container, and reached way back in the rear between the stack of black plastic bags, pulled out a duffle bag, and dropped it on the floor in front of Sarge."

"The super knelt and opened the duffle bag. Inside we saw nothing but wrapped hundred dollar bills, and he said the whole rear of the container is filled with money. Sarge told him to take out three more large brown canvas bags. He reached in and took them out one by one. Beads of perspiration are now dripping down the super's forehead, and I noticed he appeared to be a little jumpy; kind of skittish. He is caught between a rock and a hard place. If we took his supplier's cash he and his whole family would be murdered, and if he didn't give the money to us now his daughter would be killed next after him."

"I am standing motionless next to Sarge watching this go on. I put my right hand into my jacket pocket, gripped my gun, clicked off the safety, and I kept it in my pocket. The super said there are some more bags in the rear of the container, he turned around, and he reached back through the pile of plastic bags extending his arm as much as he could. But instead of a duffle bag, he started to take out a pistol. Trying to turn to face us with the gun his luck ran out. Sarge saw the gun, and without hesitation shot him twice in the upper back flinging him forward on the stuffed garbage bags of clothes. His blood splattered on the brown canvas duffle bags as he fell on them."

"Sarge said to me he shouldn't have taken a gun out from the bags, and he began to wave his pistol at me; ordering me to go in the container to pick up the duffle bags. I knew from my training as a police officer if I touched one of the duffle bags my prints or DNA would be on it. For the rest of my life, he would be able to frame me, and I would be his hack forever."

"As I somehow expected I soon found out Sarge had a different idea. He turned to me and said he is sorry but there is too much cash to share. At that moment I realized he is not going to frame me; he is going to kill me. So I didn't wait, and I pulled the trigger twice from inside my jacket pocket and shot him in his chest. His eyes flashed wide open, and he looked at me in what I thought seemed like total disbelief of him being shot; it happened to him instead of me. Falling against the side of the container, and bouncing off it, his bloody body twisted as he landed on top of the super. I knew I must get out of there. The gunshots were awfully loud, and some lights started to go on in a few of the windows high above. I grabbed one duffle bag and left the rest of the cash-filled bags where they were; inside by the bodies. I closed the container doors, and snapped shut the heavy Master locks."

"I figured the drug dealers in Puerto Rico would dispose of both men, and keep their money too. They would clean up the situation for me as far as I was concerned. I now also had the extra cash Sarge promised me. So I walked away through some interconnected alleys, and caught a cab a few blocks down on Utica Avenue; back to my apartment."

"When I got home I reloaded my gun, and put my jacket with the bullet hole by the pocket in a large paper bag I saved from the supermarket. After changing my clothes I took a short walk to the rear of a nearby diner. I threw the bag into their dumpster, and shoved it in deep amongst their smelly garbage."

Eloise sat silent, absorbing everything Khara told her. "Weren't you concerned the customs officials would open the shipping container to inspect it?"

"No. I knew since its being shipped to Puerto Rico, and the island is a United States Commonwealth, customs would not open it, and the container would be sent along to the location on the island where it is going as a regular shipment."

After listening to this Eloise, being curious, asked: "and what happened when your partner never showed up for work the next day?"

"The next day my captain did ask me if Sarge said anything to me after we left work the day before. I told him he didn't say a word about anything, and I went right home. It is bad enough he was going to kill me. I didn't want to be anywhere close to a missing police officer's investigation, including Sarge's."

"Wow, that's unbelievable, and his body never turned up?"

Eloise is sitting there in total disbelief.

"Nope, they never found him. They discovered Sarge's car double parked a day later, but the container is long gone, and en route to Puerto Rico. The perp we arrested is released for lack of evidence since Sarge brought him in, and he disappeared. The guy knew better than to say anything about the super to anyone else."

Khara continued her story "he must have heard the buzz on the street about a missing Brooklyn narcotics detective, the one who busted him and had been pictured on television as missing. He knew something went down. His supplier also disappeared so I figured he put one and one together and was smart enough to stay away from the police investigation. I guess he wanted to live. Soon after Internal Affairs went to Sarge's house as part of the missing person's investigation and they found over two hundred thousand dollars in cash in his basement. He must have been ripping off drug dealers for quite a while."

For a moment neither of them said a word.

Eloise anticipated what the answer would be, but asked anyway; "so how did you feel when you shot your Sergeant? And what did you do with the cash?"

"I didn't feel anything at all. He was going to kill me so I killed him. As for the money, I leased a small storage unit the size of a walk-in closet and hid it in there. The thing with cash is you can't spend the money on anything traceable; like a car, boat or anything which must get registered. I took short two-day vacations, bought nicer clothes, and I made sure to keep a low profile."

Eloise, wanting to bring her back to the present, told her to "remember what I told you. How to answer any questions the department's psychologist might ask you tomorrow. My information will get you back to work sooner."

Khara thanked her for the help. It seemed to take a small burden off her mind. Not that she is too worried about the investigation, but she wanted to get back to work and didn't want to say the wrong thing.

Eloise stood and glanced down at her sitting on the sofa. "It's almost noon Khara. Would you like to come upstairs to my apartment for lunch? Maybe after we eat we can spend some time together in bed."

"According to you Eloise I'm always seeking carnal excitement...so why not? I think it sounds like a good way to spend the afternoon today. Let's go."

They left the office and together took the elevator to Eloise's residential apartment on the sixth floor. Khara had been in her personal place many times before in the past, and she always enjoyed staying with Eloise when the opportunity came up. The building is located in midtown Manhattan, and when she slept over Eloise would take her out for dinner and a Broadway show.

"Wait till you see what I did with my apartment Khara. I hired an interior designer to completely redo it. I met him through a client of mine, and he's wonderful. I told him I only had two or three weeks to shop with him and everything must be in within one week after the purchases are made. I didn't want this to be drawn out forever. I needed the place finished in a timely manner."

"So tell me, Eloise, how long did it really take to redo this place?"

"He had everything organized, scheduled to come in, and be installed within one week. The carpenters, painters, and electricians only had three days to install what he ordered. Next, the furniture and carpeting came in during the next two days. How do you like it?"

"It looks great, authentically old world looking with plenty of wood and gold stuff all over. Why did you go with this type of decor?"

"You're not going to believe this Khara, but after Joan Rivers died they are showing pictures of her apartment, and I fell in love with the glitz of it."

"I must say in all honesty I do think it's nice and tacky, but cool in a way. Glad you're happy with it. Show me the new bedroom furniture you bought. I can't wait to try it out."

Later in the afternoon Khara left Eloise and took the subway back to Brooklyn, and her own apartment.

Chapter 3 -

The next morning Khara placed her clothes on the bed, getting ready to visit the department's shrink. Still tired she put on her sneakers instead of boots and she strapped on the ankle holster for her snub nose .38. In her left coat pocket, she stuffed some extra bullets and a filled quick speed loader for her revolver. Whenever she bought a new jacket she insisted on having Velcro sewn in all the exterior pockets by the store, or she would not buy it. To her way of thinking this helped prevent pickpockets; since she always carried her .38 in one of them. Khara understood the detectives' badge she wore around her neck on a chain still made her a police officer; though the department's Internal Affairs had secured her service pistol. Due to her martial arts training, she did not need to carry a gun but the thought of carrying it gave her some comfort; a security blanket of sorts.

The train ride to Manhattan is uneventful, but it is still crowded as usual. The subway car is full, and people are packed in tummy to tummy. Khara didn't need to hold onto a pole as the moving subway cars shook from side to side. The strangers standing against her held her upright, and pretty still. As usual Khara's sensitivities are ignited by some of the people on the train being so close to her, but unfortunately she had no choice in the matter. Driving into the city is a bitch, as is parking, so as a rule, she took the subway.

Boarding the jam-packed train right behind her as she entered is a tall, nice looking, middle-aged gentleman. The man ended up holding a pole which was in front of her, and he faced her. Being so close Khara is able to whiff his cologne, and the scent is alluring to her. With salt and pepper gray hair, and wearing a suit which is cut fashionably tight and fitting, she became enticed. This morning she decided to put on her body-hugging white sweater under her unbuttoned and opened brown leather jacket with stone washed blue jeans which fit her body like a tight glove. Both of them smiled at each other as the train shuffled along on the steel rails under the East River with the lights flickering on and off, but neither said anything. The subway, at last, stopped at her station as both of them left the train, and walked in different directions when they reached the street.

Being observant due to her training as a police officer she did not notice a wedding ring on his hand. There is a possibility, she hoped, they would run into each other again on the train, and this time she'll take the first step if he doesn't. "Could it be Eloise is right" she thought to herself. "If he can keep up with me, I'd stick with him."

She realized it is a daydream. She knew in her heart not many men are able to manage that feat.

Turning the corner she saw her destination is only steps away, and she entered the lobby of a large modern office building. Shimmering glass rose into the sky while white marble glistened on the highly waxed tiles. Going to the building's directory she found the psychology groups name she'd been looking for, and headed for the elevators. There are banks of them on each side of the lobby hallway. Some are express to the top floors, and others are local, stopping on every floor if you pushed the floor's button.

The elevator doors opened, she walked in and turned to press the numbered button to where she wanted to go to. Once inside she looked around and noticed this short, Latino looking man with a pencil thin mustache entering and standing beside her in the elevator. Thinking nothing of it Khara pressed the button first, and the short man pushed his after, but on a higher floor. Together they took the elevator up.

Arriving at the tenth floor the elevator doors opened, and straight ahead of her is the suite she needed to go to. Khara walked out, and the short man held the doors open for her and observed which office she is going in before the elevator door closed again.

Upon entering the office she caught sight of a young perky receptionist with polished nails and flowing tresses. The girl is sitting behind a contemporary bleached wooden desktop with a large cut-out opening on the bottom so her legs could be seen unhindered. The receptionist asked Khara which doctor she had an appointment to speak with. Glancing behind where the receptionist is sitting is an alphabetical list of almost ten different names of psychologists.

"My name is Khara Bennett, and I am here for a counseling appointment. The police department sent me, and I don't know which doctor I am supposed to be seeing. My captain told me to make an appointment with this office."

"Please take a seat Miss Bennett; I will let the doctor know you are here."

Khara walked over to a modern looking chair situated against the wall and sat next to an end table with a bunch of psychology magazines stacked on top. As she relaxed on the chair she noticed the receptionist smiling at her while under the desk she spread her legs apart while pulling up her dress a little over her knees. Noticing this Khara picked up on the let's meet later signals, but temporarily ignored them. Knowing better than to screw up this appointment for some crazy reason like sex; although she thought the young receptionist would be hot and amazing to romp with, Khara did not respond at that exact moment.

It is surprising to her as she sat because the odd-looking chair is rather comfortable. While waiting Khara began to peer at the headlines on the magazines and started to read one which included an article on psychopathic people. The title said, "How to treat psychopaths successfully". Curious about what the author wrote she looked at the publication date on the magazine and noted the date down on her smartphone for later reference in case she needed to obtain a copy.

As she opened the magazine and started to read the article a psychologist walked in the reception area. He recognized her from the police file he received the other day and had read the previous evening. The doctor introduced himself to Khara and asked if she could please follow him into his private office. As she stood and casually rolled the magazine up in her hand she followed behind him. When passing by the receptionist Khara nonchalantly dropped her business card on the receptionist's desk, smiled at her, and entered the psychologist's office after him. The doctor waved for her to sit on one of two club chairs grouped in the corner. Once Khara sat he placed himself in the other chair, and picked up a clipboard with papers on it. Looking at the folder he was holding she thought he wrote down a list of prepared questions he thought of before the appointment and wanted to ask her. Without hesitation, she is prepared to answer him as Eloise instructed her.

"May I call you Khara?"
"Yes, I'm not a formal person."

"That's some shootout you, and your partner were involved in Khara. Both of your pictures are in all the newspapers. The Post said you busted up a major barrio drug ring, and are considered heroes. How do you feel about the fame?"

"My nerves are generally calm, but the excitement made me hyper at the time. The shooting must've been an adrenalin thing, I suppose. Right now I don't feel jittery nor do I think about what happened that afternoon. The shooting is over, and I have to get on with my life. Five people died in the gunfight. Matt and I were investigating a death from the day before, and we had no intention of pursuing a drug bust. The shooting evolved, it wasn't planned. And yes, I feel bad because so many people died"

Khara put her emotions in check while she tried to keep a straight face as she lied to him.

Both of them spoke for almost an hour, and when he finished the interview he told Khara she would be off the job for at least two weeks, maybe more, and needed to relax. After some time elapsed she could go back to the precinct to do paperwork, but not to go out on the street until all the investigations had been completed. The doctor is worried about her coming down with PTSD and said he knew it is not unusual for police in those kinds of situations to be affected by using their weapon in a deadly shooting. Khara thought to herself she in truth didn't give a shit about the assholes she killed, but thought better about it, and didn't want to verbalize those thoughts to the psychologist.

The doctor asked her to come back in a week for a follow-up visit to ascertain how she is doing. Thanking him for his concern she left the office and walked into the hallway to wait for the elevator.

Standing by the elevator doors she noticed two men appearing from around a corner at the far end of the hall. The men are walking at a slow pace towards her. Recognizing one of them is the good looking handsome man she stood across from on the subway that morning she is both surprised, and pleased, to see him again. When he is close enough to her Khara thought he still smelled fresh. Smiling at him she hoped it might lead to a conversation, and maybe something more. The good-looking man smiled back. The other man is the greasy shorter fellow who followed her into the elevator when she entered the building on her way upstairs.

The good-looking gentleman had a slight yet discernable Mexican accent. "Aren't you the police detective who was on the news a few nights ago? You are the woman officer on a drug raid in Brooklyn, and shot some people also?"

"Yes, I was involved in a drug bust in Brooklyn." Still smiling she is expecting him to say something positive about it. Khara imagined everyone in the city knew she is a hero of sorts.

"Did you know the woman you killed is the sister of the head of the Ecru Cartel in Mexico City?"

Within a second Khara grew serious, and her smile disappeared. No one in the police department said anything about a cartel to her. Realizing the only way he could have known about the fat woman she shot is if he worked for the Ecru Cartel. In a flash, she understood why he reappeared again and is looking for her. These two men must have been following her since she left her apartment in the morning.

Now they are all standing so close to each other she began to smell their breath. In a split second the man in the suit charged at her placing both his hands around Khara's neck and tried to choke her. She realized the game is on.

Instinctively Khara raised her arms upwards between his extended arms and dislodged his hands from her throat. In a split second her training kicked in again and she twisted to her right side and with her left elbow hit him full force in the jaw; knocking one of his teeth onto the floor, and cutting his upper lip. Blood began to flow down his chin, and onto his suit. Khara kicked him in the groin followed by a forceful series of clenched fists to the face; smashing his nose almost flat. In tremendous pain, he fell backward hitting the wall and started to slide to the floor.

The greasy looking man, who is smaller, jumped on her from behind, straining and trying to place his arm around her neck. Khara raised her right leg, and stomped down on his foot; she thought she definitely broke bones. In pain, he let go of her as she stood straight, and with her left heel kicked behind her hitting him in the kneecap. In agony, he is forced to release his grip on her, and as she turned her right elbow hit him on the side of his face. Visibly shaken and wincing he fell to the floor doubled over in excruciating pain.

Khara turned, and with fire in her eyes glanced over to the handsome first assailant who fell to one knee; his jaw broken and drooping. With one hand he reached into his pocket and pulled out a large switchblade knife. Using his wrist he flicked the handle, and the long serrated knife swung open. Waving the steel blade from left to right while kneeling he tried to slash at her. Frustrated, he dived at her legs attempting to stab her in the thigh. Khara realized he is trying to cut her femoral artery, and have her bleed to death. She thought he is a professional hitman because of the way he handled his knife.

Fortunately, Khara is quicker than he is as she grabbed his forearm, and bent his wrist back snapping small bones and tearing ligaments. As he released the knife from his hand she picked it up, plunging it into his chest through his suit jacket, and between his ribs; piercing the heart. Reeling backward again he slammed his head into the hallway wall, this time with a soft thud. Slowly he slid to the floor in a sitting position and looking directly at Khara expired at her feet.

"Asshole" she sputtered looking down at him. "You missed having one hell of a good time with me."

Now she turned her attention to the shorter man who by now is able to sit upright on the tiled floor. Khara is totally pissed they tried to kill her. Walking over to him she grabbed his throat with three fingers, and with all her might she pinched them together, as he thrashed about the floor trying to release her grip on his neck, and get away. When his eyes started to roll back into his head she heard a gurgling sound coming from him. Out of the corner of her eye, she saw two women at the opposite end of the hallway walking towards her and aiming their guns in her direction.

Khara, yanking him by his hair and throat jerked the shorter man to his feet and using him as a shield to absorb the bullets they are shooting at her. The elevator reached her floor, the doors opened, and she rushed in while dragging his body along. Once inside she dropped his dead body on the floor of the elevator as the doors closed. Pushing two buttons; the second floor and the lobby, she executed a plan she thought up on the spot.

Opening on the second floor she hurried, ran out, and rushed to the hall stairwell exit. Entering the exit door to the stairs she quietly closed the steel door behind her and tried to listen for them running down the stairs from above. Khara strained to catch her breath and control her breathing. Feeling her heart beating she tried to calm her nerves. Listening to the silence by the steps she soon expected to hear the women as they would be coming down the stairs after her to the lobby.

Like a tidal wave rushing into the shore she is alerted to the muffled sound of footsteps coming from the higher stairs getting louder. As the two women descended the stairs and came close to the second floor, the sounds of their advance grew thunderous.

Surmising what is soon going to happen she took out her .38 and positioned herself in the far corner of the stairwell by the hinges of the door. Figuring when they turned, in haste, on the landing to come down the stairs they would not see her until it is way too late.

Khara raised her arms holding her .38 and took aim at where she thought they would be soon standing. The girls turned on the landing as Khara expected. As they both are on the first top step down from the landing to go towards the second floor, and without hesitation, she shot each of them in the chest area. Neither of the girls foresaw the deadly surprise waiting for them as their eyes sprung open when they heard Khara's gun, and looked at her standing right below them. Tumbling to where Khara is waiting at the bottom steps they landed in a pile of arms and legs, and not moving. Looking at them tangled together she perceived they are younger girls; maybe not even eighteen. There are no emotions about their wasted youth, and death, on her part.

Bending to check their pulse Khara determined one of them is now dead. The other is moaning and opened one eye. Khara bent closer to her, and asked her in Spanish "who sent you here?"

Gurgling blood, the woman is barely able to tell her, "Gonzalez boxes." The girl's eyes rolled back, and her voice trailed off; she stopped breathing. Now she had two dying women tell her the same name.

Each of the bodies at the landing in front of her is holding two guns so she picked up one of the dead girl's .45's, and put it in her belt. From experience, she knew when the police came she would be forced to give up her personal .38. She realized it is not safe to be without a weapon now she had become a walking target. Standing, she made sure the .45 is secure and walked down the stairs to the lobby to await the police.

By now the elevator reached the entrance lobby. When it opened a crowd of people waiting for it saw the dead man inside; slumped in the middle of the floor in a pool of bright red blood. The crowd started yelling and attracted the building's security, and they called 911 for an ambulance.

The police came at last, along with the commanding officer on duty, and set up a perimeter in the lobby hallway, and second-floor stairwell. When everything is under control, the area commander personally escorted Khara downtown to police headquarters. In the car, she related what the suited good-looking assassin said to her in the hall; word for word but not what the dying young girl told her.

The commander and Khara both acknowledged her life is now in imminent danger, and she is a target for revenge. When they spoke to the police intelligence unit in the afternoon at One Police Plaza she is at once given a security detail. Two detectives are assigned to protect her, and Matt, until things quieted down. Khara is taken to a hotel in Manhattan where she could be watched and kept safe for the time being. Another security detail is sent to Matt's home in Queens to safely secure it, and his family.

Chapter 4 -

The hotel suite they secured for Khara is decorated pretty nicely. There are two bedrooms and a large bathroom with a glass-enclosed walk-in shower stall. It was a recently refurbished, from top to bottom, older hotel in Manhattan situated on a side street off Broadway, but the view from the window is not too interesting. The Chief of Police allowed her to go home the next day with an escort to retrieve some clothes, but that is to be the extent of her going out in public for a while. At least that is what the Chief of Police thought.

The next morning after she showered and dressed her security detail went with her to retrieve what she needed from her apartment. Her two detective security team escorted her to pick up some clothes and toiletries. In haste, she had been brought to the hotel with only the clothes she was wearing, and she needed fresh outfits. Fortunately, the hotel supplied a small bottle of citrus-scented body wash to its guests so she smelled fresh.

Khara unlocked the front door and entered her apartment with the two detectives behind her. Instantly she noticed some of her furniture had been moved a little and is out of place. She froze, put out her arms to warn the detectives to stop, and not to follow her. The three of them stood in the entry doorway motionless for a few seconds. Without a sound, they backed out of the apartment into the hallway.

"Someone was in my apartment" Khara whispered to them. "I am an OCD neat freak, and noticed some of my furniture has been moved."

The taller of the two detectives is wearing a bulletproof vest under his jacket. He said he is going in first, and the other officer would follow him. The detectives drew their weapons. Khara is ordered to stay back in the hallway, and wait for an all clear from them. They thought Khara is unarmed so they left her alone in the hall for her safety.

The detectives reopened the door and peered in. There are no sounds or movements of any kind inside so they walked in slowly. Standing in the middle of her living room with their guns drawn they each decided to go into a different room to search for possibly an intruder. While one detective entered her kitchen he unknowingly kicked a thin tripwire on the floor; igniting an explosion which killed him. Shrapnel from the bomb flew through the plasterboard wall hitting the other detective who is in her bedroom. He is severely wounded.

Khara, standing in the hall felt the rush of dust and plaster particles fly out her front door due to the bomb blast and splashed on the hallway walls and floor. This reinforced her belief she must find Gonzalez boxes before they found her. Without hesitation, she ran inside to aid the detectives who were with her. The taller detective in the kitchen had one leg blown to pieces and is dead from the shrapnel. Khara took out her phone and called 911 for assistance. Charging into her bedroom she tried as best she could to stem the bleeding from the disabled detective who is lying on her floor.

The ambulance arrived only minutes before the bomb squad did, and satisfied the wounded detective is being medically well cared for, Khara decided to leave the apartment to look for Gonzalez boxes. Noticing the dead detective's gun on the floor she bent, picked up his Sig .45 and placed it in her backpack between her clothes. Walking to her bedroom closet she reached for the top shelf and grabbed some spare .45 clips that were loaded with hollow point bullets. Then she put them in her backpack with other stuff before leaving the apartment. Now she is carrying two .45 caliber pistols in her backpack. Khara had a score to settle now; they messed up her home really bad with a bomb, and it didn't smell too great either.

Sneaking out the rear basement entrance of her building she is confronted by two uniformed police officers who are running to seal off the back exits. She identified herself as a detective, and they escorted her back inside where she is met by the officer in charge.

Explaining what happened she is ordered to be placed back into protective custody by the area commander.

Khara walked out the front of her apartment house with her escorts, and they entered two marked police cars to go back to the hotel. She is in the second car and is being brought to the hotel again this time with uniformed officers. No one noticed she possessed the deceased detective's gun, and the young girl's also hidden in her backpack with her clothes.

It is a time-honored procedure for officers to stake out a place, and watch who leaves and enters it. The police are not the only ones to do this. The security detail escorted Khara out the front door of her apartment building. The Cartel had stationed a person, who is hidden and watching Khara's apartment house from down the block. A signal is given by the lookout, and three cars filled with Cartel gunmen started to follow her to the secured hotel room.

The first Cartel vehicle, loaded with gunmen, pulled alongside the first police car when it stopped at Broadway and Forty-Eight Street for a traffic light. Before the red light turned green another car filled with gunmen stopped in front of the first police car, and prevented any forward movement. It is blocked in the rear by the second police car directly behind it with

Khara sitting in the rear seat. There are now four cars in a straight line all locked in place.

The gunmen in the blocking vehicle rolled down their windows, and started to fire automatic weapons towards the first squad car; shooting the two officers sitting in the front seat. In total disregard, to being in an extremely heavy pedestrian midtown area they are intent on killing Khara, and anyone else who is in their way.

The officers in the second car jumped out of their vehicle, drew their weapons, and started to shoot at the gunmen in front who are blocking the first police car. They are taken by surprise when they are shot at from behind by the Cartel gunmen from the car behind them. Seeing what is going on Khara opened her backpack, took out both of her .45's and clicked the safeties off. Having a gun in each hand, she is alone in the back seat of the squad car, and she glanced back from where the gunfire is coming from.

Soon the rear gunmen approached Khara's car and she started to shoot through the closed side windows, hitting the gunman on her left. The second Cartel man who is on her right started to shoot at her head, but his first bullet missed and shattered the right side window to the car. She turned to face him as he continued to shoot grazing her scalp and taking some of her hair out with the skin attached. Bleeding profusely with blood running down her cheek she returned fire. Khara shot him in his chest several times; knocking him off his feet onto the black asphalt of New York City.

The gunmen in the first car jumped out of their vehicle and began to approach Khara; firing automatic weapons at her as they walked towards the police car she is in. The Cartel gunmen ignored the fact they started to shoot at the beginning of the Times Square area, and it is overflowing with police on patrol.

Dozens of police officers in Times Square heard the shooting and ran to where the police squad cars are stopped. Without waiting they began shooting at the remaining gunmen when they spotted them with automatic weapons in their hands firing at a police car. This started an intense firefight in the Times Square area, similar to a war zone. Many innocent people walking on the sidewalk, some over a dozen blocks away are hit by stray bullets and fell to the concrete wounded or dead.

Khara who is still in the back of the police car turned around to face forward and continued firing at the approaching gunmen. Besides a head wound, she is also shot in the upper thigh. The burning sensation is intense. She realized this is an active shooting situation, and if the police saw her with a gun they would shoot first and ask questions later. When the Cartel's men are soon neutralized by the approaching police she dropped her weapons on the floor of the car and placed them under her backpack out of the direct sight of the police. At the sight of the officers advancing to her car, and in great pain, she is able to raise her hands in the air flashing her gold detective's shield that is hanging by a chain around her neck. Khara stayed still on the car seat until she was ordered by the officers to exit the vehicle. In pain, she could not move due to her wounds.

The officers in the second car, when the shooting started called for backup, and in minutes all mayhem broke out. Fire engines, ambulances, and squad cars all converged at the location with sirens blaring. Wounded in her thigh, and bleeding heavily from the side of her head, she did not hesitate to identify herself when the police saw her and opened the back door of the car. The medics lifted her out, and onto a stretcher from one of the emergency services ambulances which arrived on the scene.

The news crews are not far behind. Only a few blocks away near Times Square CNBC have their financial studios located at the NYNEX building. Mr. Bradley, the New York City Director of Technical Operations for CNBC sent his cameramen carrying remote units to film everything for the news division. The tourists must have thought it is a movie scene being filmed. There are bodies strewn about in the street, on the sidewalks, and in and out of cars. Guns fully loaded are lying next to the dead bodies of both police and Cartel gunmen. The many draped and covered corpses of the dead gave it a sense of the surreal.

Khara and one of the uniformed officers who escorted her, and also survived the shooting, are rushed to NYU Medical Center emergency room on 34th street. The officer and she are operated on as soon as they arrived, and kept under tight security on an upper floor while recuperating.

Matt and his wife are one of the first ones to visit her, after the mayor and police commissioner, in the hospital when she is feeling better. One Police Plaza requested they be informed of her condition by the hospital. The day Matt signed into the hospital as a visitor he said he is going to see the uniformed officer who is also shot, not Khara, as a safety precaution in case he is being followed.

***

The time came when she is feeling better so her rehabilitation is ordered to start. The doctors recommended she be brought to physical therapy on the fourth floor. The FBI came to the hospital to speak to her. The FBI is concerned the Ecru Cartel had now become a terrorist organization since they shot up Times Square without regard to innocent civilians.

"Miss Bennet, I am FBI special agent Don Weber with the FBI Terrorism Task Force. When you are finished with your physical therapy today I would like to speak to you for a few minutes about the shooting in Times Square."

Khara looked up from the floor mat, peering around the kneeling therapist in front of her, and saw a handsome middle-aged man. He has wavy brown hair combed back with a touch of gray, is wearing a light blue suit and tie, wore no wedding ring on his left hand, and is smiling at her. She smiled back at him.

"If you want to talk to me you'd better sit down next to me so I don't need to speak loudly."

Don knelt slowly, sat next to her on the same mat, and started to question her about the deadly assault. They spoke for roughly twenty minutes about the incident while Khara went through some strengthening routines with the therapist. After she is finished she is placed back in a wheelchair, and an orderly returned her to her hospital room with her police security detail tagging along.

Don also accompanied her through the hospital hallways until she reached her room. The orderly told him to wait in the hall until she is in her bed. "Her gown is not too tight, and for her privacy would you mind please waiting outside."

"No, I don't care if he comes in while you help me to bed. He might see something he likes."

Don stayed in the room while Khara is gently placed back on the bed. Once she is seated in bed he stood beside her and started to ask her questions again.

"Don, why don't you get comfortable, and sit next to me on my bed? No one is here to report you. And besides, I think you are cute."

"Thank you Miss Bennett, but I can't-do that. It would be unprofessional for me to sit on your bed in the hospital. But when you get out of here I wouldn't mind meeting you for coffee sometime."

"You can call me Khara. That Miss Bennett shit can stop."

"Okay Khara, I'll call you on your cell phone in a few weeks when you get home. Maybe then we can grab a bite to eat?"

"Why wait. I am going to order my lunch in a little while. Stay and I'll order something for you too."

"That sounds like an interesting lunch offer. Thanks, I think I can manage eating lunch with you today."

The police public relations department announced to the news media she was killed in the shooting to throw the cartel off her trail. The police department intelligence unit needed time to figure out what to do with her next. But they did not count on Khara continuing her pursuit of Gonzalez boxes.

Chapter 5 -

After a thorough investigation, the district attorney decided her actions were in self-defense, as did the police commissioner. Unfortunately, Khara and Matt will not be allowed to report back to their Manhattan precinct. For their safety, she is secretly transferred to a police station on Staten Island, and he is placed in Bayside Queens. The Chief of Police thought they would be safer out of sight in case the Cartel tried to find them at their former precinct. What the department did not know is Khara had a lead regarding the case. Now she decided she is going to follow up on it since she is out of the hospital, back on active duty, and almost completely physically rehabilitated.

Staten Island is a relatively quiet borough compared to Manhattan. There are the usual minor drug busts, domestic disturbances, and every now and then some organized crime guy would beat up on his neighbor; or be found stretched out on the street somewhere by the docks of the Kill Van Kull bloody, and beaten almost to death, if not dead.

The precinct commander where she is stationed, for her security, is ordered to make sure two other detectives are with her when she went out on a call. The plan is to do this for a few weeks until her captain knew things are going smoothly. Eventually, she would be going out with a new single partner. Khara is not satisfied with this security arrangement because the fact of the matter is she had no choice in the decision. She'd rather have one solid person she knew well with her, or go out alone. The two-person security detail felt like babysitters to her, and she did not appreciate them being with her all the time.

Her recuperation is now over, and she is back in the gym almost daily. Since her last apartment is destroyed she started searching for a new place to stay. This time she chose Staten Island because it takes a short time to get to work, and the commute is much easier for her in the mornings. Her PBA union representative quietly helped her search for an affordable apartment in the area to rent. He soon found a place for her and left a deposit on an apartment in an established development on the island. The apartment is in a two family home which is owned by a retired police officer whose wife had died recently, and who understood why she needed a secure dwelling to call home. There are plenty of his own guns in the house, and he knows how to use them. The captain asked him to be the unofficial security watchman for Khara who would live in the downstairs apartment of his house. She appreciated the fact she didn't need to squeeze into a subway to Manhattan anymore. Now she could leisurely drive to her precinct.

On her first few days off from work she is supposed to go looking for furniture but decided she didn't have the time, or patience, for going from store to store. Instead, she leased an apartment full of stuff including a sofa to a complete bedroom set from a rental firm. Televisions, tables, and chairs are also included in the rental lease. This is much easier and quicker for her, she couldn't be bothered shopping around.

The time now came for her to find Gonzalez Boxes.

***

Don Weber started to call her almost every week while she is hospitalized, or he would stop in to visit with her. They would always talk for a long time when they were together. Both of them are trying to know each other a little better hoping to start a relationship. Although he did try to drop in to see her as often as he could the agency had him traveling on a lot of different terrorism cases.

Once she settled into her new apartment she is able to make a real date with Don. Now she is at last home, he is in town, and Khara is ready to start a steamy romance. After she woke up Don called her in the early morning to try and make a date to take her out one evening. Thinking he is a good looking man with chiseled facial features she had anticipated dating him after she was released from the hospital. Maybe, she thought, he would be the man Eloise suggested she should find. Or in the future, he could become a steady boyfriend for her. An evening is chosen they both were available, and she could not wait to go on their first date.

Don drove into Staten Island to pick her up at her apartment. His car is parked only a few houses down from hers due to a scarcity of parking spots, and he walked to her door. Being a terrorism expert he is always aware of his surroundings, and her notoriety. To her surprise, he brought a bouquet of beautiful flowers and a large golden box of Godiva chocolates with a pink ribbon tied into a bow on top. Don wanted to make a good first impression on his first real date with Khara.

When she opened the door and saw him, she smiled and invited him into her home.

Her face beamed with joy as he gave her the flowers and candy. This is the first time in her life a man gratuitously did anything kind for her. Even her former husband never bought her any gifts, all he wanted was sex for his gratification; she obliged every time. Granted, tonight she is smiling for another reason. Don is in her apartment, and available to satisfy her desires, and not only his.

The flowers are artfully arranged in a glass vase she found in a closet, and she put the candy down on her cocktail table after opening it and sampling a piece or two. Khara stood in front of him, placed her arms around his neck while she pulled him in closer to her body, and passionately kissed him. His smelling fresh also made her happy Don, at the moment, is there for her. She liked the aroma of his cologne so she took him by his hand, and he followed her into her bedroom.

About three hours later, after both finished showering together, they dressed and left her place and headed out for a late night dinner.

Don started to drive to Victory Boulevard where the famous Italian Gardens of Greater Venice restaurant is located. They sat at a rear table at Khara's request with her back to the wall. Khara ordered the veal saltimbocca over angel hair pasta, and he asked the waiter about their eggplant rollatini. The question he wanted to answer is if it is served on a plate or in a hot dish from the oven surrounded by sauce. They also drank a bottle of imported white wine to go with their meals.

In her mind, Khara is now dating an FBI agent and hoped he would be a long-term boyfriend, an understanding and safe man for her to be with. The bonus in the situation for her is Don is an expert on terrorism, and he is hers when he would not be traveling for the FBI. To Khara, he represented the stability Eloise often requested she should search for in a relationship.

***

Once she is ensconced and satisfied with her new place she went out on her days off walking around Port Richmond on Staten Island asking everyone about Gonzalez Boxes. This part of the island is a major Mexican population center, and she thought she would start inquiring around there first. Khara understood if she could not obtain any information on Staten Island her next stop would be in Park Slope which an older section of Brooklyn where another large Mexican enclave lives in the city.

Some days, if her landlord did not have any errands to do, he would travel with her "just to blow the stink off him" and get out of the house, as he is often fond of saying. After he retired from the police force he registered as a licensed private investigator by New York State. Now he is able to do part-time investigative work for insurance companies on those days they gave him an assignment. If the insurance company has a workers compensation claim in Staten Island or Brooklyn he is usually hired to investigate it and make sure the claimant is not faking an injury. His hours are of his own making, and he enjoyed doing it. When he is not working he becomes bored, and he would often trek along with Khara to keep her company. He knew better from his years as an investigator than to be involved in her search, and he kept his distance; since it is in Spanish, and he only spoke Brooklynese. As her unpaid security escort he would always sit in the car and listen; his hands on his lap, his coat unzipped, ready to draw his gun if needed.

Although retired he is a good looking mature man and still actively fit. Early mornings he goes out every day to walk the neighborhood for exercise, and he is always armed at the waist. Khara learned his wife passed away only two years before, and on some evenings when the weather is not too hot or cool, he would invite her upstairs to enjoy a barbeque on his second story rear deck. They drank some beers and relaxed together watching television after supper. They did this a few times, but she did not want to make it a habit. Khara didn't want to ruin a good situation by getting frisky with him and having to move out because he couldn't keep up sexually with her. So it is only an occasional type of thing for her to meet with him for barbecues in the evenings.

It is a Thursday at work when Khara asked around the precinct if there are any dance clubs on the island she could go to. Feeling the urge, she occasionally needed some romance when Don is out of town on an FBI assignment, and she is tired of sitting home alone at night and weekends. One of the detectives told her of a place off Victory Boulevard he heard is a hot dance club so she is anxious to go there.

One afternoon after finishing her shift she arrived home, took a nice scolding shower, used her favorite coconut body wash, and ironed the clothes she is going to wear for her evening out at the club. Tonight she is looking forward to a fun night of dancing and conceivably meeting someone new for a quick hook up. After getting dressed she ate a light snack of six Oreos and a beer at dinner time. For an hour or so she sat on her sofa and read the day's newspaper. After finishing her Heineken she glanced at her wrist to see the time and rose to leave. She put on her jacket and took her time walking downstairs to the garage. Entering her used M3 that she recently bought she drove to the dance club by the back Route 440 highway.

The sun set a while ago and the place is illuminated with huge spotlights beaming onto the building. As she pulled into the parking lot she stopped at the front door next to an awning where the valet sign is situated. A young man ran over to her driver's side door and opened it for her. Khara gave him the keys to the M3 and a five dollar tip.

"Please be careful when you park it, okay?"

"I will thank you."

With great care, he took it to the side of the building in full view of the entrance where other high-end cars are placed. This gave a positive impression to people who are coming to the club. Management wanted guests to feel it is an upscale atmosphere, and to come for an evening of dancing, entertainment, and drinking.

Wearing tight jeans that looked as if they are painted on her, a pink cotton form-fitting sweater which highlighted her figure, her leather jacket hiding her gun, and her now trademark boots she entered the main lobby with an air of confidence. Her hair is not in a true afro style but flared out enough to give the effect of one.

The music is loud, the people on the dance floor are squeezed shoulder to shoulder jumping to the music, and she had to wait to find an opening between the crowds standing at the packed bar three rows deep. After a few minutes, someone walked away, and she leaned into the polished mahogany bar ready to order a beer. Khara did not waste a second and told the bartender when he looked at her what she wanted to drink while this good-looking man approached her from her side. She looked at him and placed him somewhere in his mid to late thirties. He appeared to be over the threshold she made for herself to be with a man. The real young guys she only bothered with when she needed someone with stamina. This evening she wanted to relax, take in some casual fun dancing, and see if there is someone who she could relate to. This man seemed old enough to her so she answered him when he moved even closer to her.

"Hey, great looking outfit you're wearing," he said to her.

With a wise-ass reply she dryly responded to him; "thank you, I never heard a pickup line like it before, that's an original."

He smiled at her and stood to the right side of Khara at the bar. She liked the fact this man has an intriguingly pleasant smile. Khara thought to herself he smelled like he used the right amount of a better man's cologne, and he didn't have bad breath. He is dressed in a dark navy blue sports coat with his collared print shirt opened about three buttons worth exposing his moderately hairy muscular chest, and wearing nicely pressed and straight pleated slacks. His hair is full and brushed back with a slight touch of gray at the temples.

"Can I compliment you? I think you are pretty, can I buy you a drink?"

"I'll have a Heineken, thank you."

"Is this your first time here? I don't remember seeing you at the club before."

"A friend at work recommended this place to me. I moved to Staten Island recently, and I needed to get out a little. What's your name?"

"Alfonse, but you can call me Al. My friends call me Al."

The noise from the music is booming out of the huge speaker's suspended from the walls, and they must speak up to be heard.

"My name is Khara. My friends call me Khara."

She said it to him with a smile while showing her white teeth, and an assertive attitude.

"I like a girl with balls."

"What is amazing Al... is that's also how I like my men."

He smiled back at her when she responded with a smartass answer.

"Listen Khara, I manage this club for my uncle. How about we go sit on the balcony where it's a little quieter, and we can talk. What do you say?"

"I would like that Al. Lead the way."

They took their drinks with them as he escorted Khara with her hand in his, and led her through the jammed dance floor to the elevator at the back of the room. It is not a big one, as elevators go. It holds around six people if it is packed full, and they are alone in it. As the elevator took its time traveling up to the second level she wrapped her arms around his neck, pressed it against his body pressing him to the wall, and lustfully placed her lips against his. He enjoyed the passionate smooch, and put his arms tightly around her waist, and reciprocated the kiss.

In a few seconds, the door opened and he took her to a curved high walled tufted dark blue leather booth overlooking the crowded floor below. He motioned for her to slide in first. He waited for Khara to sit, and following her Al slid over towards the middle of the booth next to her, their shoulders touching as they sat watching the people dance to the music.

The dance crowd beneath them is moving to the loud beat of the music, the strobe lights are flashing, but it is a bit quieter where they are sitting due to the high-walled booth keeping a lot of the background noise out so they could talk. The lighting in the balcony is subdued, and Khara felt somewhat relaxed in the semi-enclosed booth. From where she has situated her back is to the wall so she could see the elevator door and the stairway next to it. She found it hard to totally relax.

"So Khara, tell me why do you carry a gun on you? I would like to know how you walked past my security guys out front. When we kissed in the elevator I felt your shoulder holster under your jacket."

Khara smiled at him.

"Getting in is the easy part, finding a man I like is much harder. As I approached the front entrance the big bouncer guy you employ by the large glass doors blocked me from coming in. He asked if he could pat me down. So I got real close to him, put my hand on his pants zipper, gently squeezed while I smiled at him, and I asked if he would like to talk two octaves higher? He said I could go in now. Oh, and by the way Al...He's not that big" Khara told him with a smirk on her face.

"What an asshole and I'll bet Big Boy never searched in your pocketbook either."

"Nope, I sometimes carry my detective's badge in it if I don't wear it around my neck and a .38 snub nose in it too. My .45 I wear under my jacket. Sometimes I need them for self-defense. There are some crazy drug dealers out there who want me dead."

"I can relate to what you said. My uncle, who owns this dance club, has a problem similar to yours at times. However, he has friends who protect him. So why is a cop who is carrying coming into my club? If you are here to shoot someone you would have done it by now."

"I don't want to knock off anyone at the moment Al. I'm just looking for some fun tonight. You married?"

"Nope never was. I can't find the right girl I'm meant to be with. Plus I'm having a fantastic time managing this club. I'm able to meet gorgeous girls like you all the time. Why would I want to be married?"

"I don't know either. My shrink keeps telling me to look for the right one and to settle down with a steady guy, except I didn't find him yet."

A young waitress in a tight-fitting sequined red outfit walked over to them bringing two more beers to their table with a bowl of popcorn. She left them and took the elevator back downstairs. Khara reached over, took a handful of popcorn, and sat back to munch on them. Al picked up a bottle of beer, took a swig or two, and turned to face her. He put the bottle down, held her face between his two hands bringing her closer to him, and started to kiss her.

While they embraced in the booth Khara ran her fingers through his hair, and she whispered in his ear if they could "go somewhere more private."

He still smelled good to her so she is still interested in him.

Al smiled, stood, and again he grabbed her by the hand helping her to stand and walk away from the booth. They took the elevator down to the main floor and prepared to leave the club. They walked out the main entrance hand in hand when he stopped by the door under the awning. The head valet saw him and ran to bring Al's new red Cadillac. He didn't need to take out a ticket to retrieve his car, and in a short time, it appeared in front of the doorway where they are standing. Before they walked down the steps to get to the vehicle Al glanced at Big Boy, who stopped her on her way in. "We'll talk later," he said to him as Big Boy observed them walk to the car together. The young valet opened the passenger door for Khara, and she slid in the front bucket seat. Inhaling the rich aroma of the new car leather interior she smiled to herself while Al walked around to the driver's side, pushed the electric button to automatically bring it back to his comfort setting, and sat in his plush saddle leather bucket seat. Once he felt comfortable in his seat he drove away from the club.

***

It is an uneventful cruise into Brooklyn this night. There is no traffic to speak of on the Verrazano Bridge at two in the morning. The brightness of nighttime Manhattan is shining on the waters of New York Harbor, and Khara thought the view from the top of the bridge is pretty cool. She drove over the Verrazano so many times, but never experienced the opportunity to check out the sights of the city at night. She tilted her seat back a little, and relaxed while looking out her window.

The car's satellite radio is tuned to a Sinatra station; they are playing a lot of the soft mellow standards he made famous. During the time in his car, as she is wistfully listening, Khara confirmed to herself he is definitely somehow associated with an organized crime syndicate. At that exact moment, she didn't care. She felt this is a relaxing ride with a good looking man, and the world is not baying at her door.

Taking a quick right turn Al took the ramp off the bridge into the Bay Ridge section of Brooklyn. Khara saw in the side view mirror Staten Island right behind her. His condo is in an apartment house which is situated on a large hill and is in an above average tall building for the area. He stopped in front of the underground garage door, pressed the gate opener, and went into the basement; where he parked in his usual space. His three reserved parking spots are contiguous; he always took the space in the middle of the three.

This way no one could open their car door, slam it into his new car and damage or ding it.

He opened his door and walked around the rear of the car to open Khara's door. He held her hand as he helped her out of the Cadillac. They strolled arm in arm to the basement elevator door and took the lift to his floor.

They are walking in the brightly colored hallway when they soon came to his apartment. Al always kept his interior lights off. His wide picture window at the other end of the room allowed enough ambient light to enter so it is not necessary to turn on the ceiling light fixtures. Khara walked over to the glass to peer out. As she stood by the large window in his living room she realized Al's condo overlooked New York Harbor, with the floodlights shining on the Statue of Liberty as ships sailed into the harbor. Al turned on the apartment lights in the living room using a low setting with a dimmer switch. Satisfied with the mood lighting he walked over to his stereo unit on the bookcase, tuned in some slow standards music for a romantic background effect, and put his hands on her waist.

He asked Khara if she would like to dance. Before she could say anything he took her in his arms, they moved at a slow pace around the room cheek to cheek, and belly to belly as they danced to the enchanting sounds of the music. After the first Mel Tormé song is over Al embraced her close to him, and their lips met. Without saying a word he took her by her hand, and they entered his bedroom.

The next morning about eleven she awoke to the aroma of freshly brewed coffee.

"Good morning Khara are you ready for some breakfast? My housekeeper came in early this morning and made some espresso for us, some thick Challah

French toast with berries, and buttered corn muffins she freshly baked for us in the convection oven. Get up, and come get some. Please forgive me, I also meant to tell you before we went to bed there's a silk robe from Bloomingdales by your side of the bed for you to wear. You can keep it if you want. It's my gift to you."

"I don't need the robe this morning, thanks. But I may take it with me anyway. It looks nice, and the fabric is luxurious and soft. Thanks again."

Not wearing any clothes, Khara sat up in bed and looked around the room. It is handsomely decorated and is in earth-toned masculine colors. Last night it was dark and she didn't notice anything about the room. She thought he must have hired a professional interior designer do it. The plush carpet felt nice on the bottom of her feet as she stood to go to the bathroom. Khara wanted to splash some water on her face to help her wake up. After drying her face with the softest towel she ever felt in her life she walked naked into the kitchen. Confidently she entered the room while her caramel skin contrasted against the custom colored ultra-white finish of the Italian lacquered kitchen cabinets, and imported genuine white Carrera marble floor from Northern Italy.

She pulled out a chair and sat opposite him at a small round clear glass table. There is a plate full of Challah French toast waiting for her, and a cup of espresso to the right of her knife and spoon.

Raising his head up from eating, he saw her and smiled. "Thank you for a wonderful and exciting evening Khara; I enjoyed every moment. After you are dressed I'll drive you back to the club so you can get your car."

Without being asked he passed the pure Vermont maple syrup over for her to use. "It's actually

68

organic gourmet syrup. I think you'll like it. I bought it the last time I was skiing near Bennington."

"Thanks, Al. I enjoyed last night also. You are good and have a lot of stamina. Maybe we can do it again soon."

Without missing a beat he mentioned to her he is interested in getting together with her, and meeting again, maybe even that night.

"I can't tonight. I'm working the late shift since I'm still new at the precinct. I'll give you my card with my cell number on it. Call me tomorrow morning, we can set a date. You do realize I'm up to doing it again, now. Why wait, how about you Al?"

"I would like that."

Smiling from ear to ear he could not contain his pleasure.

***

After he dropped her off at the club so she could get her car Khara is driving home when Don called on her cell phone.

"Hey Khara its Don, are you doing anything today?"

"No, I don't need to be at work till later tonight. Want to come over for lunch?"

"That sounds good to me. I'll pick up a few sandwiches for us. I'm in the Midwood section of Brooklyn and there's a kosher deli on the next block. Their pastrami is out of this world, I've had it before. See you in about an hour or so. I need to travel again tomorrow, and I want to see you before I go away. I'll be gone for a while, and I'll miss you."

"I'll miss you also. I'm looking forward to having lunch with you today."

She is excited to be with him again, and not only for eating a delicious kosher hot pastrami on rye. Later when he showed up at her home they hugged and kissed hello at the door, and went into her kitchen to eat their sandwiches.

"So where is the FBI sending you this time?"

"I can't talk to you about specifics but it's a southern border state. I am investigating a cartel which has been designated a terrorist group since the Times Square shootings."

"Is it the Ecru Cartel?"

"Khara, you know I'm not supposed to comment on an investigation, but yes. There is no question they are a vicious group who has no compunction to murder whoever they want. You need to be very cautious when you deal with them."

"Tell me about it" she said sarcastically as she placed her hand on the scar under her hair where they shot her.

"Khara I am giving you my Emergency Homeland Security phone number. It will connect you to me no matter where in the world I am. It bypasses all other cell traffic. The number routes through FBI headquarters in Washington. If you are ever in a situation and need me, call this number" as he wrote it on the back of his business card.

Khara reached across the table and took the card. She looked at the number, memorized it, knowing maybe sometime in the future she might need it. She stood and bent forward over the small table to give him a thank you kiss.

After they finished lunch she and Don cleaned up in the kitchen, and she led him by the hand to her newly furnished bedroom.

***

Three days passed before Al called Khara for another date. She is on her dinner break one night when he, at last, found the time and called her.

"Hey Khara, it's Al. Sorry, I didn't call sooner but I have been busy at the club. An emergency came up and my uncle needed me to do some errands for him upstate New York."

"Hey yourself, I thought we are going to get together before now. I had a good time with you the other day. So when are we going out again?"

It is not that Khara missed him, but she missed the lustful sex. Al is able to keep up with her, and not many men have the stamina to do that, and do it on a continual basis.

"Khara I'm sorry about not calling you sooner. Tell me when you are available, and I'll be there."

"How about we hook up later tonight Al? After I get off my shift I want to go home to change, and I can be at your club around two in the morning."

"Okay, meet me there at two, and don't hurt Big Boy at the front door. He's afraid of you now. He thought you were going to rip his manhood off."

Khara laughed, confirmed the time, and hung up, ending the conversation. She knew she is playing with fire. After asking the other police officers in her precinct office when she went back to work about the club, and organized crime, the other officers validated for her it is a front for a major underworld criminal syndicate. She thought it would be okay if she is careful about what she said to him, both in person and on the phone. Khara knew the organized crime unit of the police department must be watching him, and also recording everything which is being said in his condo and his office too. But she is like a bear to honey and the honey is just too good and sweet to resist.

Chapter 6 -

The moment Khara drove up to the club the valets are waiting for her by the entry awning. Her arrival is expected. The tall young man waiting by the awning ran over to the car and grabbed her driver's side door to let her out. Giving the valet her car keys, a generous ten dollar tip, and walking to the entrance to go in she is ready to rock and roll. Big Boy, who stopped her the first time now smiled at her and opened the embossed glass front door for her to go inside. Big Boy is a long time employee of the club, and he knew better than to piss off the boss's new girlfriend.

The moment Khara arrived a waitress notified Al she is waiting in the main lobby. Al is walking at a fast clip to the entry area as he wanted to greet her when she entered the club. With tenderness, he kissed her on the lips and escorted her to the side cafe for a bite to eat. The small restaurant served a lot of finger foods, burgers, fries and Philly cheese steak sandwiches, and ten different beers on tap from the perky young waitresses. The club only took cash in the dining room and bar, but Al didn't need to pay. The food is a fringe benefit for him; now and then along with the waitresses.

After eating they sat at the table and enjoyed some small conversations about what kind of music they each enjoyed listening to. Without hesitation, Khara said she liked the oldies with some new stuff mixed in. While talking Al acknowledged he dug the old standards like Mel Tormé, Sinatra, Vic Damone and other singers of that genre. The chatter was about nothing important so he suggested they leave and go to his place for a nightcap. With a smile on her face, she agreed to go and insisted she take her car, not his. Thinking his face seemed a little puzzled she thought he must be wondering why she wanted to drive tonight, and not him. Al decided not to argue with her and agreed with her driving instead of him as she placed her hand on his lap, and rubbed his inner thigh to send a silent message to him.

The waitress came over, and he signed off on the check. They stood and left the dining area as he held her by the arm and approached the front door to leave. Again Big Boy opened the door for them, and the valet drove Al's red Cadillac to the entrance area for him to enter. Waving the car back Al asked for Khara's car to be brought up by the awning.

The car she owned is a five-year-old BMW M3 with a six-speed manual stick shift she purchased from Marko Used Cars and Trucks when she moved to Staten Island. The M3 is outfitted with enlarged custom chrome twin exhausts, an eight-cylinder engine, and is a hot looking polished midnight black color. Khara enjoys the experience of feeling the unrestrained energy when she drives her powerful car.

Both of them buckled their seat belts as she took off spinning out the rear wheels while burning rubber in the parking lot. Shifting from first to second like a pro she pressed the gas pedal to the floor and pulled onto Interstate 440 before the traffic merges from the Goethals Bridge.

"Khara I'm not used to being driven this fast. Did you insist on driving us to Brooklyn because you are experiencing suicidal tendencies tonight?"

"No Al, I am not suicidal, at least not at this moment. I wanted to ask your advice about locating a company I'm having trouble finding. Your car might be bugged, and I must be cautious about where I talk about certain things."

"That's always a possibility...what information can I help you with?"

"Do you recall about six months ago or so there was a big shootout in Brooklyn, and a housing police officer was killed along with some drug dealers? The city had a huge procession for him with the governor and mayor attending. The officer's funeral was on all the national television stations and also the newspapers."

"Yer, I do kind of remember the funeral procession. Are you telling me you are the hero cop who shot all those people?"

"Yes," Khara answered as she upshifted to fifth gear when the road merged onto the Staten Island Expressway.

"Crap, I didn't put two and two together before. Now I recognize you from the television news shows. Your face was all over the place. The papers said you were shot and killed in the Times Square ambush. A lot of cops and innocent tourists were also murdered that day. Yer, I remember now."

"Well lucky for you Al I wasn't killed. That was a false report and was released to mislead the cartel off my back; my old partner's also. No one else is aware but I have a lead on a shipping company that might be importing drugs into the country, and I am having difficulty finding them. The Cartel must be stopped before they finally figure out I'm still alive and try to kill me again. My personal search needs someone with contacts on the docks in Port Newark to find out if they are located in that area. The company could be under a different importing name. I don't know, but I'm not able to come across them."

Approaching the Verrazano Bridge Khara downshifted to third gear, and flew through the empty toll booths going about eighty miles an hour heading into Brooklyn; cruising on the upper level of the bridge. Just as she drove off the Verrazano Al is now sweating profusely from nerves, and when she made the sharp right turn off the exit ramp, and onto the Bay Ridge streets he red-knuckled the door handle. Only a red light stopped her as the car's engine rumbled with power through its twin exhaust pipes; ready to go again.

"Now I must shower when I get home," he remarked to Khara, wiping the perspiration from his brow.

"Good idea Al; think I'll join you."

There is a big smile is on his face when she answered him.

Reaching out her window to press the door opener Al told her the numbers to input into the security pad on the side of the garage entrance. The pin number worked and the huge metal door lifted up. Driving into the underground parking area she stopped in one of Al's three spots. Before she went upstairs with him she hurried around her car and opened his door for him. The passenger door opened and he stood, while Khara standing next to him pressed her body against his chest, and kissed him on the lips while wrapping her arms around his neck. Murmuring in a soft voice in his ear she said "I'm looking for Gonzalez Boxes, and I need your uncle's help. You must be careful when you speak about the name to anyone. The Ecru Cartel from Mexico is behind this company, and they want to kill me."

Bending his head back he stared right in her face. Assuring her, AL said he would be cautious when he speaks to his uncle. Taking her hand and interlocking their fingers Al led her upstairs to his condo.

***

The next day she drove back to Staten Island, dropped Al off at his club so he could get his car, and returned to her home to get ready for work. Feeling tired, yet relaxed after another satisfying evening with Al, Khara is a little anxious about what he could find out for her. The steaming morning shower helped soothe her anxiety. The scented coconut body wash she favored also appeared to calm her down, and now she is in a more serene state of mind. When she is finished drying off she reached into her medicine cabinet, grabbed the Chanel No.5, and dabbed on her favorite perfume in a few intimate places.

After getting dressed she walked out of her apartment to go to work and waved to her landlord wishing him a good day. Inspecting his lawn he is standing on the sidewalk in front of his house when she sat in her M3, and tranquility drove off like a normal person for a change.

The streets in her development are curved with the homes built too close to one another. Staten Island was developed willy nilly with as many houses as the developers wished to build with no government restraint or oversight. There is no logical reasoning for most of the street layouts in the borough. A tremendous amount of houses are clustered together due to lax zoning laws on Staten Island. In many of the developments, the builders forgot (?) to allow for adequate parking for guests so curb space is at a premium.

Children are known to run between parked vehicles out onto the street, and Khara for some unknown reason is aware of it today. There seemed to be more cars parked on the both sides of the street this day. This changed a one lane each way into a one lane only street where an oncoming car would have to pull into a driveway in order for another vehicle to pass. Khara realized this made for a perfect ambush situation. The Times Square firefight still haunted her and is on her mind often.

Being cautious she maneuvered through the curving narrow streets until she was approaching the heavily traveled main intersection directly ahead of her. The traffic light is changing to red as Khara started to drive towards it. She noticed a Latino man standing on the corner on each side of the intersection.

There is no bus stop on either corner, and she grew suspicious as to why they would be there. Stepping on the brakes she slowed her M3 down as she approached the intersection, she un-holstered her .45 and slid the safety off. With a lot of care, she held it in her right hand as she downshifted into second gear. Lowering both side windows as she reached the red light at the corner Khara raised the pistol almost to window height, yet still out of pedestrian view.

If there is going to be an ambush she felt at least one of the men are going to die. Although prepared to shoot, she is also ready to press the accelerator to the floor, and if needed zoom out into traffic; red light or not.

The two men, one on each corner seemed to glance at the black car creeping at a snail's pace down the street towards them.

Straining to hear, and from a closing distance, she saw them shouting to one another. The men yelled something in Spanish but she could not clearly understand what they are saying. The M3 is getting closer to them when they turned and started to walk away from the corner going in opposite directions.

Relaxed after noticing them leave the corners she slid the safety back on her gun and placed it on the passenger seat next to her. With trepidation, her car entered the intersection when the light turned green as she sped across the road to the other side, and drove away taking a deep slow breath to calm herself. The thought flashed across her mind she might have tipped off someone in the Spanish community when she was asking about Gonzales Boxes.

Now slightly on edge she parked her car near the precinct and ambled in only to find out she has a new partner. The desk sergeant told her he is waiting for her upstairs. Walking up to the detective's office on the second floor she is told, on the way, her new partner would be in her cubicle, and anxious to meet her.

Cautiously she turned the corner into her desk area, and there sitting in her chair is Matt. Upon seeing each other they both smiled and hugged. At his request, he transferred to her precinct to be with her again. After being partners for the past few years he missed working with her. He is aware, no matter what happened, she would have his back. Emotionally she could care less, but understood he would always be there for her; plus they worked well together.

A 911 call came in where a body had been found in a two family home. Both of them are assigned to the case, and they went to the street address in an unmarked car. The house is a typical up and down home in Staten Island. There are literally tens of thousands of the same type home all over Richmond County.

The marked squad cars were waiting there for them with uniformed officers, and they are cordoning off the entry to preserve the crime scene. Their car stopped and blocked the driveway. Seeing a uniformed officer by the entrance both of them walked into the open door of the first-floor apartment.

The uniformed officer told them the landlady, who lives upstairs, called 911 when she came down to collect the rent. The landlady said the victim's front door was not closed so she came in, and saw the body on the living room carpet.

Matt asked where the landlady is now, the officer standing by the front door told him she is in the second-floor apartment, and he hurried upstairs to speak to her. While he is talking with the landlady Khara entered the victim's apartment and began to poke around.

The victim, an as yet unidentified male, is sprawled out on the carpet with what appeared to Khara to be multiple wounds. The long blood-soaked carving knife on the floor a few feet from the body made it easier for her to ascertain as to how he died. The next question to be answered is who did it, and why they did it.

Looking around she saw it appeared to be the usual bachelor apartment. Big screen television, a stereo system with huge boom box speakers, and TV dinners in the freezer. The fridge is full of beer; there are bags of pretzels, popcorn and packaged Hostess chocolate cupcakes in the cupboard.

The apartment is a mess, and she noticed when she walked into his bedroom his bed is not made. The nightstand drawer is pulled all the way out, and in it are dozens of unused condoms. She thought it is a typical single young guys bedroom.

Turning to her left she walked into the bathroom, and it is disgusting. The tub appeared like it has not been cleaned in months, if not years, and the room smelled awful.

The shower tiles are not clean, and hanging over the shower curtain rod is a hot pink bra. Raising her arm she took it down and inspected it. The embroidery on it is from a custom bra maker, La Charita Bra. That bra is only sold in high-end department stores, or at designer trunk shows. From her past experience, Khara understood The La Charita Bra Company has two lines of bras. The company's regular high-end line and a luxury one which is hand fitted and which would have the purchasing woman's name embroidered on the back strap. The name on this bra strap is "Flor Pequeña

[Little Flower] in Spanish. Khara knew it is a costly bra because she owns a few of them herself, but only a small number of women would spend that kind of money on it themselves. In most cases, a boyfriend, or a lover, would buy one for a woman to gain favor with them.

Those bras are handmade and expensive, but she also knew they are comfortable form-fitting, and worth every penny they cost. Eloise in the past bought Khara a few of them. She was told they are a reward for not sending anyone to the hospital for a whole year. Now she felt whoever belonged to this bra, and left it there is sure to be the killer.

Of course, Khara lifted the top of the water tank on the toilet as a procedural process only, but there is nothing in it. Old habits die hard.

Matt called downstairs for her to come up and speak to the landlady. Sometimes, when a second or third person asks the same questions they could obtain somewhat of a different answer.

When Khara opened the door to the second-floor landlady's apartment the stench of filth overcame her. Walking into the living room where they are standing Matt introduced his partner to the landlady.

"Don't you ever fucking clean this place?"

There was a moment of shocked silence from the landlady. "Yes, every so often I do."

"That's bullshit and you know it."

Now Khara is standing only a foot or two from her. "You are fucking unbelievable. You stink, when was the last time you took a fucking shower?"

Matt now had to step back a few feet from the woman, he could not stand too close to her either.

"I shower, and I clean my home also!"

In a stern tone of voice, Khara told her to stay there with Matt as she walked around the place looking for something, anything she thought might be useful in the investigation. First, she opened all the windows in the apartment to have some fresh air flow through it before speaking to her.

Strolling into the bathroom she saw it is as filthy as the one downstairs. Hanging over the shower curtain bar are two unwashed bras. One is a La Charita Bra in pink with the same color, and embroidered name, as the bra downstairs in the victim's apartment.

Khara left it in the bathroom and came back to ask the woman if she knew if the victim had any girlfriends.

"My tenant is only here about a year, and we only went out together on dates a few times. I didn't keep track of his friends."

"How long ago did you date him?"

"The last time I had been intimate with him was about six months ago. Only when I have to clean or get the rent do I go down there, usually on the first of each month to collect the rent. Otherwise, I don't enter his apartment."

Khara continued the questioning.

"Do you think maybe a jealous girlfriend might have killed him?"

"Could be, he liked it rough, and sometimes he would lose it and hit me hard when we were in bed. I wouldn't be surprised if some girl had enough of the abuse, fought back, and stabbed him."

"Why do you think it is a girl?"

"Don't know, just saying."

Sensing in her bones she is the killer, Khara couldn't yet prove it.

"Do you know anybody by the name of Little Flower?"

"Yer, that's my nickname. He used to call me Little Flower in Spanish. See he even paid for me to tattoo it on my forearm."

The woman extended her arm, and on the underside, by her left wrist is the inscription Flor Pequeña.

"And you said you only dated him six months ago?"

"Yer, that's about right, I think. It's hard to remember each time when we went out together on a date."

"Do you have a copy of the lease available?" Matt asked.

"Yes sir, it's right here in the kitchen drawer. Here it is."

Matt started to read it. The lease is handwritten and is apparently not professionally prepared by a lawyer. "This is strange, I don't understand something. How come a lawyer didn't make this lease for you?"

"Why spend the money, I wrote it myself. It's kind of legal enough, and he signed it because he didn't care, and paid me two months' rent as a deposit."

In the middle of reading it, Matt stopped, and peered up at her for a moment, and made a comment regarding the lease. "The lease says you will also clean the apartment weekly as part of the rent he will be paying you."

"Yer, he was upset because I didn't do it as well as he thought I should."

Exasperated from the gabbing Khara reached her breaking point with this woman. The apartment stunk, her patience is gone, and she couldn't hold it in anymore.

"Listen bitch, I'm so pissed off at you. Tell me why you fucking killed him before I rip your tongue out of your fucking mouth!"

Startled, the woman started to tear up as Khara began to approach her in a menacing manner.

"I don't know, it is one of those things, you know, I didn't mean to kill him. That bastard was yelling at me because he accused me of giving him an STD. He is my pimp, and dealer, I'm a heroin addict. A few years ago I used to be a high-class escort for him. Last year when he bought the house he decided I should sign as the owner so he could hide his income from the IRS. Last night he started to beat me, and I freaked out. It was either him or me, I had to stab him, or I'd end up like the other two girls in the freezer."

"What freezer?"

There is a silent awkward pause to the conversation.

"Holy shit, we must to get down to the garage and see what's in there."

Matt put her in handcuffs, and the three of them walked down to the street level with a few uniformed officers tagging along to see where the other bodies are hidden.

A young probationary officer opened the large garage door and everybody walked in. Sitting at the rear of the garage against the far wall is a white lift top deep freezer chest. Putting on her latex gloves, Khara picked up the hinged top door to the freezer and peered inside.

The two uniformed officers held the killer by her arms as Matt and Khara saw at least two women's bodies intertwined in the deep chest; covered in ice. Later in the investigation, the coroner's office found three women frozen together in the freezer chest.

On the way back to the precinct when Matt and Khara are alone in the car Matt mentioned the woman was never read her rights when Khara questioned her and intimidated her into confessing.

"No you're wrong Matt. I distinctly heard you read them to her. Besides I am sure the knife which was next to the victim's body will be plastered with her fingerprints on it. The lab people will find them I'm sure. No sweat."

The police released the information of the arrest and murders to the news media later in the day but left Khara out of the limelight. Matt is publicly credited with the investigation. The department wanted to keep Khara in a low profile situation for her safety. Her personnel file recorded her with the arrest along with Matt. The television stations ran it on the six and eleven o'clock news shows, and she is never mentioned.

Chapter 7 -

Khara started writing a report about a minor incident Matt and she had been on when a call is received into the detectives' squad. Soon after the call came in they would leave the precinct before finishing their paperwork.

The call is from a parent who said her son is missing. The mother is frantic on the phone. The boy did not come home from school, and she believed something is wrong. The woman said he always gets off the bus at the corner and is home by three thirty every afternoon. The mother said she called his junior high school and was told by the attendance officer he never arrived in the morning, and she is afraid he was kidnapped. Khara told her she would be coming to her home to speak to her.

Matt is driving and he decided not to take the highway. The bumper to bumper traffic on Staten Island is horrendous, and they wanted to arrive at the call as soon as possible. So he drove through all the connecting side streets as fast as the slow traffic would allow.

The woman lived in a typical Staten Island two family house. The mother's apartment is on the first floor and she is standing in the driveway with her phone in her hand waiting for them to arrive.

With tears streaming down her face she retold her story again to both of them as quick as she is able to talk, between crying and hysterics.

The mother is asked by Matt to describe her son to them.

"My son is only ten and a half years old and is short for his age. I know he seems like he is seven or eight, not even eleven. Unfortunately, he appears to everyone as a younger boy."

Khara asked the mother "does he carry a cell phone?"

"Yes, he does. For his eleventh birthday, we bought a reconditioned iPhone from a friend of the family for him. The phone is cheap, and he is told to only use the phone in an emergency. But he didn't call me. That's why I think something terrible has happened to him."

Khara is aware the FBI would not be involved unless they thought the boy is known to be brought out of state. Without waiting she called her commanding officer and started the ball rolling with the NYPD. In the meantime, Matt approached the mother with a question.

"Can I have his cell phone number and password? I have an iPhone also, and I can track him if you use Find iPhone on his phone."

Luckily she previously set Find iPhone up. A family friend showed them how the iPhone works, and he turned the app on in case the phone is ever lost.

Given the security information by the mother, he is able to obtain a reading for the boy's iPhone in one of the developments in Staten Island.

Both of them hopped in the squad car and drove to the Route 440 back highway with their siren on, and lights flashing. Khara called in the location they are going and asked for backup to meet them at the suspect's house.

Matt turned off his siren as they approached the street they believed the boy is on. As he arrived at the house where the phone indicated the young boy should be in he pulled into the driveway, and they exited the police car.

The dwelling is a small summer bungalow type home near the Kill Van Kull which was winterized years ago and converted to year-round use. The exterior paint is peeling, roof shingles are missing or bent upwards from the result of heavy storm winds, and garbage is strewn all over the property.

In the distance as the other squad cars are approaching their location, they are able to hear their sirens wailing.

"Matt, stay in the front till the other officers arrive while I go around the rear to cover the back entrance."

Enclosing the yard is a rusted metal chain link fence. She opened the gate while hurrying to the back of the house with her gun in her hand. Her badge is hanging on a chain around her neck flapping up and down as she ran as fast as possible to the backyard.

Checking his phone again Matt wanted to make sure the signal is still in the house he is standing in front of. The phone is still indicating the boy is in the dwelling.

Believing he has probable cause he and the backup police officers broke the door in, and scrambled inside. Matt listened to a rattling in the back of the house, and he called Khara the perp would be running out the back exit.

Aware someone will be coming her way she braced herself and is ready to take down whoever ran out the back door.

Suddenly the rotting wooden door in the back-flung open, and this disheveled vagrant-looking guy lunged out of the building and right into the fist of Khara's right hand. His uncombed hair sprung out from his head due to the jolt of her striking his face. Gushing blood from his broken nose, dazed from the impact, he is knocked backward and slammed against the now closed back door. As he fell to his knees she swung her right leg around kicking him right on the jaw with her boot; spewing blood and a few teeth from his mouth. Dropping to the grass and moaning he held his mouth in both hands in apparent pain.

Approaching him to cuff his hands she bent close to him and smelled a putrid odor emanating from him, due to his not bathing. Repulsed she grabbed his hair and shirt and with all her strength she banged his head to the ground. She rolled him over and cuffed his arms behind his back while holding her breath. Still pissed off she first stomped and then started kicking him in the ribs cracking one or two of them.

In the meantime, Matt and the other officers ran through the house searching for the missing boy. In one of the small side bedrooms, they found him naked, sexually abused, and not conscious on a filthy mattress.

While Matt placed two fingers on his neck checking for a pulse, an ambulance is called to come for the boy. A portable oxygen tank is rushed in from the trunk of a police cruiser to help the child with his breathing.

Hearing the radio dispatcher on the police frequency the local news media sent photographers and television crews to wait outside the house. Focusing on the heart throbbing story they interviewed the officer in charge, and by accident caught Khara walking by in the background. Unknown to her, her image is broadcast nationwide due to the interest of the event.

Khara's cover in Staten Island is now no longer secure.

That night Don is watching the late news while in Texas as an affiliated New York television station reported a human interest story about the found missing Staten Island boy. He recognized her passing by and picked up the hotel phone to call her.

"Khara, this is Don. I recognized you on television passing by behind as your commanding officer is speaking to the local media on camera. If I recognized you, so did a lot of other people. Be extra careful... your cover has been blown."

"Shit. I must tell Matt about this call, and also my captain. This is going to cause trouble because of my picture being shown everywhere."

"Do not wait, be alert, and have a heightened awareness of your surroundings. I'm sure the cartel also recognized you."

"Okay, thanks for the heads up."

Khara decided to wait till she is back at work the next day to speak to Matt because she didn't trust her phone is not bugged. At the precinct the next day Khara called him over to her desk to tell him what she had learned.

"Matt, the FBI notified me last night my cover has been blown."

"How did they discover you?"

"I was spotted walking by in the background when the news reporters were interviewing the captain regarding the missing boy story."

"Crap, that's a big problem Khara. What do you think we should do?"

"The first thing is to tell him, or the lieutenant, about the discovery, and listen to what they recommend"

"Okay, makes sense to me. Let's go downstairs now to tell him about this."

Not wanting to be seen in the front lobby of the precinct they took the rear staircase down to tell the precinct secretary they wanted to speak with their captain. Without hesitation, she picked up her phone and rang him on the private intercom explaining to him the matter is important and both of them are here to talk to him. The captain asked they come into his office right away. He understood from experience they would not be seeing him unless their problem is a serious issue to be dealt with. Both are two experienced detectives, and he trusted them.

"Khara, what's the problem?"

"I was shown in the background on the television reports nationwide while you were interviewed by the reporter for the news yesterday. My cover is blown, and the FBI called to tell me I was recognized."

"The FBI is now on this case? Okay, I now understand the situation a little better. I have to contact the intelligence unit at One Police Plaza and try to understand how they want to handle this. If the news clip is on the all the channels nationwide last night it means the cartel only needs a few days to find out your location in the city, and they'll attempt to hunt you down. In the meantime be careful when you go out on a call. Be alert to where you are at all times."

Matt and Khara nodded in the affirmative when he said that, afterward they went back upstairs to talk about the situation. Between them, they needed to try and come up with some strategy to deflect what they worried about is possibly going to come true.

Chapter 8 -

The cell phone rang as soon as she walked into her apartment after work. Al said he is calling her early in the morning for a date, and also he has some information to tell her. Khara is tired after working a long night shift which never seemed to end. The caller ID told her who is on thee phone so she answered the call and agreed on a time to meet with him. Not wastingg any time she did not hesitate to undress, placing her clothes in the washing machine, and took a shower to try and relax. The coconut body wash, as usual, did the trick for her. After dressing she slipped on her shoulder holster, grabbed her pocketbook with the .38 tucked inside, and went to leave for the club to meet Al.

This time when she started the M3 she went out the rear entrance of the development most of the people who lived near her didn't use. The exit is a further distance from the main entrance in, but for her peace of mind and security, she left using the back way now.

Driving up to the club she stopped by the awning and the valet hopped in her car. Carefully he parked the M3 in front of the other fancy cars. Big Boy smiled at her as she came up to the entrance, and opened the glass door for her without any questions asked. After entering the lobby a hostess not wearing much came up to her and said she will take her to Al's basement office.

Khara entered his office as Al stood from behind the desk and walked over to kiss her. After thanking the girl for bringing her to the office Al quickly closed the door when the woman left.

"Listen Khara, come outside with me. I want to talk to you in a private place."

Taking her by the hand; they went out the rear exit and stood near the dumpsters behind the privacy fence which hid the garbage from view. When they approached the dumpster Al shut the swinging gate to the area and told her his uncle spoke to him in confidence about what she asked him about.

"My uncle said whoever I am helping is in deep shit with a Mexican Cartel. The Cartel wants you dead. The Cartel's leader doesn't believe you were killed in the Times Square ambush because no funeral home was ever mentioned about where your services were to be held, plus last night you were on national television. And you also murdered the Cartel leader's sister, I am told."

Khara acted as if she did not know what he was talking about. But she remembered what the good-looking assassin told her in the police department's psychologist's office hallway before she killed him.

"What sister are you talking about? Whose sister did I kill?"

"The woman you shot and killed in the Brooklyn project is the Ecru Cartel leader's sister. His family's honor is involved, and he wants to avenge her death."

"Shit... I forgot about the fat woman. Yer, I figure I must of pissed someone off that day. They have been trying to murder me for a while. I'll have to deal with the people when they show up. But I want to find out who is behind the drugs and money here in the states. I'll be safe once I find who the person is here in the states that is after me."

"Well, my uncle did ask around and he found out Gonzalez Box Company is not in the area and doesn't exist. But he did learn a load of heroin is being trucked out of Laredo Texas this week and is expected to arrive in a Newark warehouse for storage and distribution in a few days. This shit has to be coming out of Mexico. Khara this is the best information I can come up with for what you are looking for."

"One last favor Al, ask your uncle what warehouse the shipment going to. I'll owe him a big one."

"Okay. I'll tell you what information I can gather as soon as I can."

They opened the gate together and went back to the club. Once inside he took her to sit at a table in the bar area while he walked outside to speak to Big Boy at the door who is standing under the front awning. When he went back in to meet with Khara he told her he asked Big Boy to go talk to his uncle and tell him he is right. And he gets a big favor for this from you."

Big Boy acted as if he did not understand the cryptic message Al told him, but he is smart enough to do as he is told. With Al's car keys in his hand, he left in his Cadillac, drove around for a while, and about two hours later returned to the club.

By now both of them are in the restaurant section having a bite to eat when Big Boy came strolling in and waved to him to come out of the restaurant area for a second to speak to him.

Sitting at the table Khara turned her head and saw Big Boy speaking in hushed tones to Al when Al reached into his pocket and thanked Big Boy with a hundred dollar bill in his hand.

Going back to her in the dining area Al told her they should be going now. Telling her he would talk to her in her car as they went back to his place in Brooklyn.

They walked out to the valet, and Khara's M3 is brought out front for her. Khara said she reserved a "different place to go tonight night," and she drove off with Al sitting next to her.

Al is up for almost anything as he also carried a legal gun on his waist. Since the club is a large cash business he had an easy time obtaining a carry permit. New York City makes obtaining a carry permit almost impossible. But Al obtained one.

Instead of going to Brooklyn Khara pulled off the highway, and parked on the side of the road under the 440 overpass.

"Al, what did your uncle say about Gonzalez Boxes?"

"My uncle did not find out anything about the Gonzales Box Company you asked about. But since you mentioned a Mexican cartel is involved he did find out some stuff. Big Boy filled me in on the details. Next Tuesday a tractor-trailer from Laredo will be pulling into a warehouse in the Iron Bound section of Newark. The trailer will be loaded with all kinds of illegal drugs from Mexico. When we go after it this will be your chance to question someone about Gonzales Boxes."

"My uncle wants to help you. He told me to send some men with you to protect you, in case you need them. Be at my club by eight in the morning next Tuesday. Big Boy will be going with some of the guys in his crew. You'll go with them to Newark."

"I don't need any assistance, Al. I can handle myself pretty well."

"Khara sweetheart, you have no choice. I'm not sure where in Newark the building is. My uncle does, and he won't tell me until next Tuesday morning. So let's go somewhere we can be comfortable, and get the hell out of here."

Realizing he either doesn't know the answer or won't tell her till Tuesday, she decided talking to him anymore under the overpass is useless. Shifting the car into first gear, she burnt rubber heading towards the Bayonne Bridge, and a motel in Jersey City where she called before leaving the club. Khara made a reservation for their all mirrored room at the top level of the motel for the night.

***

Her morning routine, almost every day, consisted of caffeinated coffee, a handful of different vitamins, and some powdered supplements. She couldn't sleep thinking about what is about to go down in Newark in the morning. Now Tuesday is here and the time is about five in the morning when Khara awoke and went to take a shower. After dressing in her usual boots and jeans outfit she decided she would eat her regular breakfast at home instead of at a convenience store.

She put on her shoulder holster, made sure her .38 is secure in her jacket pocket as she didn't want to carry a purse, and slipped the sheath with her thin throwing knife into her right boot. Now she is ready to leave the house for the club, and the meeting in the morning.

Khara drove to the club anticipating what is going to happen. As she came up to the building two cars are parked on the side of the entrance awning with a bunch of men she never met before standing around them, plus Big Boy. She did not understand why Al is not present.

When she pulled up to them Big Boy came over to the car, said Al told him "I am going to go with you, and I'll direct you to where we're going."

When Big Boy sat in the passenger's seat of Khara's car the vehicle started to tilt ever so slightly to the right. He glanced at his wrist and told her "time to leave. Let's go."

As she drove out of the parking lot the other cars followed her onto the expressway going to the Outer Bridge, and into Elizabeth New Jersey.

Heading north on the New Jersey Turnpike Big Boy explained to Khara how they are going to do this job. "We are going to park a block away from the warehouse, and wait until the truck turns off McCarter Highway, and onto the side street. I visited here the other day, and there is only one entrance into the building with a loading dock. A tractor-trailer is too long to enter all the way in so the cab will be out on the sidewalk while they unload the trailer from inside."

Big Boy continued "once they back into the loading dock area the driver will jump out, and start to walk inside the door to the building. The first car will drive up, and block the truck from leaving. My guy in the passenger seat in the first car will jump out, kidnap the driver at gunpoint, and they'll take him a few miles or so away then let him go unharmed."

"In the meantime, a second car will come up; my guy will take the keys from the kidnapped driver and he'll climb into the tractor cab, and drive away. He'll take the trailer somewhere we think is a more secure area. After he leaves you and I pull up and we go inside, and you do what you have to do. I'll be at your side in case you need me to help."

As she is driving Khara asked Big Boy "so who gets the trailer after your guys pull away with it?"

"I don't know the answer to your question. Neither does Al. But I am told for this to go down you are repaying his uncle a favor."

Now Khara understood why she is given all this information and help. Al's uncle is stealing a trailer load of drugs from the cartel, and if anything went wrong she is going to take the fall for the theft. She now knows no one is going to walk out of the warehouse alive if they recognized her. "Shit," she thought to herself while up shifting to fourth gear, and began smiling as she realized the humor of her thoughts. "Eloise is going to be pissed off if I kill a few more people today."

When she approached the Newark Liberty Airport exit she drove off onto Route 21 North. This becomes McCarter Highway and runs through Newark. When they came to the Iron Bound section Big Boy told her what street to turn off on, and go three blocks east, and park.

The time is now a little before nine in the morning. Khara parked the M3 with the two other cars right behind her as they are waiting for the tractor-trailer to arrive.

***

About eleven thirty a truck, at last, pulls up to the building and blows the air horn in three short bursts. The rigid metal loading dock door rises, and the driver begins to back the trailer at a slow and careful pace into the dock to begin unloading the contents.

Once the back part of the trailer is in the building the cars behind Khara drove up to the warehouse. The first car stopped a little ahead of the tractor as the driver is getting out of the cab, and the second car halts right behind the first blocking any chance of the truck exiting.

One man jumps out of each car and at gunpoint kidnaps driver. They put a bag over his head, use plastic ties to secure his hands behind his back, and throw him into the back seat of the first car. The first car waits for his partner to jump in, and keep the driver on the floor of the car when they pull away. They did their part of the heist and drove off with the truck driver secured and safe in the back of the car. This took only seconds for them to do everything. The truck driver is being taken to the parking garage at Newark Airport terminal C. The driver will be released while lying on the concrete floor between two parked cars on an upper level in the rear of the garage and out of sight of video cameras.

Jumping out of the second car one of Big Boy's men took the keys from the kidnapped driver, hopped up into the driver's seat of the tractor's cab, and begins to pull away from the building with the unopened trailer.

The second car rushed to back up to let the truck leave and begins to back up into the loading dock space. Big Boy's man parks the car right under where the door would close preventing the steel gate from shutting. The driver of the car gets out and waves for Big Boy and Khara to drive to his location.

Big Boy and his crew stole a few parked cars the previous night from a commuter lot in Elizabeth. The vehicles are expendable since they are not theirs.

Now Khara drove up, stopped next to the driveway, and ran inside the building with Big Boy while his man guarded Khara's M3.

A handful of Latino men are standing in amazement on the empty concrete dock wondering why the trailer pulled away, and a car parked in the middle of the loading dock doorway. They have no idea what is happening.

With a commanding voice, Khara barked at the men in Spanish asking who is in charge and told them to lay flat face down on the floor. They pointed to a metal enclosed office with small windows at the top of a long flight of steep stairs going straight up two flights.

Being a steep stairway with no middle landing the steps led to an office overlooking the warehouse below.

Big Boy took out his gun, and by waving the pistol at them the men started to lie on the floor. They placed their heads face down, and their arms hiding their eyes.

Running up the steel stairway Khara's boots clanged with every step she took. The noise alerted a man in the office, and he went to open the door to find out who is coming up the stairs so fast. He never bothered to peer down at the loading dock. He is too busy in the back room of the office with a young Mexican girl otherwise he would have known what is happening.

As she reached the top landing the door opened, and an undressed smallish Latino man is standing in the office by the door. Without waiting, Khara lunged at him with both of her hands and pushed him on his chest so hard he fell backward, and landed about five feet away from the door. A naked young girl ran out from the back of the office yelling in Spanish "Ayuadame. Por favor, Ayuadame" [Help me. Please help me.] She told Khara in Spanish she was kidnapped from Mexico a few weeks ago, and became a sex slave for this man. The young girl told her many men are charged money to have sex with her.

Understanding what she is saying Khara raised her hand to signal for her to stop. She spoke her in Spanish to start dressing while she deals with the man on the floor.

He lifted his head and tried to sit upright.

"Who the fuck are you lady?"

Without saying a word Khara grabbed him by his hair and with all her strength smashed his face onto the floor, breaking his nose and some of his front teeth. "I didn't tell you to fuck'n' get up" she yelled at him.

Losing patience, again she yanked his head up by his hair, and asked him who his boss is in Mexico. Blood is now gushing out of his mouth, and he slurred his words as he spoke trying to inhale.

"I can't breathe, I want to stand. My asthma." He said to Khara gasping for air.

Taking his scrawny arm she twisted his forearm upwards and behind his back into a wristlock; so she would be able to control his movements. As she is holding his hand with her vice grip a small red cross tattoo on the underside of his left wrist struck her curiosity.

He is squirming and trying to stand but he needed help. As he reached to grab onto the nearby desk to assist his rising Khara flexed her muscles and slammed his face this time on the side of the metal desk. She demanded to find out who he is working for.

"If I tell you they will kill my family. I can't have my sons killed. They are ruthless." He begged her to allow him to take his asthma medication.

"You can take your meds later, but first you must tell me who your boss is. I don't give a shit if you turn blue and croak."

He began to gasp deeper for air and fell to his knees. "Better tell me or you're not getting any meds."

She screamed in his ear forcing him to wince from the pain, as she started to twist his wrist almost breaking bones. While Khara is dealing with the naked man the teenage girl is getting dressed in a hurry and is shocked at what is happening in front of her. She remained silent while continuing to put on her clothes.

As his lips began to turn blue, his eyes became glassy, and he tried to grasp the desk where his emergency inhaler is he said: "ok, I'll tell you."

Khara stood back a little and let him reach into withdraw his bronchial dilator from the bottom drawer.

On his knees, he hesitated for a second and began to pull out the drawer. Placing put his hand in the drawer to lift out his inhaler she thought he tried to lift out the inhaler with his fingers. Grasping something in his hand, instead of an inhaler, he took out a switchblade knife lunging at her. She grasped his forearm, and twisted his whole arm behind his back, grabbed his hair again, and threw him out of the opened office door. He tumbled down the two flights of steel steps. Khara thought he broke some bones in his legs, arms, and also his neck in the two stories fall. His head is slanted at a ninety-degree angle to his body on the bottom step while he is sprawled out on the hard concrete floor below the step.

The girl is now dressed in the dirty clothes she had been wearing when she came to Newark from Mexico. She stood watching everything but said nothing until Khara turned to her. In Spanish, Khara told the young girl she is safe, and she is to come with her now. Both of them scurried down the steps jumping over the body of the man as he is lying motionless. The young girl stopped long enough to spit at his still body, and she ran out right behind Khara. As they hurried past Big Boy, he turned and followed behind them out of the warehouse. They are joined by the crew member who is watching Khara's car parked outside the building. They all pile into the M3 wanting to make a fast exit. Once inside she drove off.

The young girl sat in the back while Big Boy is again in the front of the car with Khara. She floored the M3 in first and turned at the next corner and followed Big Boy's directions back to the turnpike.

As they are driving on the turnpike extension to Bayonne Khara asked the girl in Spanish how she ended up in the warehouse in Newark. The girl told her she does not understand where she is. She is from

Nuevo Laredo in Mexico, and two weeks before had applied for a job in a hotel to clean rooms.

She told her "the hotel manager told me he wanted to show me where the laundry room is in the basement. When I went in with him two men were waiting and pointed their guns at me, and tied me up. They put me in a big laundry basket and handed me down into a tunnel somewhere in the hotel's basement. A little while later I am being lifted up through a hole in a floor in someone's house. Many men are standing around me and looking at me as they gave me a drink which made me sleepy. They each took turns having sex with me until they each finished. They were laughing and drinking and passed me around to each of them. I am in a big house for many days with them. I couldn't run away because of the many security men with guns all over the place. When they tired of me they put me in the back of a car and brought me here to have sex with strange men. I don't know where I am now."

Khara told her she is in America and is safe with her, and she will be taking her back to her home where she can be with her family. Big Boy sat and said nothing. He didn't speak Spanish like Khara and did not understand the conversation. He is content to look out the window at the ships docked at Port Newark unloading their cargo of new cars as they are soon coming to the Bayonne exit.

The M3 drove off the turnpike onto the ramp to route 440 which went down the east side of Bayonne. She stayed on the highway until she went over the Bayonne Bridge into Staten Island.

She dropped Big Boy and his man off at the club and continued to her home with the girl sitting in the back seat.

Chapter 9 -

Having the girl in tow Khara needed to decide how to proceed next. Pulling up to her driveway she pressed the automatic garage door to open, and parked in the garage. She motioned for the girl to get out, and they both went upstairs to Khara's apartment.

The petite girl is dressed inappropriately for the cooler weather and still wearing the same filthy clothes she wore from Nuevo Laredo. Many weeks passed since her clothes were washed and cleaned. Taking her into the bathroom Khara turned the hot water on, gave the girl soap and a small washcloth to clean up, and handed her the container of coconut body wash on the shower shelf explaining how to use it.

While showering Khara put the girl's clothes in the washing machine while she showered, and started to search through her closet to find something for the young girl to wear. Khara's blouses and slacks she soon realized are too large for the petite girl although she is not a big woman. The decision Khara made after the girl finished her shower, and her clothes clean, would be to take the girl to the Staten Island Mall to buy her a few new outfits to wear. She loaned her a sweater to wear even though it was too large for her, but it at least kept her somewhat warm.

When she came out of the bathroom and put her clean clothes on Khara asked her if she is hungry. When she answered yes Khara gave her a peanut butter and jelly sandwich and a glass of beer; she didn't have any milk in her apartment.

About a half hour later they went downstairs to the garage and drove to the Staten Island Mall to go clothes shopping.

As Khara drove the young girl fell asleep in the car. Khara thought sheer exhaustion from her recent events knocked her out, and let her rest a bit before she woke her when they reached the mall parking lot.

Walking in, the glitz of the Staten Island Mall overwhelmed the young girl and seeing the number of people all dressed so nice. Khara took her into many different stores which catered to younger teens and bought her some tops and pants. They both stopped for some donuts, a shake, and a little downtime while at the mall.

When they finished shopping Khara drove her back to her house. On the way home, she asked the young girl a few questions in Spanish. "Did you ever overhear them talking about anything in the tunnel when they took you."

"No, they did very little talking. But they said the champ wanted to have me first. I didn't understand what they meant until I met him later in the day."

"Where did you meet him, and who is he?"

"I don't know who he is. They all called him 'Champ' and they brought me into an expensive looking house. I met him in the house with the tunnel. A lot of people worked in the fancy palace. Many people wore caps and dressed in white uniforms and opened doors and served him. Three men took me upstairs to a bedroom where the Champ stayed, and he had sex with me repeatedly. He is strong. I am not as strong as him, and I could not resist him. When he finished with me, his friends took turns with me. They then drove me for a long time in a car to the building where you found me."

Upon hearing this story Khara became determined to find who is behind this. It began to twirl in her mind everything is connected, but she couldn't yet place her finger on it. Deep down she knew, but she couldn't put the pieces together yet.

***

As evening came Khara gave the young girl a small side bedroom to sleep in. Khara told her she is going out for a while but would be back. Reassured she would be safe in her home, and not to go anywhere the girl agreed, smiled, she lay back in her bed, turned over, and went to sleep.

Khara left the house and drove over to the club to see Al. She said there are a few things to discuss with him about the day. In her heart, she knew he might not give a truthful answer to her questions, but she wanted to ask them anyway.

When she pulled up to the club's awning the valet took her car and parked it next to Al's red Cadillac. Khara didn't need a valet ticket anymore. They all knew who she is.

"Hey Biggie, how're things?"

Khara approached the front entrance. Big Boy smiled at her as he opened the door.

When Khara entered the lobby a new girl at the coat check asked if she would like to check her jacket. Khara said "no thanks, I'll keep it" and walked into the club. Even if she wanted to she couldn't. She wore her .45 under the jacket and her .38 is in her right pocket.

A waitress informed Al Khara is in the club and he seemed to appear out of nowhere to greet her. He kissed her hello and took her by the handover to a small table in the bar area set off to the side.

"I am told things went pretty well today Khara. What do you think?"

"Yes, I agree. I obtained some more information, but I'm not sure how valid it is yet. It is bothering me I feel I am so close, but not near enough to get to the answer I need."

"I heard you brought a young girl back with you. How does she fit into the picture?"

"I'm not sure yet."

"Big Boy told me you took care of a creep in the warehouse office. You threw him down a double flight of steel steps and left him dead before you and Big Boy came back to Staten Island."

There is no response or answer to his statement. Not sure if the room is bugged by the police or FBI she smiled at him and put her finger to her mouth in a gesture to be quiet.

"Let's go out back," Khara said as she stood, and he followed her to the rear exit.

When they left the club they walked to the dumpster area and closed the gate behind themselves.

Without hesitation, she turned and hugged him, and planted a big kiss right on his lips. Khara did not kiss him because she wanted to be intimate with him at the moment while standing next to a garbage dumpster. When she held him tight, while pressing herself into him, she also ran her hands around his back and chest trying to feel if he is wearing a wire. Only her firm hands landed on his chest, and nothing else; she felt no wire.

"Al, tell your uncle thank you for me. I repaid him the favor today with the trailer he took. If anything he now owes me a few favors. I might need to collect them in the future. But for now, I am grateful for his help."

"Khara how about we go out and celebrate a little tonight."

"Can't, I have to get back home. The young girl is staying with me, and I must figure out what to do with her."

"I understand, how about we get together another night?"

She kissed him and said she'll call him the next day and set a date. They closed the dumpster gate and walked around to the front of the club. The valet ran to get her car, and Al went back inside as Khara drove away.

On her way home Don called her to see how her day went. She said it is okay, things are quiet, and nothing unusual is going on. He told her "I'll be out of town for a few more weeks, maybe two or so. The project has been extended a bit and I look forward to seeing you soon. Oh, one more thing. I found out the Ecru Cartel members tattooed a small red cross on the underside of their left wrist. The higher up in the organization they are they add a red blood drop on one side of the cross. The Cartel leader is tattooed with four blood drops coming off the cross; two on each side."

"Thank for the tip Don. I'll look out for the cross with blood drops in the future. I appreciate the information. See you when you get back."

Now realizing the warehouse job stole narcotics from the Ecru Cartel, due to the tattoo she saw on the man she killed today, she started to understand things a little better. Pulling into her driveway Khara said goodnight to Don and went inside to undress and go to bed.

***

The next morning she woke up late and rushed to get to work on time. She told the young girl to stay in the house, and her landlord would come up to make her breakfast. The girl said okay and stayed in bed while Khara left.

Some mornings Khara would stop at a convenience store on Hylan Boulevard to grab a cup of black coffee, a buttered roll, and the Daily News if she is running late. But something in today's newspaper is going to set her off when she reaches her desk in the morning.

As she sat, relaxing in her cubicle to drink her morning coffee, she opened the newspaper and started to read the headlines. Khara is not a political person, but she noticed a picture of a good looking man the article announced is retiring from boxing. He is a World Boxing champion originally from Mexico, and now living in Laredo Texas. He is being hired to head the personal security detail of an American presidential candidate from Texas. The name of the retired fighter is Pablo Gonzales.

In a flash, Khara realized her thinking is wrong. It's not a company she is after. It is a boxer, Gonzales the boxer, not Gonzales Boxes.

She turned on her computer and searched his name. It showed his history and his personal background information. His family originally came from the Ecru District of Mexico City, and soon settled in Nuevo Laredo Mexico. As a young man he took up boxing in Mexico City, and later in life, he bought a home in Laredo Texas when he is recognized internationally, and successful boxing in the ring.

The search listed his family members by name. His parents, a sister, and brother are named, and who to everyone's knowledge still lived in Mexico.

He became a pillar of the community and gave generously to municipal charities. Although he is not an American citizen he found himself immersed in local and state politics, giving a lot of money to powerful right-wing political parties in Texas.

Khara did a search on the Ecru Cartel in Mexico. She discovered by reading between the lines the Cartel leader, Alejandro, and Pablo Gonzales are stepbrothers.

"Son of a bitch," she said to herself. "There's the connection. I must to talk to Matt and see what I should do next."

***

She waited patiently until he came on duty and told him she wants to speak to him confidentially. They walked outside in front of the precinct and stood between two parked police cars to talk to each other without being overheard.

Khara explained to Matt how she kept the Gonzales lead to herself. She knew if she told anyone in the department they would say it is not a valid lead, and only do a cursory investigation. She laid out for Matt the timeline on the information she found, and why she thought she is at last closing the missing link on the case. She even told him about the young Mexican girl. She felt Matt didn't need to know all the details about her killing the creep in the warehouse office, just the major facts. But she is not sure what to do next.

Matt told her "I think it's time for you to go to the intelligence unit in Manhattan to tell them what you know. Plus you are keeping a Mexican girl in your home that can corroborate everything."

"I can't use her without admitting to a felony" Khara said to him. "I aided in the theft of a trailer full of illegal narcotics by the mob, I left the scene of a major crime, and am also harboring an illegal alien in my home."

Matt repeated himself to her "the only thing which comes to mind is to go to One Police Plaza and leave out some pertinent parts of the puzzle and hope they buy into your conclusion. They know you downtown from the gang bust and the Times Square shootout. You are one of the only very few people who can access them easily."

Khara told him she is going to wait a day or so and think about her next move. "I'm not sure about the department helping me in this case without arresting me. I want to think about it for a day or two before I do anything."

Matt grudgingly agreed with her and told Khara he would not say anything about their conversation.

***

On her way home Khara stopped at a takeout place and brought home some rotisserie chicken, a side of corn and a side of mashed potatoes with bacon bits in it for the young girl and herself.

During the day her landlord came upstairs at Khara's request to check on the girl, and he made a peanut butter and jelly sandwich for her lunch. He also brought with him, for the girl, a can of soda to drink with the sandwich instead of beer.

When Khara later in the day opened the door to her apartment she saw the girl sitting on the sofa drinking a Heineken from the frig, and watching Telemundo. At first, she is put off by this and didn't expect to see her drinking a beer. She decided to ask her how old she is now. The girl answered she is seventeen, her birthday occurred three months ago. Upon hearing her age Khara shrugged her shoulders. After what the girl's been through, drinking a beer is the least of her problems. Not that Khara cared.

Khara went into her bedroom to take off her work outfit and change into jeans. She thought the girl is about thirteen or fourteen because she is so petite and youthful looking.

Placing the food on the kitchen table she called the girl to come into the kitchen to eat dinner with her. They sat on opposite ends of the small table, and Khara watched her devour her dinner. She seemed famished. When they finished eating and cleaned up the table, she phoned Al to make a date to see him in the evening. She needed some additional input on her next move, and he is the only one she thought would be able to help her.

As she is driving to the club Khara called ahead and asked him to meet her outside when she pulled up to the awning. He is standing there with Big Boy when she arrived. Al hopped into her car when she stopped in front, and Khara drove away to talk to him privately.

Her favorite spot is under the 440 overpass on the way to the Bayonne Bridge. There are never any pedestrians on the sidewalk and the cars keep whizzing by.

After listening to her tell him everything she knew about Pablo Gonzales Al said he would speak to his uncle, and see what he recommended.

"My uncle knows a lot of people and has connections. He can find out all about this guy for you. But I'll need a few days, a little time, for him to reach out... I'll get back to you. Give me two or three days, okay?"

"Is there any other choice?"

She came to the realization this case grew too big, and she needed someone to help her who would not turn her into the police. Khara knew in her heart she is about to make a deal with the devil himself. She also knew whatever his uncle suggested would, in the end, benefit him too. She felt if Al is satisfied with this solution, his uncle would help her situation.

Finished talking about the Cartel Al told her to turn around and drive to a local hotel only a few blocks away for some private time with him. Khara threw the M3 into first, almost made a U-turn on two wheels, and upshifted to second as she flew back under the overpass to go to the hotel with him.

Chapter 10 -

A few days passed since they spoke, as Al said it would when Khara received a phone call. She is to meet Big Boy at a location on the docks in the Stapleton area of Staten Island at noon the next day.

She asked her landlord to watch the girl while she went out. Khara still did not know what to do with her but felt at least the girl is safe for the time being. It is not an altruistic moment Khara is feeling. There are no feelings of concern about the situation the girl is in, but Khara knew the girl might be helpful down the road. This is why she is trying to keep her safe and hidden for now.

Bay Street is a twisty street hugging the Upper New York Bay on Staten Island. Khara kept shifting gears as the road turned, emptied of cars for a few blocks, filled again, and having to come to a stop at red traffic lights.

When she turned left onto the street where she is supposed to go to she found herself in a warehouse district on the waterfront. Down the block, she saw Big Boy standing outside the door to one of the warehouses. He waved for her to drive over to him. He pointed to where she should park her car, opened the driver's door for her, and told Khara to follow him into the warehouse.

It is a typical old wooden shipping dock warehouse sitting on the edge of the harbor. The musty scent, cobwebs hanging from the rafters, water lapping against the wooden footings below the floor, and the creaking wooden ash planks skeeved Khara's senses, but she continued to walk behind Big Boy.

They proceeded about a hundred feet or more until they reached an old rickety wooden room at the far end of the warehouse. Its paint is peeling from the salt air of the bay beneath it.

Big Boy opened the door to the room, and they walked inside a small chamber with a few filthy opaque windows on three sides. At the back end of the room is another door which is slightly ajar. Khara could see on the other side of the door a good sized cabin cruiser docked to the pilings outside and heard its engine idling.

"There is some information this guy wants to tell you," Big Boy said to Khara.

Sitting tied up in a chair is a short Latino looking man with a pencil thin mustache and perspiring profusely. His face is distended from an obvious beating, and his left eye is almost swollen shut. Khara thought she is standing in old forties black and white Hollywood crime thriller movie when she looked at the man sitting there. His feet are encased in a tub of hardened cement, and two burly men in dark navy sweat suits with white stripes running down the sides of their pants stood on each side of him. There are obvious bulges which protruded out by their waist from the guns they are wearing.

"Tell her what you told us before," Big Boy said to the little man. "And I mean everything, and don't leave any shit out."

He started to speak to Khara with a heavy Spanish accent. She noticed a small red cross tattooed on the underside of his left wrist and only one red blood drop on it. The blood drop on his wrist under the cross told her he is not a lowly soldier for the cartel. He is a little higher, but not too high up.

The hostage told Khara he worked for the Ecru Cartel and is their point man in Texas. His boss ordered him to come here after the trailer full of narcotics went missing, and their area manager was killed. His job is to find out who stole the trailer. He said he must have asked the wrong person some questions, and ended up in a warehouse in Staten Island with Big Boy and his crew.

"Do you want to ask him anything Khara?"

"Thanks, Biggie, I do want to ask him a question or two. Is Pablo Gonzales involved in the drug smuggling?"

Speaking in Spanish she began questioning him.

"Yes. He arranges for the drugs to come in, and he sends the money back to Nuevo Laredo by an underground tunnel. He gets to keep a lot of it. His brother wants him to buy his way into politics. Now you know why he is doing all the good stuff in Texas. The politician who is running for president hired him for security. But the guy owes the cartel some huge favors because they are backing him with drug money" the man told her.

He stopped talking.

"Anything else you want to tell her" Big Boy said to him.

The man shook his head from side to side indicating he is finished talking, and he asked for some water in English.

"Al's uncle wanted you to hear this. He thought up a plan to help you with your problem" Big Boy said to her. "Let's go now" as he turned to leave.

One of the men called out to Big Boy.

"Hey, what do you want me to do with him?"

"He wants some water, give him some water" Big Boy responded as he continued walking out of the room with her, and not bothering to turn around.

Khara assumed what is going to happen to the man once she left. She obtained her information, and couldn't care less about him, realizing there is nothing she could do at the moment without getting herself killed in the process. Plus he would kill her for the Cartel if he could, and not think twice about it either. So she continued to her car and drove home.

***

Not too long after she drove away Al called her. He said his uncle wanted Khara to listen to a plan he laid out for him to relay to her.

She told Al to meet her at the hotel they stayed at the other night in one hour. Khara felt in bed there would be no chance of a wire on him; or in a room which she chose specifically, yet randomly, reserved by her with the hotel.

After checking into the hotel she went to the room and took a quick shower, sat on the bed relaxing, and watching television until Al knocked on the door. She opened it and greeted him with a kiss while naked.

Khara suggested he first shower, and slip into bed with her afterward. He dried off and then pulled the covers back and snuggled next to her. They hugged and kissed, and he began to tell her his uncle's plan.

"My uncle wants you to fly down to Laredo International Airport in two weeks. Big Boy and his crew will be driving down with the young girl a little earlier. We need her to show us around Pablo's mansion to the tunnel when we go in there."

He continued with the plan telling her "once you arrive at the airport someone will meet you to drive you to a safe house. There you and Big Boy can stage my uncle's plan. Automatic weapons will be available at the safe house, plus explosives, for you to use when you go to the mansion. After you find the tunnel you are to take it to the end and find Pablo's brother. My uncle wants him and Pablo brought back here if possible."

Khara asked him "what if his brother is not there? Or Pablo is not there? What do I do in Mexico?"

Al told her "everyone will be either in Laredo or Nuevo Laredo the day you are there. My uncle is arranging for a large donation to be made by a local Laredo businessman to a presidential candidate. He knows Gonzales always brings the candidate back to his mansion to party with him when he is in Laredo. The odds are Pablo's brother might be there as well to meet the unsuspecting candidate. It is well known his ego is pretty big."

"Okay, I'll start packing, and tomorrow I'll put in for a few vacation days at work. Now, where are we?" Khara now snuggled closer to him in bed and started to play with his ear.

***

When Khara went to work the next day she called human resources to inquire about taking her unused vacation days. She did not take a vacation for over two years, and maybe even more.

On her last vacation, Eloise arranged for Khara to go on an all-expense paid cruise with her to the Caribbean. She booked a suite with a balcony for them to stay in on an older cruise ship. The cost was a lot less, and the security cameras don't exist as they do on the newer large cruise ships.

Before the cruise, both women went shopping in the city for different outfits, and Eloise treated Khara to any clothes she wanted. They shopped at Bloomingdales, Saks, and the small boutiques in Soho. They spent a few weeks together buying a lot of clothes for their vacation.

The cruise ship docked in Manhattan. When it left everything was peaceful and relaxing. It was to be a twelve-day cruise stopping at all the islands which Khara only read about in the brochures.

The food tasted great, the entertainment enjoyable and the sun-drenched pools fun to swim in. Eloise and Khara decided to go to the upper deck pool where clothing is optional. They splashed around for hours and enjoyed themselves in the water.

About the fourth night out as they sat in the bar having drinks in one of the ships bars a nice looking mature man, dressed sharply, approached and asked if he could join them at their table. Eloise said it is okay with her, and Khara nodded her head in an affirmative manner.

"Thanks for letting me sit with you. There are not many tables available, and both of you girls look great."

Khara knew it is a lie as she turned her head a little, and saw a few empty tables. But a good pickup line is a good pickup line only if it works. And his seemed to work fine with Eloise, she fell for his bullshit.

He bought continuing rounds of beer, scotch, and greasy fried finger foods. The gentleman, after a few rounds, suggested they all go back to Eloise's suite for some adult fun. Khara is always up for a ménage à trois, and she noticed Eloise drank a lot more than she should have. But Khara didn't object when Eloise also said it is a good idea. Khara felt like some conjugal action, and she looked forward to it.

They walked, and Eloise stumbled due to her drinking, to the elevator. After a few minutes, everyone, at last, arrived at Eloise's suite. Khara opened the door and they all went into the cabin.

Eloise sat, her head touched the back of the sofa, and she passed out once inside the suite. Khara and this good-looking gentleman undressed and slowly walked out to the balcony together. They started to passionately kiss, and embrace with his hands roaming all over her. Khara was starting to enjoy the moment when suddenly she heard his stomach start to rumble from all the alcohol, and greasy finger food he consumed. He again kissed Khara on her lips and belched in her face. As he turned his head and emptied his stomach over the balcony railing into the sea below, Khara was fed up and disgusted by him. She reached down, grabbed his legs in both her hands and flipped him over the railing while watching him hit the water with a small splash as the ship continued on its way to the next island.

The slight wind from the moving ship chilled her naked body. She was still pissed at him, and getting tired standing there she went back inside. Closing the glass sliding door behind her she climbed into bed and went to sleep.

The next morning when Eloise awoke she saw Khara sleeping naked by herself with a man's clothing lying on the floor next to the bed. Eloise undressed, took a quick shower, and slid next to her under the covers. They spent most of the morning not leaving the mattress.

By the time lunch was being served they decided, after hemming and hawing, to go down for a bite to eat. They showered together and dressed casually. In the elevator, Eloise whispered to Khara "when did your date leave the room last night? I saw his clothes are still there."

Khara took Eloise's hand and said: "I'll tell you later when we're in the pool." There are other people in the elevator, and she didn't want to blurt out what happened.

Eloise gently squeezed Khara's hand, smiled at her, and said "never mind. I can guess what happened to him." They went for lunch forgetting about him.

That is the last time Khara took a vacation. But this time it is work and survival for her, not pleasure.

***

There is one last thing to do before leaving for Texas. She called Don to see where he is. He mentioned to her he was going to Texas, and she wanted to make sure she didn't run into him there.

"Hi Don, its Khara, how's it going?"

"Oh hi Khara, I'm busy down here in Dallas. I missed hearing your voice."

"And I missed you too. When are you coming back to New York?"

"I'll be back soon. We are finishing up some surveillance work on the Ecru Cartel, and I'll be flying back in a week or so."

"That's great Don. I miss you. See you when you get back."

"And I miss you also. I must go now. There is a meeting with the border patrol in an hour, and I need to be there. Talk to you soon" he told her before hanging up.

Chapter 11 -

The weather is hot and muggy as usual when Khara arrived in Texas. Her flight was uneventful, and as a law enforcement officer she was able to board the plane with her two guns, and a throwing knife in her boot. Instead of her leather jacket, she is wearing a light all seasons sports jacket because of the heat. She also pulled her afro hair back into a short, tight, ponytail due to the hot southern Texas humidity.

When she disembarked from the plane and walked into the terminal a tall Latino man approached her. He is wearing cowboy boots and hat, a western style shirt with pearled buttons, and a smile as big as Texas. He had a swarthy complexion that contrasted nicely against the lighter colored western styled clothes he is wearing.

He approached Khara and asked if she had a nice flight down. The man was looking at a picture on his cell phone that Al sent to him as to what Khara looked like, and the flight number she was on.

"Miss Bennett I am going to take you to meet Big Boy. He is staying in Cotulla Texas. It's about an hour north on Interstate 35."

Khara thanked him for meeting her as she walked with him through the busy terminal. Laredo is a bustling city now that shale oil was discovered recently. Also, it is the largest inland port in Texas. They do a lot of international importing through Laredo from the American factories situated in Northern Mexico just over the border.

He arranged for someone to get her luggage and meet them by the arrivals exit. She traveled light and only carried one medium size suitcase. As they stood waiting a light beige Cadillac SUV drove up to them, the trunk popped open, and her suitcase is placed in it. Khara and the gentleman then entered the back of the car, and it drove out of the airport onto I-35 North.

The short trip to the City of Cotulla is uneventful as they drove through the flat grassy land with only a few hills every now and then. Khara felt it is a boring ride with not much to look at.

As they approached Cotulla they pulled off on a mile long dirt road and entered a small ranch. After a quick drive on the private road, they saw Big Boy's passenger van. It is parked in front of the house, and they stopped next to it.

Khara stepped out of the Cadillac and stood to stretch her legs. She is stiff from sitting for such a long time and walked to the trunk to lift her suitcase out of the back.

The planked entry door of the building opened and she is ushered into the house. Big Boy is seen relaxing on the sofa and waved hello to her. The young girl is lying on the floor reading a Spanish newspaper when Big Boy stood and asked Khara if she would like to see "what's in the barn."

"Yer, let's go I'm tired of sitting on my ass all day."

Big Boy signaled to two of his men to come with them to the barn. They walked out the rear door onto a small wooden porch that barely held the weight of everyone as they stepped on it. About fifty feet away is an old Texas horse barn that hasn't been used for many years. The doors are sagging and some of the planks on the side of the building fell off due to dry rot.

Big Boy opened one of the two doors, and they all went inside. In one of the empty horse stalls are three satchels covered with a tarp. Big Boy said "they shipped some M183 demolition charge assemblies down here for us. They are in M85 carrying cases."

Khara knew what she is looking at is armed forces grade C4 explosives. She picked up the "they" in what Big Boy said, but thought better not to ask who the "they" are, and let it drop.

In the next stall on some portable folding tables are automatic submachine guns with loaded clips. They are actual military grade caliber ones from the United States Navy. Khara didn't want to know how they ended up here in a barn in Texas; she kept silent on the issue. Big Boy picked one from the table and told her to try it. It is a NATO approved short submachine gun; a Heckler and Koch MP7 with a thirty round magazine and a Zeiss red dot sight on top. It fired special bullets that are capable of defeating personal body armor. Khara released the safety and walked out of the barn to a wooden fence about twenty feet away. Starting to shoot the gun, it blasted the wood fence to smithereens very quickly. Satisfied it would do a lot of damage she handed it back to Big Boy and smiled. Plus it could somewhat fit under a jacket and be hidden.

It is getting late, and everyone is hungry, so they all piled into the large passenger van and Big Boy drove into Cotulla. They found a local pizza place where they all ordered dinner. Big Boy ordered two large pepperoni pizzas for himself alone, and a few pies for the others sitting at the table.

After dinner, Khara excused herself and went to the ladies restroom. She is washing her hands by the sink minding her own business when a very tall heavy set woman with a deep Texas drawl walked in.

"Hey black girl, I noticed you with that bunch of nice looking white men out there. How much money are they paying you to screw all of them?"

Being the wiseass girl from New York that she is, Khara answered her. "Not as much as your daddy paid me before!"

"What the hell did you say about my daddy?"

The woman is so tall she is actually looking down at her.

Khara glanced up at this obese giant of a woman with a six foot two massive body and said to her "I just finished having your daddy lick my ass. That's what I said, bitch! Now get the hell out of my face before I have to fuck'n hurt you."

"You ain't going anywhere after I finish pounding the crap out of you."

The woman moved towards Khara and raised her arm to strike at her.

Khara quickly dodged to the left, and with two fingers on her right hand jumped up and struck the woman in both eyes. This stopped her for a moment as she is in great pain, and couldn't see.

Swinging her foot out in a wide loop Khara hit the larger woman in the back of her knee. The woman's massive leg buckled as she fell to the floor with a loud thud. Khara then swung her leg around and kicked the woman in the head full force with the heel of her right boot sending the woman reeling into the bathroom wall.

Dazed the woman is now moaning softly. Khara bent over her, grabbed her by her hair, and pounded her face into the floor numerous times until there is a massive pool of blood under her head. Then yanking, and pulling the giant woman into a restroom stall, she again picked the woman's head up by her hair and smashed it three times into the side of the toilet bowl; cracking it.

Satisfied that this is over, Khara dropped the bigot's head as it bounced off the tiled floor. Calmly she walked to the sink, finished washing her hands, adjusted her jacket and blouse, and in a calm manner walked out of the ladies room being careful not to step in the pool of blood as she went back to her table.

"Hey Biggie, I strongly suggest we leave immediately."

Big Boy didn't question her. He didn't know what she did, but he knew what she is capable of doing. The tone of her voice told him to listen to her. He finished eating few minutes before, and he stood while taking out a few hundred dollars. The money dropped in a pile on the table for the bill and tip. Then they all left and went back to the ranch for the rest of the evening.

The next morning before breakfast one of the men went into town to go food shopping. When he returned he started to cook for everyone. He made scrambled eggs with crisp country bacon and freshly baked biscuits and rolls which he placed on the dining table.

Television is on, and the local news station reported that a presidential candidate would be visiting Laredo at two in the afternoon to give a speech. Then the station switched to a live shot of a breaking news story. There is a local reporter on scene standing at the pizza place they ate at the evening before. The reporter said "that a woman, whose family name was requested not to be announced, was found in a coma in a bathroom stall in the ladies room late last night. The woman's father is the leader of a local white supremacist group that wants Texas for Texans only. The police reported that they are investigating the incident but there are no leads at the moment."

After hearing that, Big Boy and his men turned to Khara looking directly at her. Nobody said anything, they just sat silently. She smiled and said, "I guess she just slipped on a wet floor and bumped her head when she fell."

It is now time to get everything loaded into the van. They drove it up to the barn, and one of the men opened the two doors so Big Boy could back it into the horse stall area. But before he did that Big Boy went to uncover and back in an official Texas Utility van that is parked on the side of the ranch house.

The man that met Khara at the airport works for an associate of Al's uncle in Texas. He paid off a utility repairman with ten thousand dollars in cash to borrow his work van for a few days.This Texas Gas Utility van would be the one that carried in the explosives.

Al told Big Boy that as soon as he crossed over into Texas he is to turn in his rental vehicle and get one with Texas plates if he is going to drive around. He felt that this would not be as noticeable as the van with New York license plates driving around in Texas.

They planned to stage the attack in Cotulla because Laredo is a much larger city, and there are more people moving about. Out here they thought they would probably not be seen, or noticed by anyone.

Once all the weapons and explosives are loaded into the two vans they all drove away from the ranch on the dirt road leading back to the highway.

Big Boy is driving and Khara relaxed in the passenger seat next to him, and the young girl sat on the floor in the back of the utility van. The leased second van and Cadillac followed them down Interstate 35 to Laredo.

* * *

The donation ceremony was not a large affair, and it is over by the time they arrived in the city. The press had been there and the candidate did some video takes to be saved and made into a commercial for a later time.

Big Boy knew Pablo's address and used the GPS on his phone to get him there. When he came within a few blocks of the mansion he pulled over to make sure everyone knew exactly where they are going, and what they are going to do.

A few days before Khara arrived in Laredo Big Boy cased the area around the mansion with his crew. It is located in a residential area with acres of land around it. He wanted to know where every entrance and exit is located. They all knew it is only about a mile or so from the Mexican border, and the tunnel the cartel dug went directly under the Rio Grande River. It went from under the hotel's basement in Mexico to the basement of the mansion in Laredo. They have no idea what would happen above ground when they set the charges, and the tunnel exploded.

Khara asked a question.

"Hey Biggie, why blow up the tunnel?"

"Because that is how they bring the stuff into the country and his uncle wants to crush them. And that is the only way to get to the cartel leader, if he is in Mexico he will be in the hotel. He also owns it. You can't go armed into the country unless you take the tunnel. Al's uncle has that under control. When you get to the hotel in Nuevo Laredo make yourself known to the general manager. He is in the cartel, and will inform Alejandro Gonzales that you are in the hotel."

"And then what happens to me, Biggie?"

"Stay in the hotel. We'll make sure people are present to help you if you need it. The manager will tell the cartel you are there. Alejandro will probably personally come to see you. I am sure he will want to kill the person that shot his sister to death. But don't worry. We will hold his brother as insurance, just in case, something goes wrong. Just remember that every day at three in the afternoon there will be a red car behind the hotel waiting for you. They will show up there for three days only, and leave after ten minutes. You are to be there by three, or they will drive off without you."

"Shit, I hope so. I'll be in a mess if I miss it."

Chapter 12 -

Big Boy drove the Texas Utility van up to the imposing twelve-foot high black iron entry gates with polished brass spikes on top in front of the mansion.

The presidential candidate is already in the building with Pablo. His limo could be seen in the distance parked by the front double wooden doors of the building, and there are only one or two men guarding the home on the outside. The security gunman at the front gate stopped the Texas Utility van that Big Boy is driving when he pulled up to the guard house. Once Khara spoke Spanish to him he let their vehicle enter the grounds. She told him they were called by Mr. Gonzales' maintenance man to investigate a gas leak in the basement. The guard directed them to drive to a basement entrance in the rear of the mansion behind a row of hedges. The back bushes are high, thick and wide enough to hide the door from view, and the van also.

As they are driving up to the mansion they saw five foot tall white Greek style statues on thick pedestals alongside the brick-lined driveway. Ahead of them is a massive building three stories in height with open-air verandas encircling the house. Khara could see a few men with guns walking on the premises securing the mansion.

Another security guard is waiting by the back of the building for them. He opened the heavily carved wooden basement door, and let them in. Khara explained to him in Spanish they have to bring in some equipment to check for the leak otherwise the house might explode. The guard understood what she is saying and is glad that they are there to stop the gas leak. He even helped them carry some cases into the basement not knowing they are filled with explosives. He went in first and turned on the lights in the room for them. They followed him in as he led them to where the gas lines came into the building.

They found themselves in a subbasement utility room and saw the gas meter, and the main gas line that came into the house. Khara told the guard in Spanish she didn't smell any gas and that there must be another pipe coming into the house.

"Is there a tunnel or something down here also? We want to check that just in case it is leaking below ground."

He told her there is another room nearby, and he opened a small door to the right of where they are standing. It led to a much smaller room that has a tunnel situated in the middle of the room, going directly down into the earth. Khara turned to him and smiled to distract him while Big Boy approached from the rear of where the guard is standing. Suddenly a strong rope is placed around the man's neck. Big Boy garroted him from behind until he stopped struggling, and fell limply to the floor.

"Biggie we need to go upstairs, find Pablo, and the candidate. I have a score to settle. I'm tired of these assholes continually trying to kill me. I'll tell the girl to lead us to where he is in this house. Follow us."

The young girl started to lead them up the back stairway of the house. The steps are made of white marble with gold inlays set into each step. The stairway has a few landings and then stopped at another heavily carved wooden door on the third and top floor.

With her MP7 at her side, Khara slowly opened the door and saw it led into a sitting area. It turned out to be in Pablo's bedroom. Listening for any sounds she heard a man talking in the bedroom next to where they are standing. She waved for Big Boy to follow her in. But she has the young girl walk in first, ahead of them, as a distraction in case Pablo or one of his men saw them and signaled an alarm.

Khara made the young girl open the buttons on her blouse almost all the way down her chest before she started to enter the room. As the girl walked into the bedroom she saw Pablo is naked in bed with two very young Mexican girls. He saw the young girl, and her opened blouse, but obviously did not remember who she is because he motioned for her to join him in his bed.

Two steps behind her are Khara and Big Boy fully armed and ready to start shooting if needed. They stepped out from behind the door, and Khara quickly walked over to the foot of Pablo's bed. She thought he looked surprised to see them in his bedroom; especially with guns pointed at him.

"Who the hell are you? And what are you doing here?" Pablo demanded as he looked at Big Boy.

Then he looked directly at Khara and recognized her.

"You will never leave here alive, bitch."

Big Boy approached his bed from the side and pistol-whipped Pablo across his head sending him flying off of his silk sheets onto the white imported marble tiled floor; with his blood smearing across it.

"Right now Pablo" Big Boy told him, "I think it's you who might not leave here alive."

Pablo was the welterweight boxing champion before retiring, and he is used to taking hits. The blow Big Boy gave him is unexpected, and he started to get up from the floor due to his conditioning and training.

Khara ran over to where Pablo is sprawled on the floor and shot him directly in his right knee cap with her MP7 shattering his bones. This prevented him from getting up. She would have liked to kill him right then but Al's uncle wanted him brought back alive. The sound of the gunshot echoed in the room and alerted the guards. The bedroom is all marble tiles and a mirrored ceiling. There are no acoustic barriers to deaden the loud gunshot-like carpeting and drapes.

Pablo grabbed his knee, yelling out in pain, and rolled over onto his side. Khara could see the intense suffering he is experiencing, yet she felt no remorse for crippling him. To shut him up Big Boy took duct tape out from his backpack and covered Pablo's mouth while he is squirming on the floor. While he did that Khara used plastic ties to handcuff Pablo's arms behind his back. They are careful not to slip on Pablo's blood that is now covering most of the marble tiled floor in the area where he is lying.

Khara looked at the two girls in his bed and asked them in Spanish "how old are you."

The older looking of the girls answered in Spanish that "I am fifteen, and my friend is fourteen.

We were taken from our town in Mexico and brought here last week for sex parties with Pablo and his friends. Can you help us get back home?"

"Okay, I will try, get dressed and come with us."

Together Khara and Big Boy turned Pablo over onto his back, and Big Boy started dragging him by the back of his shirt to go down the stairway to the basement. Pablo's legs and shattered knee are bouncing on the marble stairs while leaving a trail of blood.

While they were still in the bedroom Khara by chance looked out the window, and saw the limo with the candidate drive down the tree-lined esplanade to the black iron and brass entry gates. She called out to Big Boy what she saw. He stopped, called his crew with his phone at the front entry, and told them what to do.

Before Big Boy's call, the other van drove up to the Iron Gate and asked the security guard if he has any cigarettes. When the armed man came over to talk to them the side door opened, he is pulled into the van, overpowered and killed. One of Big Boy's men then took his place at the gate. The van backed up, out of the driveway, and staying on the outside of the tall adobe wall with the van's engine idling.

The limo carrying the candidate reached the front iron gates when it stopped, and waited for the tall gates to open. The gates didn't open, and the van that is idling on the side of the wall drove up to the entrance blocking the chauffeured vehicle from leaving. The iron gates are now opened and two of Big Boys men from the van ran towards the limo with their MP7's ready to fire at the car.

They ordered the driver to open his window and turn off the car which he did without hesitation as a machine gun is in his face.

The driver is told to open the locks on the rear doors and keep his hands out the driver's side window where they could be seen at all times. They opened the rear door to the limo, and one gunman looked in. He saw the presidential candidate with his pants down, and a totally undressed young Mexican girl that looked like she is twelve years old in the back seat in flagrante delicto.

The candidate is ordered to completely undress and hand his clothes out the door. Once he is naked, except for his thick dark-colored rimmed eyeglasses, the other gunman took all their clothing and asked the driver to flip the trunk lid open. When he walked to the rear of the limo to throw the clothes in the back he saw four large duffle bags in the trunk. He slid the zipper open on one to look inside. He saw hundred dollar bills wrapped and stacked neatly in rows. He took the bags out of the car, threw the clothes in, and then closed the lid of the limo's trunk.

Then he quickly carried the duffle bags as fast as he could to their van. When the bags are safely secured in the back of the van he walked to the open rear window where the candidate and the girl are sitting. He took out his cell phone, took a lot of pictures of them being close together in the back of the limo with his phone. These pictures would be used as blackmail against a married presidential candidate in the foreseeable future.

***

The gunshot in the bedroom alerted Pablo's private security men, and Khara could hear them running up the front marble stairway to Pablo's upstairs private bedroom.

Khara shouted to Big Boy and the girls to leave the bedroom using the back stairs they came up. She walked over to the side wall, and set herself up in a corner where they couldn't see her as they entered the room until it is too late.

She surprised them when she started shooting at two of them in a very fast and deadly gunfight. Two more men are in the stairwell and they ducked down when they heard the automatic machine gun fire coming from the room. They returned fire by bending down and holding their guns over the steps; firing blindly. Bullets flew everywhere in the room shattering mirrors and some marble floor tiles. There are so many bullet casings on the steps that one of the cartel gunmen slipped on them and fell to the floor when he rose to charge into the room. The shooting continued for another few seconds until the last security gunman fled down the front stairway to the level below. When there are no more cartel men coming up the front stairway into the bedroom Khara ran down the back staircase following after Big Boy to the basement.

Once they reached the basement room where they had entered Big Boy told Khara she has only twenty minutes to get down the tunnel, set the explosives in it to detonate before he set off his in the mansion.

She asked Big Boy about Pablo's brother. How do they know if he is somewhere in the house with Pablo?

"We don't know that. But if he is in the mansion he's going to die once we set off the C4. Now get going. You only have fifteen minutes."

Khara saw there is a light switch at the top of the tunnel and she flipped it on. The whole cement walled tunnel is electrified with lights and a fresh air blower. The young girl went down the ladder first followed by Khara who carried the explosives and radio activated detonator with her. The other two girls then stepped down the steep ladder following her.

The tunnel is very humid, and damp, but everyone climbed down the shaft as quickly as they could. At the bottom of the ladder, Khara found a small platform on wheels sitting on what looked like tiny rail tracks. She realized that the smugglers used the tracks to transport drugs easily into the United States. Khara placed her explosives on the platform, and all of them began pushing it on the tracks into the tunnel. They started to run as fast as they could. The tunnel is cement walled, seemed to go on forever, and they all could stand erect in it. They didn't need to bend over to clear the ceiling of the tunnel.

When they reached a point that is about halfway to Mexico Khara saw a marking on the wall. It is a vertical line with the letter M on one side and a U on the other. She figured this is the halfway mark in the tunnel. Carefully she set down the M85 and attached the detonator to it with the radio transmitter. She looked at her watch and realized they have very little time left to get to the other side. She hurried to finish setting the detonator properly. When she is done attaching it Khara started to run with the girls while carefully holding the transmitter in her hand. She did not want to detonate the explosives until they all climbed out of the tunnel.

Big Boy set his explosives, dragged Pablo out of the mansion leaving a trail of blood on the ground, and literally threw him into the back of the van. He started the engine, began to slowly drive down a shorter back driveway to the rear exit, and didn't look back.

The gate where Big Boy headed for is a much smaller wooden one, and he went right through it smashing in the front of the Texas Utility's van. When he reached the street the Cadillac pulled around to pick him up. They lifted Pablo out of the van and into the Cadillac's trunk, shut the lid, abandoned the van, and drove back to Cotulla.

The men that stopped the candidate's limo made sure they have everything. Then they hopped into their van and drove off to follow Big Boy's Cadillac that is around back with Big Boy in it.

As they put some space between themselves and the mansion the building exploded about fifteen minutes later. It actually lifted up off its foundation. Windows blew out with glass flying everywhere, then fell back down collapsing inward, and completely falling apart.

Khara heard the explosion go off at the mansion while she is in the tunnel, and she is almost to the other side when Big Boy set it to blast the place apart.

There is a rush of air through the tunnel, whirling dust and pieces of light gravel in front of the forced air from the explosion. It caught up with Khara and the girls and knocked them to the floor. Covered with a fine dust they stood, and again started to run to the Mexican side of the tunnel using the battery-powered emergency lights that were installed in the tunnel to see where they are going. The explosion at the mansion destroyed the electric, the fans blowing air into the tunnel failed, and the lights stopped working.

There is a tall ladder at the other end of the tunnel that would lead up to the hotel in Nuevo Laredo. When they reached it Khara let the girls go up first, then she followed.

Once they all lifted themselves out of the tunnel Khara pressed the button on her transmitter and listened for the explosives to be set off.

There is silence.

Nothing happened.

"Shit, this sucks big time. It didn't go off" she said to herself.

Khara started to go back down the steep ladder. She is careful taking only one step down at a time.

When her hand holding the transmitter is below the top of the tunnel she inadvertently pressed the transmission button again.

Immediately there is a huge sound of explosives going off deep in the tunnel. A blast of air coming from beneath where she is standing on the ladder actually lifted her up and pushed her out of the tunnel. Again pieces of dirt, dust, and rocks flew up out of the tunnel entrance right after Khara is pushed and lifted out. It is so forceful she almost hit her head on the basement ceiling the air draft was so strong.

The Rio Grande River above the tunnel rose into the air due to the explosion underground. Then as the tunnel collapsed the water rushed down into it creating a temporary whirlpool. The border police on both sides of the river heard all of the explosions; especially the tunnel explosion. They saw the water rise almost fifty feet into the air, and then saw it being sucked down into the swirling water.

Now she is in the hotel's basement in Mexico and Khara wanted to find the hotel manager that kidnapped the young girl she saved in Newark.

She turned to the twoo girls she had justst rescued from Pablo's bedroom and told them to be quiet. Then she looked at the young girl who worked at the hotel and told her to come with her. "But don't tell anyone I speak Spanish. Do you understand?" The girl answered yes.

Slowly she opened the door to the tunnel room and it led into a storage room in the hotel laundry machine area. Khara entered that room and then tried to listen by the next door to hear if somebody is working with the machines. There is no noise or people talking.

Looking at her watch she realized it is siesta time, and the workers are off for lunch. All of them scooted into the laundry room, and then out to a hallway leading to the rear exit of the building. Once outside she looked around to get her bearings and saw a small gate that led to the street. Khara told the two girls to go leave the hotel property and try to get home. She gave them twenty dollars in American currency so they could get a taxi to the police station for help in getting home.

Chapter 13 -

Khara is alone in the back alley of the hotel with only the young girl. She reloaded her MP7 then hid it behind a thick row of hedges that hugged the rear wall. She is satisfied it is out of sight and well hidden. Opening her jacket she put a fresh magazine into her Sig .45 then went back into the building with the girl walking right behind her.

Following the hall signs to the lobby, Khara eventually saw the front desk. She walked up to it and asked in English "can I have a room for two people for three nights please?"

Being so close to the Texas border and having a large number of American business travelers often stay at the hotel, the desk clerks spoke fluent English.

"Do you have a reservation?"

"No, I didn't plan on staying in town but something came up, and I need a place to sleep."

"I am sorry, but I think we are booked full."

"I understand. Can I please speak to the general manager? Perhaps the manager might be able to help me find a room."

"Yes, of course, one moment please, while I call him."

Khara knew that if they are fully booked the woman would have said so, not that she thinks they are fully booked. She thought to herself that a bribe is going to have to be paid to the manager in order to stay there tonight.

The clerk, then speaking in Spanish, dialed for the hotel manager to come out from his back office to talk to Khara.

In a few minutes, the manager walked out from a rear office to speak to the prospective guest. He is well dressed in a blue suit and tie and stopped at the front desk where Khara is standing, with the young girl motionless hiding behind her.

"Good afternoon señorita, how can I help you today?"

"My daughter and I need a room for three nights. I would appreciate it if there is some way you could arrange that."

"My clerk said that she thinks we are fully booked. I am not sure that we can accommodate you tonight."

Then she reached behind her and tugged at the young girl to come forward to stand next to her; which she did.

Khara could see on the manager's face that he remembered the young girl. He stood there speechless for a moment, and Khara thought he appeared to have a slightly dazed look on his face. He apparently is confused as to what is going on with that girl back here in his lobby.

"Can I speak to you privately in your office?"

Khara is smiling at him as she said it.

"Si, Si. Come around the desk over here, and follow me please."

Khara and the girl walked behind him to his office. She felt that something is going to happen, but she isn't sure yet what it would be. When all three of them are in the back room, and the door closed, the general manager turned to face Khara. "Who are you and what is she doing here?"

Putting her hand inside her jacket she reached in and took out her Sig .45 from its holster, and touched his forehead with the gun barrel. "I am your worst nightmare come to life. Now you are going to do two things before I blow your fuck'n brains all over this room. Take out your wallet, and give it to the girl."

He started to perspire. This never happened to him before. The cartel always protected him, and he is very nervous at that moment. Slowly he reached into his pocket, took out his billfold, and handed it to the young girl.

"In Spanish I want you to tell the girl to open it and take all your money."

The girl flipped the wallet open, removed a thick handful of bills, and put them in her pocket. The expensive Rolex watch on his left wrist did not go unnoticed by Khara.

"Take off your watch and give it to her also."

When he did this she saw a small red cross tattooed on the underside of his wrist. There is one blood droplet tattooed falling off the cross. He is more than an underling.

Whispering in the young girl's ear Khara said she "should walk out of the office, and leave through the main lobby out to the street. Then go home the best way you can."

The young girl said "okay", put her arms around Khara's waist, and hugged her thank you. Khara looked down at her and patted her on her back gently. Then the young girl left and she turned her attention to the general manager.

"How many suites do you have here?"

"We have two and a penthouse on the roof. But they are all reserved already."

"I'll take the penthouse suite. Cancel the other reservation."

Khara holstered her gun then took one step back from the general manager. "And now we'll both go for an early dinner together in your restaurant. Just remember that if I feel you are trying to warn someone I will kill you where you stand."

The manager nodded his head affirmatively and then walked out of the office first with Khara walking directly behind him. They stopped at the front desk, and he asked the desk clerk to bring him the key to the penthouse suite while he is dining in the restaurant.

As they entered the restaurant greeting area she told the maître d' she wanted a table by a wall and not a window seat. He said that table number eighteen is available. She is not interested in the view that the restaurant has to overlook a plush manicured Mexican garden. The maître d' led them past tall floor to ceiling windows over to a table in the rear of the restaurant. Khara sat in the chair where her back is to a solid wall. She wanted to see who is approaching her table at all times.

This is a fine dining restaurant that the hotel runs, and the double linen tablecloths hung over the edge of the table almost touch the floor. Once seated, she reached into her jacket pocket, gently and slowly took out her .38 snub nose, and placed it on her lap. Then covered it with the tablecloth, and not visible to anyone passing the table.

A waiter walked over and started to pour water into both glasses on the table. Khara waved him off, and asked for two organic bottles of water, unopened. She knew better than to drink the tap water, and especially if it could have been drugged to knock her out. Unopened bottles are safer.

She is handed a menu and it is in both English and Spanish.

"What do you recommend?"

She looked at the hotel manager and asked him in English. No one yet heard her speak Spanish.

"The twelve-ounce sirloin steak, cooked medium, with a demi glaze is very good. It comes with small roasted white potatoes and candied sweet carrots in a reduced butter sauce. Our restaurant is a four-star establishment?"

"I really don't care. But I am looking forward to the free meal. Thank you in advance."

The waiter is standing next to the table waiting to take their order. The manager told him that they will both be having the sirloin dinner. He wrote it down and asked if they would like a shrimp cocktail or a salad.

Khara said "we will both have the shrimp cocktail. Thank you." The waiter then went into the kitchen to place the orders.

"It's amazing what drug money can accomplish." She dryly said to the general manager as he sat back his chair, and said nothing.

One of the front desk clerks came over to the table and gave the manager the electronic key to the penthouse suite. He thanked her and passed it over the table to Khara who is sitting directly opposite from him. "Thank you," she said as she took the key. "After we finish dinner you will come with me to the elevator as we go to the penthouse." He shook his head in agreement and said nothing more.

When the food was served the waiter placed the dishes on the table in front of each of them. Khara looked up at the waiter, smiled, and said: "thank you." The waiter turned and left. Then she reached across the table and exchanged plates with the hotel manager. He stared at her for a second, then picked up his knife and fork and started to cut his steak into small pieces.

When they are finished eating the manager signed the check for the meal. Khara lifted the tablecloth slightly, put her snub nose .38 back in her jacket pocket, then they walked out to the elevators to go upstairs to the penthouse.

Reaching the top floor there are three heavily carved wooden doors in a small elegant lobby. Khara asked if he carries a passkey to all the rooms. He said he did.

"I want it now."

She looked at the key the desk clerk brought him and it is for suite number three. He opened his wallet, took out his passkey, and gave it to her. Khara went to door number two and opened it. She waved for him to go in first, which he did. She followed him in.

"Are the other suites filled yet?"

"No. They are rarely used."

"Okay, now call downstairs for room service. I want some packaged cookies and soda brought up." The manager picked up the phone, and in Spanish ordered the food and drinks. Then he said to call his boss that "the murderer is here with me." Then he hung up the phone.

He did not know that she spoke fluent Spanish. She had only spoken in English to him, and Khara heard and understood everything he said.

"Come with me next door," Khara told him. Using his passkey she opened the door to the penthouse that is situated on the opposite side of the building where she is staying. They both walked in, and Khara told him to stop by the balcony door, which he did.

Now speaking to him in Spanish she told him "I warned you not to say anything about me being here."

She saw the look of panic on his face. He didn't know she spoke Spanish, and Khara thought he must have finally recognized her when he said that on the phone. She told him to open the door leading to the balcony. They walked slowly outside when he suddenly turned to her and begged for his life.

"Please let me go. I will not tell anyone you are here. I am married with a wife and three small children at home. Please don't kill me."

She looked at him with tears running down his cheeks.

"Tell me, how many young girls did you send to Pablo to be raped and sold as sex slaves in Texas?"

She saw him start to shake. Khara knew that he is aware she is a killer. Her reputation from New York is probably now a legend in the Ecru Cartel.

At first, she thought of throwing him over the balcony from twelve floors up. But she changed her mind. Someone might find him, and she isn't yet finished in Nuevo Laredo. She ordered him inside, and they went into the bathroom where she told him "fill the tube all the way up."

She observed him shaking from nerves. The manager suddenly turned to her and attacked Khara. He is able to hit her in the face with a glancing blow as she shifted to the right trying to deflect his punch. She reached over and grabbed his forearm, twisted it behind his back until she heard a bone snap, then grabbed him by the back of his shirt. While still holding his arm behind him, Khara tripped him and pushed his face down flat into the tub as it is filling with water. His legs are flailing wildly beneath her until she grabbed his other arm and twisted it behind his backbreaking it also.

His face is now flush to the bottom of the tub as the water started to rise, seep into his nose, and began to flow into his lungs. When the air bubbles finally ceased Khara let go of his limp body as he fell backward onto the shiny Aztec mosaic tiled floor. She lifted him into the tub and filled it until his body is covered. She turned off the water, closed the bathroom door, and left that penthouse suite while putting a do not disturb sign on the handle.

Going back into her suite she locked the door, put the chain on it after taking the desk chair and wedging it under the door handle. Exhausted from a hectic day she undressed, took a hot steamy shower, and then fell asleep on a fabulously luxurious king-sized bed. It is now only a little past eight in the evening.

About midnight she awoke, decided to go to the hotel lounge, drink a cold bottle of beer, and chill out listening to some music. Putting on her jacket again, and with both her guns on her, she took the elevator downstairs to the lobby.

The lounge is crowded, the bar is full of young people drinking and talking, while she sat at a small table in the rear of the lounge. A nice looking young man approached her and in Spanish asked if he could sit with her. She liked his looks and said yes. He is staying in Nuevo Laredo for business. They both ordered a beer, and Khara ordered her usual, Heineken in a bottle. She looked at his wrist as he lifted the bottle to drink from it. There is no red tattoo of a cross on his left wrist.

After a few minutes of small talk, he asked her to dance. The small lounge trio is playing a slow tune, and she held him tightly against herself to see if he is armed under his jacket. He is not armed.

He smelled fresh and clean so after dancing that night Khara invited him upstairs to her suite for more intimate relaxation. He left about two hours later, and she went back to sleep.

Chapter 14 -

The next morning Khara awoke to the sun shining into her room through the sheer linen drapes. She sat up in bed, placed her feet on the floor while picking up her Sig .45 from the nightstand, and carrying it into the bathroom while she showered.

While the water splashed all over her she dabbed on some of the body wash the hotel placed on the vanity next to the two sinks. Then she dressed and decided to go downstairs for a nice Sunday morning breakfast in the restaurant. She looked through the peephole on the door to make sure there is nobody waiting to ambush her in the small lobby.

Seeing the hall is empty she took the elevator down to the main lobby and walked into the restaurant. She asked to be seated at table eighteen and took the seat where her back is to the wall. Again she placed the excess tablecloth over her snub nose .38 that is resting on her lap and hidden from sight.

When the waiter came to her table to take her breakfast order she decided to order the crepes from the moving cart while the chef makes it at your table. She also ordered two bottles of unopened water.

While she is waiting for the cart to come over Khara saw a very handsome man in a white linen sports suit enter the restaurant. His floral shirt is unbuttoned about half way and his toned hairy chest is clearly visible. He walked directly to table eighteen and politely asked if he could sit down with her. She nodded her head, yes, and he pulled out a chair and sat at the opposite side of the table from her.

"Good morning Khara," he said to her in English with a heavy Spanish accent. When he greeted her by the name she knew they found her. That is what she wanted, and she is what the cartel wanted.

After greeting her he waved to the waiter to bring him some coffee by pointing to his empty cup. As he did that she noticed a small red cross on the underside of his left wrist, and there are three red blood droplets falling off of it. He is not Alejandro, but he is a very senior member of the Ecru Cartel.

"Did you enjoy yourself in the penthouse suite last night?"

"It is quiet. I might recommend it to friends when I return to New York."

"I am glad that you enjoyed a relaxing night. We would like to make sure you also enjoy a long restful sleep."

"I'm sure that piece of human shit Alejandro wants me to have a long sleep."

"He is very upset that you killed his sister. I would like you to finish your breakfast, and then come with me outside by the front lobby. I have a blue taxi waiting for us there. I'd like you to join me for a short ride. Alejandro would like to personally kill you."

He smiled as he looked at her.

"And if I don't go with you, then what?"

"I will order you killed right here in the restaurant. There are men at the surrounding tables waiting for me to signal them, and you will not leave this table alive."

Khara answered him in a softer voice this time.

"Please listen very carefully. I want you to hear a very small sound".

Slowly, with her thumb, she cocked the hammer on her snub-nosed .38 that is sitting on her lap; causing him to hear a very faint clicking noise. "Did you hear that? You will be the first one to die. I don't miss."

"You are a very brave woman. I believe that in your country they call this a Mexican standoff. The next move is up to you Miss Bennett."

Khara glanced to her right, and then to her left. Two clean-cut businessmen in suits are having breakfast by themselves at two nearby tables on a slightly elevated platform. At a table directly to her left is a nicely dressed young Spanish woman in casual business attire that walked in after Khara. She is reading the morning newspaper and has a very thin scar running down the right side of her face from her ear curving to under her chin. She thought that the scar looked like it might have been caused by a razor blade. She now must decide if he is bluffing, or are there one to three cartel thugs ready to kill her.

From the speakers in the ceiling soft relaxing music is playing in the restaurant. The waiters are bringing food to the tables, and Khara is sitting there looking at this very handsome man at her table. She is trying to decide her next move.

She sat back in her chair and looked directly at him.

"Slowly place your hands on the table, palms facing down. If you as much as blink I will kill you right now."

He put his coffee down, leaned forward in his chair, and smiled at her. In a slow manner he did as she said, then he told her "you have nowhere to go. The minute you stand to leave without me you will be killed."

They sat there facing each other for a while until most of the other guests left the restaurant. Waiters are walking around cleaning off tables. New people are now entering the restaurant taking tables nearby. It is a packed place to be eating in the morning. One young waiter came over with the crepe cart to make crepes for the lady with the scar on her face that is sitting at the table to Khara's left. He positioned himself between her and Khara. Suddenly he lifted the linen cloth covering the bottom of the cart and took out a pistol, and twice shot the handsome man in the head who is sitting with Khara.

In Spanish, he yelled out at the falling body "this is for killing my father and brother."

The two businessmen Khara noticed sitting at nearby tables took out guns from under their jackets and shot the waiter multiple times. He fell back onto the lady's table and then slid onto the floor.

Khara raised her gun and shot one of the men in the chest twice then ducked down behind the crepe cart. The remaining gunman started to shoot blindly at the cart and unintentionally shot the lady with the scar. She fell onto Khara and her body absorbed multiple bullets from the shooting businessman that was intended for her.

He is approaching her and is only a few feet from Khara when she heard a dry shot. He started to drop an empty magazine from his gun and reload. She pushed the dead body of the woman off of her, and kneeling Khara looked up and shot him three times in the chest. He fell backward onto the floor dead.

Khara quickly looked around and saw everyone running out of the restaurant. She put the .38 in her jacket pocket and ran out hidden in the middle of the mass exodus into the main lobby.

People are screaming in the lobby that there is a shooting inside the restaurant. It is total chaos and Khara is able to run unnoticed out of the hotel lobby with them. She saw the blue taxi that is waiting at the back of the taxi line for her and the dead cartel guy that was just shot in the head at her table and headed towards it.

She opened the front passenger door and slid in. The driver looked at her with a puzzled expression. In Spanish, he asked her "where is he?" referencing the dead cartel bigwig. "Muerto. Unidad en torno a la parte trasera del hotel" [Dead. Drive around to the back of the hotel] Khara told him. Obediently he started the car and pulled out of the taxi line into the congested street traffic.

Taking her .38 out of her jacket she pointed it at him. Khara knew she only has one shot left but felt reassured that her Sig .45 is still loaded, still in her shoulder holster, and she has two clips for it in her other inside jacket pocket.

The blue taxi made two turns and when it arrived at the rear of the hotel stopped. Khara told him in Spanish to wait two minutes. She hopped out and ran to the thick hedges against the back of the hotel and retrieved her MP7. Then re-entered the blue car through the rear door, and sat in the back seat while the taxi started to drive.

The driver did not say another word to her while he is taking her to an unknown destination. He is bringing her to a warehouse district where Alejandro is waiting to kill her. Driving on the Boulevard de Campanario he turned off onto a small side street, stopped at a small door in the rear of a monstrous warehouse building, and she stepped out. The blue cab drove away in a rush leaving her standing there alone.

Holding her MP7 Khara turned the handle to the door, slowly opening it, while peering in, as best she could, to the darkened interior of the building. The sun is bright and making the interior hard to see. There is no noise coming out of the warehouse, and this made her very suspicious. She knew that someone must be inside, or why would the blue taxi drop her off at that location.

Khara flung the door open, it slammed against the other side of the building, and gunfire erupted from inside. She hugged the exterior cinderblock wall as the bullets flew out the door hitting the sides of the entrance, and others bouncing off the opposing warehouse wall across the empty street from where she is standing.

Looking down at the ground she saw two black shadows on the dirt road. She pointed her MP7 upwards and started to shoot. One body dropped to the ground, and the gun from the other shadow fell also; dripping blood onto the hot dry pavement.

Khara ran about fifty feet to the corner of the building and stopped. She knew she could not stay where she is outside. Luckily it is a Sunday and most of the manufacturing and distribution businesses are closed.

Noticing there are large over the road tractor trailers with sleepers in the tractor cab parked in the next warehouse lot, diagonally across the street, Khara started running towards them. She is able to reach them before anyone stepped out of Alejandro's warehouse looking for her. In her haste, she did not realize that there are cameras on all the building's roofs, and watchmen in the building, who saw her get into the truck.

Grabbing onto the cab's chrome sidebar she opened the door to the tractor and jumped up into the driver's seat. The keys are in the ignition. Khara started the engine and stepped on the right pedal trying to quickly warm it up. She did not need a lot of time to get the diesel warmed up and going. Finally, she depressed the clutch, put it in gear, and it crept forward slowly. Increasing the truck's speed, she up-shifted the transmissions gears, while driving back to the warehouse door and past it to the end of the block.

She stopped the tractor-trailer, put it in reverse, and drove back toward the open rear warehouse door while picking up speed. As the truck is going almost forty miles an hour in reverse and the rear of the trailer is almost even with the warehouse door, she turned the wheel hard and crashed the trailer through the wall of the building by the opened door.

The back of the trailer smashed into the entry with such force the cinderblocks fell away, and the truck continued into the bowels of the warehouse.

Khara held her MP7 as she steered back into the dark warehouse. She saw the flashes from the cartel guns brighten the darkness. She returned fire aiming at the barrel flashes of their guns.

As the trailer bounced up and down she thought it is going over the bodies of cartel gunmen who didn't get out of the way fast enough. Khara kept gunning the engine and didn't apply the brakes. Finally, the truck stopped when it hit another interior wall and could go no further. The cartel shooters came charging the truck's cab firing their guns as they approached.

When there is no return gunfire from the truck they stopped shooting, and slowly walked towards the truck's cab. Khara jumped into the back of the cab when it no longer moved in reverse, and it halted its rearward motion. She sat back on a mattress where the driver would normally sleep on long hauls. Silently she waited. In the darkness of the warehouse, no one could see her wedged between the two high back seats of the cab.

Suddenly gunmen scrambled up on the running boards, grabbed the chrome pull-up bar handles on the side of the tractor, and opened both doors on each side of the cab. They awkwardly climbed into the cab of the truck. Khara made no sounds and continued to wait. She held her Sig .45 in her left hand, the MP7 in her right one, and she opened fire at point-blank range once they climbed in and advanced onto the cab's seats.

Two men died at her feet, then two more right behind them. The truck's interior is now filling with dead and bleeding bodies. The men below the cab started to shoot into it. Khara pulled a body into the rear of the sleeper where she is, and onto the mattress. Wrapping his dead torso around her back the dead cartel gunman absorbed the incoming bullets, and none hit her. She realized that due to the height of the trucks' cab the gunmen are too close, and are shooting up into the roof of the cab completely missing her. She stopped firing as she did not have a clear line of sight to shoot at anyone. The Cartel bodies are piled too high in front of her on the seats, and gear shifter.

After a few seconds, the gunmen also ceased shooting at her. She heard a man yelling in Spanish for her to come out, and she would not be killed. Khara sat silently and listened.

Men on either side of the truck cab reached up and grabbed the ankles of the dead men that are hanging out of the open doors. They started to pull on their legs to bring them down and out of the truck. One after the other the bodies fell on the ground with a dull thump. Khara did nothing. She stayed silently still.

"Go up there, and get her body" she heard someone yell in Spanish.

Releasing the spent clip onto the mattress she reloaded her pistol. She is now down to her last clips, and if they continue to attack she will be out of ammunition soon. Khara remained quiet and waited.

Again gunmen climbed up into the truck's cab, like an army of ants on the march, from each side door they tried to come inside. Khara waited, and then she again opened fire at point-blank range killing them instantly as they began to climb into the cab again. The shooting started all over.

Khara faintly heard sirens in the distance. The sound began to get louder, and closer. The gunshots stopped, and she could hear them yell in Spanish to leave the building; the police are coming.

She kicked the remaining dead bodies out of the cab and climbed back into the driver's seat. Downshifting the gears to pull out of the warehouse she wanted to go forward. The truck would not move. In the shooting, some bullets must have damaged either the transmission or engine. The cab is full of bullet holes, and not knowing what happened to the engine she decided to climb down out of it, and go on foot.

Khara ran to the other end of the warehouse where the offices are situated. As she exited the entry door by the building's lobby she saw the gunmen drive off. She knew it is only a minute or two before the police would arrive, and she must try to get as far away as she could. Slipping the MP7 under a desk she left the building and started to run in the opposite direction from the coming sirens.

She made it to the Boulevard de Campanario after the police cars passed her by. She waited at the side of the highway for a vehicle to come along. There are some smaller trucks driving towards her. She pulled her jacket back a little over her shoulders, pushed her chest out, and smiled. The first truck to come by her stopped, and she hopped in.

She offered the truck driver a hundred American dollars to drive her back to the hotel. He smiled to himself and is probably very happy that he stopped for her. Driving her to the hotel he took her around to the back entrance. It is almost two in the afternoon. She couldn't walk out of the small cargo truck yet, and chance being recognized. Another hundred dollar tip and she is able to sit with him in an air-conditioned cab till three o'clock came.

Exactly at three a red car pulled up by the back of the hotel and stopped. Khara thanked the truck driver and ran to the waiting car. Big Boy kept his word to her.

Chapter 15 -

The red car sped off to a pleasant looking house nestled in a quiet residential area of the city. Stopping at the rear of the driveway, the back door to the house opened, and Khara is waved to come inside. She hurriedly opens the car door and runs toward the man who is waving to her.

When she entered he introduced himself to her and explained that they are the Grupo Marte [secret police] and also secretly worked with certain members of organized American crime organizations. Their main interest is in Mexico, but the Americans seem to help out whenever there is a need on either party's part for assistance.

Being asked for her passport, Khara took it out of her left boot and handed it to him. One of the other policemen took it over to a room in the front of the house, and it is stamped with an entry mark. She is now legally in Mexico.

It is explained to her that they were apprised of what is going on by their American contacts, tried to follow her, but the shooting and chaos in the restaurant threw them off. They did not count on that happening and lost her when she ran out of the hotel in the craziness of the moment. The only reason we found you is the tractor-trailer you stole set off a silent motion alarm in the parking lot. The security guards also called in they heard a tremendous amount of shooting in the area. We knew it had to be a cartel matter so we came to investigate.

"Do you know what happened to the hotel's general manager? We have been following him for a while and thought we had him for kidnapping young girls. But when you entered the hotel he disappeared."

Khara smiled at him, shrugged her shoulders, and said nothing. She saw his face and understood that they are now not going to look for him. In unspoken words, they knew she must have killed him.

The police officer she is speaking to had a phone call and excused himself for a moment. When he returned he said to her "my men counted fifteen dead cartel gunmen in that warehouse. It is now a certain guarantee Alejandro definitely wants to kill you. He will not stop at anything to have it done. We want to get you across the border before tonight for your safety."

A rusting older car pulled into the driveway, and an officer went out to meet the driver. He returned in a few minutes with Khara's MP7 in his hand. In Spanish, he said to her "I think you forgot this at the warehouse." She took it and thanked him. She had a few loose bullets in her jacket pocket, and she inserted it into the weapon's clip. "You must go now Miss Bennett, We can't wait any longer."

They ushered Khara into the garage and asked her to sit in the back of a large SUV with dark tinted windows. On each side of her are armed Grupo Marte policemen, one sitting behind her in the trunk area, and two in the front. She sat in the middle of them with the MP7 on her lap. Then they pulled out onto the street and headed for the border crossing.

When they reached the avenue leading to the long bridge over the Rio Grande they pulled over to the side of the road and waited. A Mexican border patrol vehicle came to meet them and waved for them to follow it to Texas.

When they arrived at the United States border an American border patrol vehicle approached and stopped the two unit Mexican caravan, and an American agent came over to speak to them.

A tall red-headed American agent with a Boston accent spoke to the driver of Khara's car and peered in the back seat to look at her. The back window is rolled down and he asked to see her passport. Khara handed it to him and he saw it is properly stamped. He also noticed the MP7 on her lap. "Where did you get that weapon?"

"It's a long story but I am a New York City Police Detective, and here is my identification." She smiled, took out her ID wallet with a badge, and handed it to him. He looked at it, smiled back at her, and then returned the wallet.

"Okay, get out and come into my vehicle. I'll take you the rest of the way." She thanked the Mexican officers for their help and slipped into the back of the American border agents SUV.

As she is being driven over the Rio Grande she noticed that there are several small armed boats patrolling the American side of the river. It is a very tight border crossing, and she is glad it is being handled for her benefit.

Once on American soil, she thanked the border patrol agent and told him to look her up if he is ever in New York. He thanked her for the offer and asked if there is something else she needs in order to get back home.

"No, I just need to call a rental agency and get a car so I can drive back home."

"The airport is not far from the border, and I can drive you there to rent one. All of the big car rental companies are there. When I get off duty in an hour or so I can take you."

"Thank you for the offer. I'd be very grateful if you could do that for me."

Khara waited at the agent's office till he is finished with his shift. She is now in the passenger seat of his personal car and he is driving her to the airport. When they arrived he said "it's too bad you aren't leaving tomorrow. I would have liked to have taken you out for dinner tonight, and show you the sights in Laredo while you are here."

"You know what? I think I can wait a day to return home. Let me make a call and arrange that. I'm still on vacation time and don't need to be back so soon."

"Great. Come back to my place with me, and I'll let you use my computer at home to book a flight out tomorrow instead of driving. If you like you can stay over tonight with me. That way you can save the expense of a hotel room."

Khara understood the implied no strings attached offer, though he is a good looking younger man, and she is ready to chill with him. "That sounds good to me, let's go see the sights." She still carried the loaded MP7 on her lap when she said that.

It was late in the afternoon as he drove her around Laredo showing her different churches and plazas. He asked her if she would like to go into one of the churches and say a prayer. He stopped at San Augustin Church and offered to go in with her, but she declined.

"I'm not a holy roller type of person. I really have no interest going in a church."

"Did your parents ever go to church with you?"

"No. I was raised in abusive foster homes till I was eighteen. My father was a drunk who was killed in a bar fight, and my mother committed suicide in front of me when I was six. I never went to church, and I have no use for it either. That upbringing kind of hardened me to life."

"I'm sorry to hear that Khara. I think you might be missing out on something good."

"Don't be, I get by just fine in the world, I think."

"Anyway, how about having dinner with me tonight? It's getting late and there's a great BBQ place right near where we are, dinner's on me."

"Sounds good, let's go. Then I'd like to go back to your place, wash the clothes I'm wearing, and take a nice hot shower while they're drying. Care to join me?"

***

The next morning before getting dressed she showered again, and after a cup of caffeinated coffee is ready to go to the airport. Her host gave her an old backpack he owned so she could put her MP7 machine gun in it. He didn't think it would look good with her toting a submachine gun through an American airport in plain sight. Then he offered to drive her to the airport, and when they arrived she thanked him with a big kiss. "I had a great time yesterday with you. If you ever get to New York make sure you look me up" she said as she opened her wallet, and gave him her police business card with her contact information on it.

When she walked into the airport she knew she had to go to the airline's security office to check in as an armed law enforcement officer. That way she is allowed to bring her weapons on the airplane, and also enjoy priority boarding. Her MP7 is in a small backpack on her back that the border patrol agent gave to her to keep it in.

As Khara is waiting by the gate for the plane to arrive she called Don Weber on her cell phone. She didn't use the special number he gave her because she didn't feel it is needed at this moment.

"Hello Don, this is Khara. Are you still in Texas?"

"No, I'm in New York right now but I'll be leaving soon. I had to fly back for the weekend to clear up some old casework. Where are you?"

"I was in Mexico for a few days' vacation time by myself. I will be flying in from Laredo in a few hours. Can you meet me at Newark Airport?"

"Okay, I'll look up your flight. And I'll see you at the gate. You weren't going after the Ecru Cartel were you?"

"It's a long story, Don. I'll explain it to you when I get back home. Just please be there for me when I arrive at the airport, I missed you."

"Okay Khara, look forward to seeing you. Have a good flight.

Khara is still nervous about the cartel. The secret police in Mexico had been trailing her, and she wasn't aware of it. That made her uneasy. She liked to know what is going on so she could protect herself. Having Don meet her at the airport is like having a little security blanket for herself. She is ready to board the plane, settle in quietly, and enjoy the few hours of solitude.

There is an announcement in the gate area where she is sitting that the plane was delayed at its previous stop, and a new crew would have to be boarded. The old flight crew is over their FAA allowed day's flight time. As she sat watching the plane taxi to the terminal she noticed the new pilots and crew waiting together by the gate to board the plane.

When the ticket agents opened the gates and the plane is ready for boarding by passengers Khara is able to pre-board with the first people allowed on the airplane. She sat in an aisle seat on the right side of the plane.

She placed her backpack under the seat between her legs where she could keep an eye on it. Although the MP7's safety is on she didn't want it falling out of an overhead compartment and going off on the plane. Khara sat back and waited for the rest of the people to board the airplane.

When they are ready to take off she looked around at the other passengers and noticed it is not a full flight. There is an empty seat in almost every row. She did not think too much of it and is buckled in ready to get airborne.

After the takeoff, Khara took a magazine out of the zippered pouch from the backpack at her feet and started to read. A stewardess came down the aisle with a beverage cart asking if any of the passengers would like a soft drink. She asked for a ginger ale. The stewardess handed her a cup with her right hand and a can of soda with her left hand. Khara noticed a small red cross on the underside of her wrist.

"Shit," she thought to herself. "Now I can't take a nap. I have to watch out for her. It's almost a seven-hour flight, and I won't be landing until dinner time."

The flight is uneventful and the plane is now about an hour out of Newark Liberty Airport in New Jersey. It is beginning to set up a landing pattern to descend when the stewardess approached her and asked if she is Khara Bennett. The stewardess told her there is a call for her from New York in the rear galley.

Khara stood thinking it has to be Don calling her and walked after the stewardess to the rear of the plane. As they approached the galley the woman turned into the kitchen area and reached for the wall phone to hand it to her. Khara closely followed her into the small space when without warning the stewardess took the handle of the phone and smashed Khara on the side of the head. Reeling backward, and slightly dazed, she banged into the bathroom door causing it to swing open; falling into it.

Starting the final landing approach into Newark Airport the plane banked to the right, and Khara fell on the aluminum toilet seat with the cartel stewardess careening on top of her with a knife in her hand trying to stab her. Quickly Khara lifted her legs up, placed her arms under and then around the stewardess's arms, pinning her knees to the floor with her head resting on Khara's lap, and her arms upright into the air behind her back, and the knife dangling in the air.

Reaching up Khara grabbed the stewardess's knife out of her hand and placed the sharp blade against the neck of her assailant.

"How did you know I am on this flight?"

The stewardess looked up at her with a sneer on her lips, and spit in Khara's face.

The plane pitched back the other way, and the bathroom door slammed shut.

"One last time, I want to know how you knew I am on this airplane. If you don't tell me I'm going to cut your ears off one by one, then your tongue. You know who I am, and you know I'll do it."

There is silence. Khara grabbed hold of her right ear and placed the knife behind it when she heard the stewardess start to speak in Spanish.

"We have people in the airport that see all the manifests of passengers flying in and out. They were alerted to watch out for you. When they saw your name they switched the flight crew, and sent me here to kill you."

"Thank you." Then she grabbed the woman's hair in her powerful hands, released her leg hold on her torso, and stood while turning the stewardess's head in a downward motion plunging it into the waterless toilet. Khara held her head there while she plunged her knife into the woman's throat twisting it several times. She held her head in the toilet while she bled out, flushing it when the bowl became filled with blood. When the woman stopped struggling Khara let the stewardess's body fall to the floor. Calmly she turned the sink water on, washed some blood off of her hands, closed the door behind her, and in a calm manner walked back to her seat to put on her seatbelt getting ready for the landing.

As the plane is coming into Newark the other stewardesses are looking for their missing coworker. But the landing had started, and they quickly sat and buckled into their jump seats at the forward part of the plane.

With only one small bounce it landed safely and taxied to the gate for the passengers to disembark. Khara grabbed her backpack and stood while heading for the front of the plane to leave.

As Khara walked into the airport terminal she spotted Don waiting for her by the gate as she left the mobile gangplank and entered the main terminal.

"Welcome home, Khara."

"Thank you, Don."

She held his hand in hers and kissed him hello on his lips. "I'm happy to be back, and really glad you met me here this evening. I just want to wait a few minutes before we leave the gate area."

"Is there a reason?"

"Yes. The Ecru Cartel knew I was on this plane, and they tried to kill me. I want to wait till the crowd thins out so I can see who is hanging around, and who is not."

Meanwhile, she took his hand then backed both of them against a wall so no one could come up behind them.

"Khara, no one is allowed in this section of the airport if they are armed. What makes you think they could have someone armed in here?"

"Don, they have people in the airport in Laredo who work for them. They bribe ordinary people with lots of money to get what they want. They are ruthless."

"I am well aware of that. They would have to bribe a Federal official to get a gun in here. But if it will make you feel any better I'll go along with what you said." Subconsciously he then felt for his pistol through his sports jacket.

They watched for a few minutes as the Newark police rushed in the terminal and to the plane. The dead stewardess's body must have been discovered after the plane landed.

After a few minutes when almost all the passengers had left the gate she nodded her head, and they started to walk to the terminal exit. Don followed the signs to the parking garage to get his car. Walking across the enclosed bridge over the street below them they entered the garage on the second floor by terminal C.

Don saw someone in the corner of his eye standing by a car, and not entering it. He nudged Khara and told her to look to her left. "Do you see that guy over there by the gray car? I don't think he belongs there."

They didn't stop walking to his car and tried to ignore him. Khara instinctively reached inside her jacket and placed her hand on her Sig .45, and then she continued to walk alongside Don to his car.

Finally reaching his car in the middle of the second level she threw her backpack into the foot area of the front seat, slid in, and sat down next to Don. She opened the backpack and took out her MP7 putting it on her lap turning off the safety. She placed the backpack over it while Don backed out of the spot, and left the garage to drive her home.

In the car, Don had some questions he wanted to ask her.

"Khara, you do remember I am a terrorism specialist with the FBI?"

"Yes Don, I know you are. Why do you ask?"

"We had a few reports from The Federal Ministerial Police of Mexico [the Mexican version of the FBI] that recently there was a gun battle at a hotel in Nuevo Laredo involving the Ecru Cartel, and a dark-skinned Spanish woman. The report also said a lot of Cartel gunmen were killed in a warehouse shooting too. You by chance didn't have anything to do with that, did you?"

Khara knew better than to admit to anything.

"I was in Mexico for a short sightseeing vacation. I'll show you that my passport is stamped properly by the Mexican authorities when I get home. Don, you know I can't bring any weapons into Mexico."

Not getting the answers he thought he would get he persisted in asking her one more question. "Please explain to me why you are traveling from Laredo Texas with a Navy issued MP7? You know, the one sitting on your lap."

"I bought it when I was in Texas and thought I'd bring it back with me for self-defense. In the lone start state, you can buy almost any type of weapon. You know that. Plus the Cartel wants to kill me, remember?"

Don is not satisfied and continues his questioning of her.

"Did you have anything to do with that champion boxer's mansion being blown up in Laredo? The news reports said it was a gas line leak. But with you down there I have my doubts. Trouble seems to follow you everywhere you go."

"Don, I may be an adrenaline junky, but I don't go around blowing up homes of famous men or shooting gunmen in a warehouse somewhere in Mexico. I never even rented a car when I was down there. Besides I won't have any idea on how to do that anyway."

"I don't know Khara. It just gives the impression like it is too much of a coincidence to me. Plus they found some of his security men at the mansion in Laredo dead, and not from the explosion. They were shot."

"Don, I dig you. I really do, but I have no good answers for you at this time. Right now let's not talk about things we might not want to know about. I'm hungry, let's stop and grab a bite to eat."

He stopped the conversation and continued silently driving.

It is early evening now, and Khara hadn't eaten all day. She suggested they eat at an Italian restaurant on Hylan Boulevard that she discovered before she left when she was on a date with Al.

Don pulled into their parking lot while she placed her MP7 in the backpack. When they closed their doors he popped open the trunk so she could place the backpack in it for security reasons. But Khara insisted on bringing it in with her. Don is too tired and hungry to argue with her. So she carried it in hidden in her backpack. Then they went inside for dinner.

Khara asked for a table near a wall, and she sat with her back to it. Warm bread and olive oil with freshly ground pepper in it are brought to the table for them.

Don ordered an Amstel Light and Khara said she would like a Heineken on tap in an iced glass. For appetizers, he felt like the fried ravioli with a zesty dipping sauce, and she ordered eggplant rollatini with extra tomato sauce over it.

The dining room manager came over to their table and welcomed them to the restaurant. He smiled and welcomed them then asked: "how did you hear about us?"

"A good friend of mine, Al at the club by the back highway, recommended it to me."

The manager smiled and said "please say hello to Al for me. I know him very well and thank you for coming here tonight."

After he walked away the waiter brought them their dinners. Khara ordered chicken balsamico over angel hair pasta. Don is more plebian, and he ordered the veal parmigiana with a side of spaghetti.

Their conversation during dinner touched on a lot of meaningless things; weather, vacation time allowed, and the New York Mets. "In case you didn't know it, Don, I am a huge Mets fan."

"No, I didn't realize that. Hope they have a good season next year. I read they might sign that Brooklyn kid named Levy for second base. What do you think?"

"I'm not sure. I know he played for his high school team while also playing in a semi-pro league during the summer. He has a lot of talent but the Yankees might draft him first. Just don't know."

They avoided speaking of the obvious issue, Khara's Texas trip, and the cartel killings in Mexico.

When they finished eating the waiter asked if they would like to order dessert. Khara said no. Then she looked at Don. "Would you like to come back to my place for dessert, Don?" winking at him as she said it.

The waiter thanked them for coming in and instead of giving them a check told them "the manager said the dinner is on him as the lady is a friend of Al's from the club."

Khara noticed that Don looked a little puzzled when the waiter said that, but he took out his wallet and left a nice cash tip. Then they walked out of the restaurant, and he started his car for the drive to her apartment.

While Don is driving to her place she sat up front next to him and began to twirl the hair on the back of his neck. He had a question for her. "Who is this Al, and from what club?"

"He is the manager at a club in my precinct. I dated him a while back, but he is in the past."

"Listen Khara, from my experience these clubs are run by criminal organizations. The less you have to do with them the better off you are. I think you know that already."

"Don I completely understand what you're saying. I don't see him anymore." She lied to him, and trying to reassure him she continued rubbing the back of his neck softly.

He drove into her driveway, parked the car, and popped the trunk. She took her backpack out, and they both went inside.

"Don, I want to take a shower. It is a long trip I took on that plane from Laredo. Want to join me?"

Chapter 16 -

Don woke up early, before Khara, about five in the morning to shower and dress. He had to return to his apartment in Manhattan to pack then catch a flight out of LaGuardia Airport around noon. He kissed her on the forehead, and she opened her eyes and smiled at him. Then he went downstairs to his car and drove home.

Now she is awake, it's early in the morning and Khara decided to shower, swab on her coconut body wash, and get dressed. She is always armed when she leaves her house. Slowly she walked down to her garage, looked down her street both ways, and then backed the M3 down the driveway to the street and left home. She is going to Dunkin Donuts to get a large coffee and a toasted bagel with egg and cheese for breakfast.

She tried not to take a regular route out of her development. There are two roads in and out, and she never made a steady pattern of how she used those exits. But there are still only two ways in and out.

This morning, as she was a few blocks away from the main intersection, she saw in the distance the same two Latino men, standing on different corners that she saw previously. This time they are two blocks into her development, and not on the exit corners as before.

This unnerved her. She intuitively experienced a bad feeling about them, but at that moment she could do nothing about it.

When she entered the Dunkin Donuts lot, as a safety precaution, she used the drive up window. She bought her coffee and sandwich then drove three blocks away, and parked on a side street keeping her engine running. The radio is on an oldies station playing Bruce Springsteen's "Jersey Girl". She relaxed a little and drank her morning coffee slowly while it is hot. When she finished her breakfast she drove to the gym where she usually worked out and changed into a pair of pink cotton sweats that she kept in her small gym bag in the car trunk.

After the workout, self-defense training class, and a shower she dressed back into street clothes then returned home to get ready for work.

***

When she arrived at the precinct Matt just left his car and is walking to the front door when he greeted her on the sidewalk before going inside together.

"How was Texas? I heard there was some trouble in Laredo this past weekend. The boxing champ's mansion exploded from a gas leak. It made the late news broadcast last night. Is there any truth to the reports it was a gas leak?" He looked at her knowing something she must have been involved somehow.

"Nobody died that shouldn't have. Now let's go inside."

Khara didn't want to discuss it at the moment. She trusted Matt but is tired and not in a talkative mood that morning.

When they walked into the precinct lobby the desk sergeant told them there is a domestic dispute and that a squad car had responded, and they asked for a detective to come over to the house. The officers thought it is more than what appeared to be a domestic argument.

Matt drove, and while they are in the car he again asked her about Texas.

"So really Khara, I know you told me about Gonzales the boxer before you left for Laredo. Did you kill him, and then blow up the house to cover the murder?"

"No, Matt. I didn't kill him, I don't think. I just kneecapped him with a bullet when I was in his bedroom. Then I left with the young girl I told you about and brought her back to Mexico with me. He was alive the last time I saw him. That's the truth."

"You were in the champ's bedroom... and you also took the girl back to Mexico? How did you do that? She is an illegal alien here without a passport."

"I found a drug runners tunnel under his mansion that went into Nuevo Laredo under the Rio Grande River. I took her back using that tunnel."

"Khara, don't tell me any more. I know more than I should." Matt is about to turn onto the street where the squad cars were stopped. He saw them double parked with their lights flashing, and he pulled behind one of the cruisers and parked. Khara walked up to the first officer she saw, identified herself, and asked what the problem is that they needed a detective. He informed her that social services are also called, and they are on their way to pick up the children. Then two ambulances drove up the street and stopped by the house.

She figured there must have been some really abusive guy in that house. She walked in the opened front door, and saw a younger man sitting on a living room chair; covered in blood. He is holding a kitchen paper towel to the side of his head and wearing a torn tee shirt and jeans. A police officer is standing next to him wearing latex gloves trying to apply pressure to the head wound.

Khara questioned the officer. "Who is he?"

"He is the victim. His wife is cuffed in the other room lying on the floor. The husband told us she went out last night and scored some meth that set her off. She came home late this morning, became violent, took a frying pan, and beat him senseless when he woke up and started to question her. We are waiting for an ambulance to take him to the hospital for stitches and to see if he has a concussion"

Khara noticed dust balls under the sofa, lamp tables, and the housekeeping is not being kept up. She walked into the kitchen and saw a tall gaunt woman almost five foot eleven, maybe one hundred fifteen pounds. There is blood on her blouse, slacks and splattered all over on the kitchen cabinets and floor.

"Can you lift her up, and sit her on a chair? I want to speak to her if I can." Khara asked the officers in the kitchen.

"We are waiting for the ambulance to arrive before we get her up" the officer standing guard over her replied. "We had to use physical force to subdue her when we walked in the house. Once she is strapped onto the stretcher, and immobile, then you can speak to her. She can be very violent. She took some drugs last night, and we don't know what she ingested; just what the husband told us. We need a blood test at the hospital to find out."

Matt went upstairs to see the children. There are two little girls guarded by an officer who is waiting until social services arrive. He noticed that their clothes are unwashed; their hair is stringy and knotted. Khara was asked to come up to see the girls. When she saw them she immediately knew they are being neglected. It brought back memories of her as a young girl in foster care. She turned and walked out of the room without saying a word.

Going back downstairs into the kitchen she saw emergency services are already lifting the mother onto a gurney, and strapping and restraining her securely.

Khara walked up to the woman. "What is your name?"

The woman turned her head at her and yelled: "who the fuck are you to ask me my name?" Her fists are clenched, and she is trying to wiggle out of the restraining straps. "I'll fucking kill you. Get me out of this!" the woman cursed at the medics.

Khara noticed that her hair is sticking to her scalp due to sweat, and her clothes are filthy. Her blouse has black dirt rings around the collar and on the cuffs of her sleeves by the wrists. This woman is filthy, and it turned Khara's stomach. She hoped the medics would just leave the room for a minute so she could pound the shit out of her. She knew that would never happen, though she wished it would.

Khara saw she is missing a lot of teeth, and the ones she had left are dark brown from neglect and rotting out. She saw her gums are inflamed, and knew that most of her other teeth would eventually be falling out. She had to be a big-time drug addict.

With nothing to be discovered in the kitchen, Khara waked back to the living room to ask the husband the names of the family members for her report.

Satisfied that there is nothing meaningful to do after that, they drove back to the precinct to do some paperwork on the call. While driving their radio had a dispatch code 10-24 [officer needs help] at an address on Victory Boulevard.

There is a holdup in progress at a small jewelry store. A police officer was walking out of a luncheonette next door when he glanced over and saw a gunman through the front window pointing his weapon at the sales clerks inside.

The patrolman called in the robbery. Then he went back inside the luncheonette and yelled for everyone to leave by the rear door for safety reasons. The walls are paper thin and if there is any gunfire he didn't want innocent people being shot. The officer then walked out the front door and stood behind his parked patrol car, took out his gun, and waited for backup.

Matt drove to the strip mall and saw there is another patrol car already there assisting the original officer. He steered the car to the back of the shopping center to block any escape from the rear door of the jewelry store.

As he is pulling around behind the stores, and starting to slow down, Khara jumped out of the car. She ran over to the back door of the jewelry store. She noticed a sand-filled cigarette stand next to the back door for the employees to smoke. She turned the handle, it is unlocked, and she figured one of the clerks didn't lock it when they came back out for a smoke. With great care not to make a sound, she opened the door. With great care, Khara pulled it towards herself and peered inside. It opened to a storage room with racks of boxes and wrapping paper stacked on both sides of an aisle.

Without hesitation, she walked in with her pistol drawn and facing up. She could hear some talking in the front of the store and quietly tried to listen. She overheard the gunman tell the clerks that he saw the police outside and that he is going to use one of them as a hostage to escape.

The robber ordered one of the two female employees sit on the floor, and he told the other one to open the back door for him. He had asked where they parked their cars and was told in the rear behind the store. He demanded her car keys and forced one lady to walk in front of him to her car. The hostage opened the door to the back room and the gunman followed her with his gun pointed at the back of her head. Khara heard what is going on. Silently she hid behind one of the tall racks with boxes stored on it.

The gunman walked into the storage room, and he is looking forward towards the rear door. He did not notice Khara standing only a few feet from him to the side, as he passed in front of her.

Carefully she aimed her Sig .45 and took one shot to the side of his head killing him instantly. His brains flew out the opposite side of his head onto the light brown cardboard boxes that are stacked neatly on the racks; his body fell to the floor. The loud gunshot startled the woman hostage as she started to yell, cry, and wave her arms in the air frantically while her body shook violently from nerves and shock. She fell to the floor in tears. Khara knew the woman freaked out from the sound of the gunshot but otherwise, is not injured.

Matt, after he heard the gunshot, came running into the storeroom wearing his badge on his chest. Khara told him what just happened, and he took her gun and gave her his. He is going to take the credit for the shooting because he knew that the supervising officer is going to confiscate her gun if she said she shot the gunman. He didn't want her to be unarmed again after the Mexican killings he assumed she did.

The news media came and again he is the hero that is on the late broadcasts that day. Khara is not mentioned, and this time she lowered her head when she walked by any reporters.

***

That afternoon after work she showered at home then called Al at the club. "Hey, this is Khara Bennett, can I please speak to Al."

The woman in his office answered. "One moment please, I'll page him for you."

"Hi Khara, when did you get back?"

"I flew in the other day. Would you like some company tonight?"

"Sure, come on by. I want to talk to you anyway."

"I'll be there in an hour or so. Bye."

She put her shoulder holster on and checked the clips in her left inside jacket pocket. In keeping with her protocol, she kept two of them there at all times. In her right outside jacket pocket, she placed her small snub nose .38 when she didn't take a pocketbook with her. Walking into the bathroom she sprayed Chanel No.5 on her wrists and neck. Now she is ready to go out for the evening.

As Khara is about to open her front door to leave there is a knock on it. Her landlord wanted to speak to her.

"I heard you walking around before and knew that you had to be back. The shower was running for a long time, and only you do that at least twice a day. I wanted to tell you there have been two Spanish looking guys walking around the area asking people if they know a colored lady who owns a black BMW. They said she lost something, and they wanted to return it. I think its bullshit. I told them you moved from across the street about a week ago. But I don't think they believed me."

"Thanks, keep your guns loaded, and if they come on your property again shoot to kill. Try to see if they have a small red cross tattooed on their left wrist; they work for the Ecru Cartel if they do have one. They'll kill you, and me, without blinking an eye. Be careful." Then she went downstairs to the garage to start her car.

After opening her car door in the garage she flipped the remote, and the large garage door opened. She backed out at speed and took off shifting into second gear heading to the club.

As she approached the exit ramp on the highway she kept thinking about what her landlord told her. "They must know I live in the area. How did they find out?"

This information started to bug her.

Pulling up to the valet parking she stopped at the awning and the young boy took her key and again parked the BMW next to Al's Cadillac. Khara walked up the stairs to the front door, and Big Boy smiled at her. "Nice to see you again Khara," he said as he opened the door to let her in. "Thanks, Biggie" as she walked past him, and kept going. Nothing is said about Texas.

Al met her in the lobby and kissed her on the lips. "Khara you smell delicious." He is smiling at her while placing his hands on her hips. Then took her by the hand, and brought her to the upstairs lounge where they sat in a curved booth again; very privately snuggling against each other.

"I missed you while you were in Texas."

With a smile on her face, she told him "Al, that's bullshit, and you know it. You have so many girls here to fool around with, how can you miss me?"

"Listen Khara, yes there are a lot of girls here for me. But I'm crazy about you. I don't want to get married, I went through a hellish divorce many years ago, but I do want to be with you. I did miss you."

She remembered he told her when they first met he was never married. He couldn't find the right girl. Another bullshit lies she thought to herself.

"That's very sweet of you to say Al" as she kissed him on his neck, and began to nibble on his ear. "Let's go somewhere we can talk about private stuff."

They walked to the elevator, went down to the ground floor, and out the front door. Khara said she would drive so the valet brought her M3 around for them to get in.

"Please drive normally this time" Al requested as he snapped his seat belt in, tightened the straps, and said a quick prayer to Jesus under his breath, but slightly audible.

Khara looked at him and smiled. "Pussy," she said in a whisper. She slammed the gas pedal to the floor, popped the clutch, and took off onto the back highway burning rubber in his parking lot. This time she went directly to the hotel that they usually signed into for the night and skipped stopping under the overpass to talk.

Khara had called ahead and requested a certain room number. She didn't want to stay in the same hotel room consistently. This is a safety precaution against bugging the room, or who knows what else could happen if she fell into a routine.

After parking the M3, and checking in under an assumed name, they went upstairs to the reserved room. She went in first and sat on the edge of the bed. Al followed her in and sat next to her.

"Khara I want to speak to you about what is going down. It affects you, and I don't want you to be hurt."

"I'm a big girl Al. I've been in a lot of dangerous situations in the past year or two. So tell me, what's up?"

In a hushed voice he turned his head to her and told her about Big Boy, and what happened to Pablo Gonzales.

"After Big Boy stuffed the champ into his car trunk he drove back to Cotulla to pick up the rest of his stuff. Pablo was bleeding heavily so Big Boy called my uncles associate in Laredo, and a private doctor was sent to the house to treat him."

"When you shot Pablo you shattered his kneecap, and almost severed an artery. The doctor gave him propofol and benzodiazepine to put him asleep while he worked on him. When the doctor was finished temporarily patching him up for the trip Big Boy placed him in the back seat of the Cadillac and drove back to New York. An IV was placed in Pablo's arm, and one of Big Boys men was instructed on how to keep him alive, and asleep, during the drive back here."

"So Pablo survived? He's on Staten Island right now?"

"No. He needed major surgery. My uncle arranged with an associate of his in New York to have him brought to Brooklyn where a Russian surgeon worked on his knee. My uncle's Russian associate also owns an outpatient surgical center in Brooklyn where he rips off insurance companies for millions. He has a use for Pablo once he stabilized him. Pablo can't die before we monetized him. Alive he is worth millions, dead nothing."

"Who is this Russian man?"

"He runs the biggest Russian organization in New York City, an old-time KGB officer. He's located in Brooklyn with his live-in girlfriend Olga Levinsky. She is a former Russian secret police assassin and is very deadly to deal with. She's a lot like you in many ways; very versatile and knows how to handle herself in difficult situations."

"So what do the Russians have to do with all of this?"

"My uncle and his friend in Brooklyn have worked together in the past. They have a plan to extort millions from Alejandro, and the Ecru Cartel, using Pablo and you as bait."

"I'm a piece of fucking bait to be thrown away?" Khara is starting to slowly fume.

"Not at all, they want to set up an exchange with Pablo for fifty million dollars, and they are going to tell Alejandro that you will be there to hand him over. They feel the lure of you, and Pablo together will be too much for him to resist. He'll probably want to show up himself to personally kill you. My sources tell me he really hates your guts."

"Fuck him, and your uncle. What's in it for me besides getting killed?"

"You're not going to get killed. You'll live without fear of them anymore. Plus I'll be here to take care of you in the future. And that's why Olga will be with you. Between the two of you, Alejandro has no chance of surviving the meeting. Once he's out of the picture my uncle, and his Russian friend, have major contacts in Mexico who will take over Alejandro's operations. Everyone involved gets to split the money from his business evenly."

"I'd like to meet with Olga before I agree to anything." She knew better than to ask for any of the money. Khara knows organized crime doesn't play nicely, and if she is to get any cash from this operation she probably would never live to spend it. She felt she was in enough trouble with the Cartel at her heels, and didn't want to have to deal with the local hitmen also.

"The meeting with Olga can be arranged. Let me make a call tomorrow to my uncle, and he'll set it up."

"Okay Al, now get up, and turn off the lights while I go to the bathroom to shower and get ready. Care to join me?" she seductively told him after lightly kissing him on the cheek, and pulling him up by his hand.

Chapter 17 -

While driving Al back to the club a few hours later to get his car Khara is thinking about what he said to her earlier that night.

She realized that this is going to be a very risky exchange as Alejandro is not stupid. He would probably show up with dozens of his crazed gunmen to ambush and try to kill her. Khara went through that once already in Mexico and is not keen on doing it again.

Olga is an unknown quantity to her, and before she put her life on the line with her Khara wanted to meet with her personally.

Turning off the Memorial Highway on Staten Island, and onto Richmond, Avenue Khara decided to stop by a small strip center where there is a McDonalds and order her breakfast.

She ordered black coffee and the oatmeal cereal with brown sugar. She went to the drive-in window then as is her habit drove a few blocks away to park, relax a bit, and eat her food in peace before starting her day. As she is drinking her coffee the phone rang, and it is Don on her caller ID.

"Hi Don, missed you."

"Good morning Khara. I don't have a lot of time to talk, but we found out the Ecru Cartel knows where you live. They have an informant in Police Plaza that they bribed for your home address, and which precinct you work in."

"Shit, that sucks. How did the FBI find out about this person?"

"They are wiretapping known Ecru Cartel member's phones in Laredo, Mexico City, and Dallas when this police clerk's name came up. They discussed personnel records on what she found out about you. The cartel bribed her with one hundred thousand dollars in cash, and a threat to rape and kill her teenage daughters if she did not rat you out."

"Okay, thanks for telling me. I need to get home to warn my landlord before they kill him." With that, she started to drive, but she kept him on her Bluetooth so she could continue talking.

"Just be careful Khara. The chatter from the cartel is that you were in a gunfight in Nuevo Laredo, and also killed Pablo Gonzales by blowing up his house. Tell me the truth Khara, is what was overheard the truth?"

"I honestly had nothing to do with blowing up his house or killing him. And by the way, I was in

Mexico at the time on vacation in Nuevo Laredo. Check my passport stamp. And I really didn't kill him, honestly, I didn't."

"Khara, you do remember that I'm on the FBI's terrorism task force, don't you? I heard from my sources that there was a gunfight in a hotel between cartel members, and a black girl with an afro, shooting up the place. That girl wouldn't be you, would it?"

"Don, I told you this before. How could I shoot up a Mexican hotel if I can't bring a gun into Mexico? Don't be silly. I need to go, see you when you get back in town. Bye"

She immediately asked Siri on her iPhone to dial her landlord and told him not to answer the door under any conditions. There are killers out to get her, and they would not blink an eye shooting him also.

"Thanks for calling me Khara, but I'm not worried about them. I have my pump-action shotguns fully loaded, and I'm not moving away from them. They come up my stairs I'll blow the shit out of them."

Khara immediately decided that she is going home to escort him out of harm's way after she picks up Matt at the precinct. She dialed Matt and told him to immediately meet her outside the precinct. She explained what is going on at the house, and how they must get her landlord out of there quickly. When she saw him waiting outside the building she stopped, ran back to the trunk of her car, and retrieved her backpack with her MP7 inside. Matt had the keys to an unmarked squad car and they jumped in it and took off with sirens blaring and lights flashing.

On the drive back to her house Matt told Khara that "I informed the captain that you have a tip that the Ecru Cartel knew where you live. The captain told me that he received a call from the police terrorism task force this morning. A clerk in Police Plaza has been arrested. She told the cartel where your apartment is located. The department is sending a swat team to your home right now as we speak."

"Matt, I hope my landlord doesn't take a nap. I know he stays up late, and sometimes takes a nap during the day."

He sped as fast as he could to her home. As Matt pulled into the driveway they saw a lot of men with guns approaching the house from both sides of the street.

He slammed on the brakes and she opened the garage door as he drove inside. Quickly they exited the car, ran up to the front door, and Khara unlocked it. She called upstairs to her landlord that she is coming up to see him. He rang her in, and both of them scurried to get into his second-floor apartment.

Once inside she saw the guns he owned. There are handguns, 12 gauge pump shotguns, #4 buck cartridges with 27 .24 inch lead balls in each, and boxes full of ammunition on his coffee table. There is a lot of potential death in that small room.

"Here, you and Matt take one and use it. He handed them each a loaded pump-action shotgun, a sidearm with extra clips, and a large box of shotgun cartridges to reload with.

Khara took her MP7 out of her bag and swung the strap around her shoulder as she walked to the top of the stairway with her mini arsenal.

Matt said he is going to the back door of the landlord's apartment, and prop himself in a corner. The rear door led to a wooden deck that had a steel spiral staircase leading downstairs to the backyard. He said he is sure they would also try to also come in that way. If they did he wanted to be ready for them.

Khara looked out the front window and saw about ten men with guns drawn running down the block to her house. "They are coming" she yelled out and went to the landing at the top stairs leading up to her landlord's apartment. She is ready for them. At that moment she grabbed her MP7, unlocked the safety, and placed it on the floor beside her. Her landlord handed her a headset to deafen the noise from the guns, and a pump action shotgun to use. She put the headset down deciding not to use it. She wanted to hear them coming for her.

She sat on the top of the steps with her right leg against the wall to buttress the blowback from the shotgun. Khara aimed the gun barrel directly at the front door. Her landlord stood on the side behind her ready to give Khara another loaded shotgun if she emptied hers.

There is a loud banging on the front door like a hammer is hitting it until it swung open, and the locked handle flew off onto the floor. Khara heard them shouting in Spanish to one another to kill the black bitch and everyone in the house.

As the first man started to run through the doorway Khara blasted away at the front entrance. He fell backward with a huge splatter of blood spurting out of his chest. Khara pumped the shotgun and ejected the cartridge while reloading the chamber. Another man jumped over the first body, and he too ran into the hallway. He met the same fate, is shot, and slammed backward into the hallway wall as he collapsed in the doorway. Khara kept pumping and shooting without stopping. Body after body started to pile up blocking the entry to the house. Massive amounts of blood are splattered all over the cream-colored hallway walls and floor.

They continued coming and shooting blindly because they couldn't see her sitting on the top of the stairs. If they are wounded and tried to get up they slipped on the blood, then fell over. Some of them had their arms ripped off from the buckshot; others had massive head wounds killing them instantly. The gunmen then started to shoot blindly upwards towards the second floor; hiding behind the front doorway wall.

Realizing that the front walls are only made from plasterboard with a thin aluminum exterior siding Khara started to blast away at the wall; penetrating it with deadly buckshot. She saw two men fall forwards on the concrete landing behind the pile of Cartel bodies.

Meanwhile, Matt began to shoot at them when they reached the top of the spiral steps in the rear of the house; trying to step onto the deck. They couldn't see him from below the deck, and every time they tried to step on it he fired his shotgun and killed them.

After only two or three minutes of total mayhem and chaos, there is silence.

No sounds are coming from anywhere. Just dead silence.

Khara is given a fully loaded shotgun by her landlord while he reloaded hers. They are certain that there would be another attempt at killing them. But the silence persisted.

Sirens could be heard approaching the house from both sides of the street. The landlord ran to the front window and gingerly peered out. He saw the swat team arrive as they deployed in front of his home.

The officer in charge spoke through the loudspeaker on the armored personnel carrier to the people in the house. "There is a C4 charge wired, and placed on the top of the garage door."

He ordered everyone on the street to get back from the house, and as far away as possible. The police at the scene are then ordered to go house to house and evacuate the entire street. The bomb squad is ordered to come and disarm the C4 charge.

Khara heard that, and both she and the landlord ran to Matt. They opened the back door to get to the spiral steps on the deck. But there are too many dead bodies on the metal stairs, and their descent is blocked.

Matt and the landlord took two dead bodies that are already on the deck and quickly threw them over the railing onto the ground beneath the deck. They told Khara to jump first, and the gunmen's dead bodies would cushion her fall. It is about fifteen feet or so below them.

She jumped, landed feet first with a dead body absorbing the impact of her fall. Khara then tucked and rolled safely off onto the backyard grass. She is okay. Matt and the landlord are the next to jump off the deck following her lead.

Khara knew it is too dangerous to run to the front using the side alley if the explosive charge went off. She looked around, and there is a six-foot tall wooden picket fence all around the yard. Matt and the landlord started to kick off some boards from the rear section of fence so they could climb through it. As they tore off enough boards to scamper through into the next yard the C4 charge exploded in the front of the house.

All three of them ran as fast as they could through the backyard neighbor's yard stopping when they reached the front of the home. Then the gas line in the Khara's house ignited, setting off a secondary massive blast that sent the remaining parts of the house flying into the sky.

The three of them are finally on the street with no place to take cover. Matt saw a 26-foot truck making a furniture delivery across from where they are standing. It is high enough off the ground for the three of them to hide under the chassis as pieces of wood, piping, and sections of furniture started to fall into the street. They are all safe at the moment.

Later that night Matt and Khara, exhausted, returned to their precinct to finish writing their reports on what happened that day. He said goodnight and went home, and she drove her M3 to the club to see Al. She had no place to stay, or any clothes to wear other than what is on her body, and she thought he might be able to help her until she is settled in somewhere again.

That afternoon the police public relations department announced a gas explosion is responsible for the house on Staten Island blowing up. The news media let that story fly except for one reporter who saw some bodies that landed on the front lawn. He approached the officer in charge and inquired about what he saw. He is told nothing of the shooting, and that the bodies are from the people who lived in the home.

The only media company that ran the dead bodies story is a small newspaper on Staten Island itself. No other news outlet picked up on that story, and it died out the next day.

Her captain gave her two weeks off and told her to see a shrink. It is standard department policy after an officer is involved in using a firearm on duty; even though it is not her personal weapon.

As Khara drove her M3 to the club that night looking for Al she heard the news reports on her car radio. When she left her car for the valet to park and started to walk into the club she saw Big Boy is at the entrance as usual.

"Hey Khara, I was having a few cheeseburgers for my first dinner at the bar when a breaking news flash came on the television. Is that your house that blew up?"

"Shit yes."

"Khara, you're one dangerous mother fucker to be around. Try not to blow up this place. I like the job."

"Screw you, Biggie." He laughed and opened the door for her to enter.

Al is informed she has arrived at the club. He is not expecting her but he dropped what he is doing, went to the front lobby, and hugged her hello.

He kissed her on her cheek.

"Come with me to my office."

Taking Khara by the arm they walked downstairs to his private office and closed the door once inside.

Turning to her he said "tell me what happened, and how I can be of help. I saw there was a gas explosion at your house. It is breaking news on the television this afternoon. Are you okay?"

"Yes, I'm alright, but it is not caused by a gas explosion. The Ecru Cartel found out where I lived, and came after me. They blew up the house hoping to kill me, but they failed. I need a safe place to stay, and I need to buy all new clothes. I lost everything I owned in the blast."

"Don't worry about a thing. There's a brand new residential hotel in Bayonne. I know the owner, and he owes me a favor or two since I invested in it. I'll ask Big Boy to drive you there tonight so you can rest. He'll pick you up early in the morning, and take you to the Short Hills Mall to go shopping with my credit card. I want you to get whatever you need. Tomorrow I'll tell my secretary to look for an apartment for you in Brooklyn. You can easily get lost in the crowd there, and not be noticed."

"Thanks, Al. I appreciate your helping me out this way."

"Not a problem. You're my girl, why shouldn't I help you? Come upstairs with me and leave your car here. I'll have Big Boy drive you to Bayonne right now with my car. I'll call you as soon as I finish here tonight. I'll try to stop by later to see you."

"Okay, thanks, Al. I'd like that."

***

The next day Big Boy picked her up at the hotel about two in the afternoon. He drove her to the Short Hills Mall and parked by Bloomingdales Department Store.

Khara went on a shopping expedition with Al's credit card. She bought all new clothes, and Big Boy paid for it with his American Express card. When she is finally finished buying everything she wants they place all the overflowing bags full of clothes in the trunk, the backseat, and one or two smaller ones on her lap in the front seat of the Cadillac. The winter coats and jackets she arranged to be shipped by UPS to the club. She told Big Boy to store them in Al's office for her until she could get there to pick them up.

She also bought some hair products, Chanel No.5, and cosmetics which she placed in her new oversized pocketbook that she just purchased in the accessories department. She also arranged for the other new pocketbooks to be shipped with the coats.

"Hey Khara, I'm hungry. Let's get something to eat. This shopping is exhausting."

"Okay Biggie, I saw the Hilton Hotel is across the street. Let's go there for lunch."

Big Boy drove out of the mall onto JFK Boulevard and crossed over to the hotel. He let valet parking take the car while Khara and he went into the restaurant for lunch. He gave the valet a twenty dollar tip to watch the car carefully because he had clothes in it.

They are seated at a rear table and the waiter walked over to explain the specials for the day. But neither of them are interested; they ordered from the menu. Khara tried the chicken salad wrap with hazelnuts, cucumber, apricot jam, on a whole wheat wrap, and a Heineken beer.

Big Boy ordered two 8 oz. Certified Angus Beef burgers with bacon jam, cheddar cheese on a brioche bun; with a 20 oz. Coors Light beer because he is trying to lose weight. For dessert he ordered the PB & J chocolate cake sandwich with peanut butter mousse, raspberry jam on devil's food cake. Khara declined to order dessert; she is full.

When they are finished eating Big Boy drove her back to the hotel in Bayonne and helped her carry her new clothes back to her room.

Al called and reserved a room on the upper level of the hotel for her for security reasons. She asked for one that high up. Khara always requested the top floor so nobody could come down the stairs when she is in the hallway. She only needed to be careful of someone walking up the stairs. One stairwell is easier for her to watch, not two.

Big Boy said goodbye as she locked the door, took her backpack out of the closet, and opened it. She placed the MP7 on her dresser so it is available in case she needed it.

After carefully hanging her new outfits in the closet she opened the drawers to the dresser and emptied the shopping bags. Slowly folding and placing clothes in the dresser she is very satisfied with her purchases. She phoned Al to thank him and invited him to her hotel room before he went to work so she could personally show him her appreciation.

About an hour later he called that he is coming up to see her, and would be there in thirty minutes or so. Khara told him she is waiting for him and to knock three times at her door so she would know it is him.

When she heard the knocks on the door she didn't walk directly to the door but stood in the bathroom doorway next to the entry door holding her .45.

"Who is it?"

"It's me, Khara. Who else would be knocking on this stupid door three times?"

"Just being safe Al." She unlocked the door and let him in; holding her Sig .45 in her right hand.

"Hey, I have some good news for you. My uncle arranged for you to stay in an apartment in Brighton Beach Brooklyn. It's in the same building that his Russian friend lives in with Olga. There are two doormen at all times and a concierge in the lobby. They are all armed, and nobody gets in there unless he wants them in. You'll be very safe in that apartment."

"Do they also own a parking garage? I can't leave my BMW on the street. It'll get ripped off."

"Better than a garage, there is a valet that will take it, and park in an attended parking lot he owns a block away. It has twenty-four hours a day security on duty watching the cars. You don't need to worry about your precious suicide car being ripped off. Plus you'll get to meet Olga. She will explain the exchange we're doing with Pablo and Alejandro, and how it's going to go down."

Al held up a gift-wrapped small box. "Look what I bought for you. I picked up your favorite coconut body wash to shower with. Want to use it now?"

"Sure, c'mon join me" as she undressed, and headed for the shower.

***

That evening, about six o'clock, Big Boy drove to the hotel with her M3 and waited for her to come down to the lobby. He is going to take her to Brooklyn to meet Olga for dinner. When Khara met him she said she preferred to drive, and told Big Boy to get in the passenger seat of her BMW.

She drove to the Bayonne Bridge and is on Staten Island in only a few minutes heading for the Verrazano Bridge. Her M3 roared with the power of a V8 engine as she pressed the gas pedal to the floor pushing Big Boy back into his seat. Khara placed her portable police light on top of her car and took the restricted high-density traffic lanes for cars with three passengers because it is almost empty. She bypassed the stop and go traffic on the regular lanes to her right.

Big Boy gave her the address in Brooklyn and she turned off the Belt Parkway onto Coney Island Avenue. She made a right and is in Brighton Beach under the elevated train. With a turn or two, she ended up in front of the apartment house that she is going to stay in.

There is a wide covered canvas walkway extending from the building to the curb with a valet waiting for cars to pull up and stop. Khara opened her door and flipped her keys to the valet while Big Boy slowly stood, squeezing out of the car, and stretched his legs.

They walked to the entry doors and the doorman, in a heavy Russian accent welcomed them and said they are expected. The concierge came out from behind a polished brass and marble counter and asked them to wait a moment while he called upstairs to let Olga know her guests arrived.

"Please wait a moment," the concierge asked them. "Someone will be down shortly to escort you upstairs."

It is a short time until the polished art deco brass elevator doors opened, and a man who looked like a typical gym rat bodybuilder walked out with his muscles bulging from under a tight sports jacket. "Please come with me and I will explain the security of our buildings to you before your meeting."

As the elevator doors closed he pushed the top button for the penthouse. "You should be aware that every room, every hallway, every inch of this building is equipped with a video camera with sound in it. In the basement, there are three people watching everything that goes on in this apartment house. Everything is noticed. Plus we hid motion sensors in the blind spots. This is the most secure building in New York City."

Upon reaching the penthouse floor the doors opened into a sumptuous lobby with marble tiles, and mirrors on every wall. Khara felt it was very disconcerting to stand in a wholly mirrored room, and not see a door to leave. Only the elevator door behind her was visible.

Suddenly a mirrored door, without a sound, opened to Khara's right, and she saw this tall thin brunette with long flowing hair walking out to greet them. Her long skirt is swirling and her blouse is nothing short of elegant and expensive. Khara thought she could have been one of those high fashion models she sees in magazines like Vogue. With a Russian accent, she introduced herself as Olga and asked them to please come into her apartment.

Olga apologized that her boyfriend is out of the country at the moment. "He is flying to Cuba for some important business dealings with the communist government."

Khara asked her "how can he be doing business with Cuba. There is an embargo for over fifty years by the United States?"

"Oh, that doesn't matter to him. He has close friends and high-level contacts there from when he was in the KGB years ago. Both of us were stationed there for a while. Cuba is a fun place to live. I enjoyed the years we spent there. Can I get you something to eat or drink?" She smiled while walking to a fully stocked bar in the living room.

Big Boy requested a cold beer, and Olga excused herself as she went into the kitchen to get him one. While she is gone Khara looked around and tried to see the hidden cameras. She spotted two small ones, but they are well disguised in a bookcase. There is a medium-sized wall at one end of the room that is totally mirrored, and she suspected that it is also a two-way mirror with cameras behind it.

Olga reentered the room, gave Big Boy his beer, and then she suggested that she and Khara go for dinner, and get to know one another. Big Boy knew his work there is finished. He thanked her for the beer, and as he turned to leave the muscular man that brought them upstairs is there ready to escort him back to the lobby.

"Olga he can't leave. I drove him here in my car. He has no way to get back to Staten Island."

"No problem." In Russian, she told the muscular man to drive him back to Staten Island. Turning to Khara she told her that Big Boy would be driven back safely in one of her Cadillac Escalades.

"Khara I would like you to come with me now for dinner. We are going to stop in the basement first. I want to show you something we are saving there for Alejandro."

They left the penthouse and took the elevator down to the basement. Once the doors opened a group of unshaved burley looking men are waiting for them. One man opened a second door leading into an inner room with no windows. "This is our secure room," Olga told her. "The cameras see who it is, and if it is okay they will let us enter the next door; come" as the door buzzed to let them open it.

Khara followed her through a series of short hallways that seemed to her to be a mini maze; until they turned into a somewhat darkened room. There handcuffed to a bed is Pablo Gonzales. His left leg is cut off from just above the knee. Upon seeing Khara he started to curse at her in Spanish. He accused her of ruining his career by shooting his knee. She answered him.

"Usted debe ser agradecido que no te maté lugar."[You should be grateful I didn't kill you instead."]

"So that's where this piece of human shit ended up." Khara turned around, and they both exited the room.

"Yes, we needed to remove his leg to save his life. It had gangrene, and it was easier to remove it than to try and save it. Anyway, we are going to kill him at the exchange with Alejandro. Come, I'm hungry." Olga took Khara by the arm and they left the basement to go for dinner.

Chapter 18 -

When Olga and Khara walked out onto the street there are four bodyguards walking discreetly behind them, and two in front. The two women are safely escorted to a Russian restaurant in Brighton Beach where Olga is greeted at the door by her name.

The owner rushed out from the back when he heard Olga is there, and he personally brought them to a table in the rear of the restaurant that is relatively private. It is a very tall booth that no one could see over. Olga and Khara slid in together, and their bodyguards sat at a nearby table out of earshot. Olga cautiously bent over and looked under the table for a microphone. Satisfied that their conversation would be secure she sat upright and waved for a waiter.

A cocktail waitress quickly approached and asked in Russian if they would like something to drink. Olga ordered in English a sour apple martini, and Khara asked for a Heineken beer. After the woman left with their drink orders Olga asked her how she liked the MP7 she used in Mexico.

"How did you know about that?"

"Through our Cuban contacts, we obtained the weapons for Al. We are in on the whole thing. If we can stop the Ecru Cartel then we will split the business between us, Al's organization and our Mexican contacts. It's a no-brainer, plus we did business ventures together in the past."

"So you also arranged with the Mexican secret police? I thought it is his uncle that dealt with them."

Olga laughed lightly when she heard that. "Al's uncle died a few years ago. Al runs the whole operation now. He's run it for years. And he also is very successful at it. He's not greedy, and he shares the profits."

Khara sat back with a poker face not betraying her surprise at the new information. She now realized that she is dating the head of a major crime organization. Then the waitress came back to the table with their drinks.

Olga raised her glass and toasted to the end of the Ecru Cartel. They each took a drink and are ready to place their dinner orders. A waiter walked over and looked at Olga, and he waited for her to order. "I will have the crepes with red caviar to start, and then I'll have the grilled sturgeon with two side dishes for dinner. One will be the pan-fried potatoes, and the other the pan-fried vegetables." Khara ordered the homestyle beef stew served in a clay pot. The waiter thanked them for their orders and went to the kitchen to place it.

After taking a few sips of their drinks they sat back in the booth and started to talk about relationships.

The conversation is started by Olga saying that she knows "Al has a soft spot for you."

"Olga, why would you say that? There are plenty of girls at the club I'm sure he's sleeping with."

"Yes, I'm sure he is, but I know he thinks of you as his number one girl. He told us that you are the only one he could think of that is capable of doing this job. And he entrusted us to protect you. Al is very attracted to you, and he is also very afraid of you. I think he likes walking on the thin edge of danger by dating you. He told us about that Newark warehouse thing that you did with the guy in the upstairs office. Big Boy told him what he saw. Not many people can intimidate Big Boy, but you do."

"He's just a big pussy. Grab him by the balls, and he'll squeal like a pig. All men are like that."

"I'd rather just shoot him. I'm not interested in his balls." They both chuckled at that statement, and Olga offered to share her red caviar appetizer the waiter now brought to their table.

As they started to eat the caviar Olga told her that "Al arranged with us for an apartment on the fourth floor of my building for you. There is twenty-four hour security, and you will be safe living there."

"Thank you. I now need to go out and buy new furniture for the apartment. I never saw the rooms. Can we go back after dinner to look at it?"

"Of course you can, but it is not necessary. Tomorrow bring all your clothes to the apartment after lunch. In the morning I'll arrange for all your new furniture to be delivered. And here is the key for your front door. If you ever lose it don't worry, the concierge always can make an extra one."

"I am not sure if I can afford to buy all new furniture again. I just bought some recently for my Staten Island apartment. But it was blown up by the Ecru Cartel."

"Don't be concerned about the money. Al is paying for it. I purchased it for you this morning when he called me. It's all taken care of already. I hope you like what I selected for you?"

Khara is pleased with that news, but she is now realizing that she is slowly becoming fully enmeshed in an organized crime operation. It is now more than just self-defense against the Ecru Cartel. She is right in the middle of a battle between two major crime syndicates and a Mexican drug cartel and felt that she needs to speak to Eloise about this. She believed in her guidance. Khara decided as she is driving back to the Bayonne hotel after dinner she'll call Eloise for an appointment for tomorrow.

Their dinner arrived in a normal time frame, and Khara said hers is delicious. She ordered the beef stew on Olga's suggestion. After finishing their dinners she wanted to know about the exchange with Alejandro.

"Here's how it's going to go down. We are going to send Alejandro a video of his brother, with you standing behind him together with our demands. This will drive him crazy. We will arrange the exchange in Far Rockaway then we will lead him to the Kennedy Bay Sanctuary where we will kill both of them."

"Olga, how do I come into this exchange after the video?"

"You will be driving the car with Pablo in it. Alejandro will follow you to the sanctuary where they both will meet their death. Tomorrow we will make the video after you move in."

"Okay, it sounds like a plan. And where are you going to be while I am driving Pablo around in my M3?"

"I'll be in the car sitting right behind you, and next to Pablo. We are going to sedate him a little so he doesn't get too frisky. If he does I will just kill him in the car while you are driving."

Khara finished her beer and thanked her for dinner. The two walked back to the building, and Olga gave her the key to her new apartment.

When they arrived at the building the valet brought Khara's M3 to the front entrance. She noticed that the curb is painted bright yellow by the entrance. Olga told her "we reserved the space for our valet. No one parks there anymore."

Khara knew it wasn't legal, but she thought who wanted to get themselves killed over a parking space? When her car arrived she tipped the valet and began to drive to the Belt Parkway on her way to Staten Island.

Her mind is unsettled and running all kinds of shooting scenarios with Alejandro. Khara more than before needs to speak to Eloise.

She pulled off the highway at Bay 8th Street and stopped her car. Dialing Eloise, she wants to make an appointment to settle her nerves.

"Hello Eloise, this is Khara."

"Hi darling, how are you? Why are you calling so late tonight?"

"I want to see you tomorrow. It's important."

"You don't need to wait. I'll see you tonight, I'm lonely. Park around the corner in the second garage on the left, and tell them you are seeing me. They will park your car even if they are full."

"Okay, I'll be there soon." She drove back onto the highway heading for the midtown tunnel.

***

After she parked and entered the building's lobby the concierge called Eloise as is usual. Khara is told to go to her office, and Eloise would meet her there.

She only had to ring the bell once, and Eloise opened the door to let her in. She is waiting for her, and they went into her private office to sit and talk.

Khara explained what happened to her apartment, and what is going on with Olga, Al, and Dan while Eloise listened intently. When she is finished speaking Eloise tried to put everything in a perspective that gave Khara her choices.

"I believe that you are safest with Al and Olga right now. They want you alive because you are a New York City detective that is working with them. You are very valuable to them for now, and probably into the future. If you stop now then you will have them, and the Ecru Cartel, trying to kill you. You have no choice but to go through with this plan. I can imagine that it is nerve-racking, but I know you for many years, and I believe you are capable of handling this."

"I know, but I needed to talk to you about it. I can't tell Don or Matt because I don't want to drag them into this. Besides Don would probably arrest me; he's a goody two shoes if I ever met one."

"I know. You told me before all about him. Khara, I would like to hypnotize you to help you focus. It will take a lot of the stress away. I promise you that it will work. I've done it before too many of my patients."

'Eloise you know I trust you. Go ahead, I'm ready."

Khara sat back on the sofa, lowered her arms to her side, her legs are limp, and Eloise then started to put her under. In a short time, she is finished with her post-hypnotic suggestions and brought Khara out of the hypnosis.

"Are you feeling better now Khara?"

"Yes, thank you. I really do, and thanks for seeing me so late."

"Khara, you know I'm always here for you. It's late already, why don't you stay here with me tonight? You're staying in a hotel anyway, and you know you are always welcome here with me."

Khara said okay, and they both went upstairs to Eloise's apartment.

***

After leaving Eloise early the next morning Khara is driving back to Bayonne to pack her clothes when her phone rang. Don is on the line.

"Hi Khara its Don, how are you? I saw on the evening news shows your home had a gas explosion. I don't think it is due to a gas leak. Were you near it when it exploded?"

"Don it wasn't a gas explosion. The Ecru Cartel is still trying to kill me. Your tip saved my landlord's life."

"I thought that is what it was about. Our New York office investigated the explosion when they heard you are involved. I am calling to tell you that Alejandro is intent on killing you. He'll stop at nothing to get his revenge. He lost a lot of men because of you and he's not happy about it. I can arrange a protective detail for you. Or I can put you in a Federal safe house."

"No Don, that won't be needed. I'll be okay."

"Are you sure? I'll be back in New York in a few hours and we can discuss it further. I'll see you then. Be careful."

"Alright, thanks for the information. I'll definitely see you when you get back. Have to run, I'm driving and talking at the same time. Bye."

"Shit," she said to herself. "He must know I was in Nuevo Laredo and is somehow involved in that shootout, and also Pablo's home exploding. He's not stupid, he must have figured it out. Now I need to finish this one way or the other. Either I kill Alejandro or he kills me."

Driving south on the East River Drive she swung around the battery and is on the West Side Highway heading for the Holland Tunnel to New Jersey. Bayonne is only a ten-minute ride from the tunnel, and she didn't hit any traffic to speak of.

Exiting off the turnpike she is about to park at her hotel when Al called her on her phone. "Khara, how did it go with Olga last night?"

"She is very helpful, thanks. I appreciate you buying me all that new furniture for the apartment. I'm just now arriving back to Bayonne, and I am going to pack my things so I can move in this afternoon."

"That's great. I'm getting into bed now. We hosted a big party at the club last night, and I couldn't leave. Maybe I'll see you tonight before I go to work?"

"That'll be a sure thing, Al. Call me when you wake up."

"Okay, talk to you later."

Khara stopped at a local supermarket in Bayonne and bought a box of trash bags to put her new clothes in for the move to Brooklyn. She does not own any suitcases so this is the only way to transfer everything she has in the hotel. On her way to the elevator she grabbed a cart that is standing in the lobby so she could place her things on it when she is leaving.

It took her only an hour or so to pack everything. She closed the door to her room and headed downstairs to the lobby. Checking out is easy, and then she drove her car around to the front entrance. She is not able to place all the bags in the back seat, front passenger seat, and the trunk. Walking back inside she asked the hotel manager to please hold her extra bags for later. Al will send Big Boy later for them.

Khara did take her backpack out of the trunk to place it on the floor by her front passenger seat opening the zipper to make reaching her MP7 easier.

Once she is settled in the car she drove to the end of the parking lot then stopped to make a call. She needed to let Matt know where she is going to live just in case she disappeared. And she sent a text to Don also. Although she felt safe in the Brooklyn apartment house she did not fully trust Olga yet, or even Al now that she knew he lied to her about himself and his divorce. He had told her at first he never married because he couldn't find the right girl.

***

It is now midafternoon when she drove up to the valet by her building. The doorman spoke in Russian to the two burly men standing in the lobby. They rushed out to help Khara with her garbage bags full of clothes and shoes. In only a few minutes she is in the elevator going to her apartment on the fourth floor.

Opening the door she walked in to see a fully furnished apartment with all modern designed furniture. She is surprised and the fact it is really nicely designed, and she especially liked the red leather sofa that is facing a large flat screen television.

Khara told the men to follow her, and drop her bags in the bedroom. She saw a king size bed with sheets, pillows, and comforter already on it. The wood dresser is all naturally finished and contrasted nicely against the deep green color of the plush carpeting that she is walking on.

She put her hand in her pants pocket and took out two twenty dollar bills to tip the men. They smiled thank you, and politely refused the money. Khara thanked them again for helping her, and they left the apartment.

Grabbing a full garbage bag by the top she placed the bag of clothes on her bed. She opened it to start putting her items away in the dresser. Pulling one draw open she is surprised when she saw it is filled with fully loaded clips for her MP7, and her Sig .45. She closed that drawer and then pulled open the drawer directly below it. That drawer is stuffed with circulated twenty and fifty dollar bills. The drawer under the money one is also filled with money, only it is used hundred dollar bills. Khara knew why they have used bills; they could not be traced. She took out a handful of the twenties and stuffed them in her pants pocket, then she finished unpacking.

When most of the clothes are all placed in the proper drawers, at least the empty ones, she walked into her living room and sat on the leather sofa to relax a little. But it is short lived. There is a knocking on her door, and she walked barefoot on her new soft carpet to see who is there. It is Olga coming to talk to her.

"Olga, come on in." Standing in the hallway she told her "not now, please come with me. We want to take a video with Pablo, and we need you to piss Alejandro off enough that he will want to come here personally to kill you."

The Adrenalin started to rush through Khara's body when she heard that. "Okay wait a second." She walked back inside her apartment to get her jacket and put her boots on. "I'm ready now, let's go."

Khara locked her door and took the elevator to the basement room with her to where they are keeping Pablo. In the elevator, Olga handed Khara a cheap cell phone. "This is a burner phone Khara. It's untraceable. You will tell Alejandro the number to call you when you do the video. He will call for the location of the exchange. When he does make contact you must give him only one day to be there at six in the morning. And tell him you will also text him the bank he is to wire transfer the funds, or we will kill Pablo. Don't forget."

Although Khara is an experienced cop she is not intimately familiar with money wire transfers between banks. "He can't stop or trace the funds once it's wired to your bank?"

"No, we use a small bank in Asia that immediately transfers it out to our secure wire account in Cuba. Once it gets in that account nobody except a certain government official or us can touch it. We worked out an arrangement, that's all I can tell you about it."

Olga then opened the basement door and they walked into the first room. Two men are sitting there guarding the room that Pablo is in. One of them opened the next door, and she and Khara entered.

Pablo is already sitting in a chair wearing shorts exposing his cut off leg from above the knee. There is a digital video camera on a tripod facing him, and a cement wall behind him as a backdrop. Three men are guarding him in the room. Olga handed Pablo the daily Spanish newspaper and told him to hold it upright directly in front of him. The video camera started to record as Olga told him to tell his brother that the New York black detective did this to him. She also instructed him to tell Alejandro they are going to kill him if he didn't give them the fifty million dollars they wanted.

Then Khara is told to walk behind him and place her hand on his shoulder. She held her detective's badge in her other hand and exposed it to the camera so Alejandro would see it.

Standing there Khara said in Spanish to the camera to call her cell for further instructions, giving him the number, and that if Alejandro is not man enough to come save his brother then she'll cut off Pablo's balls and send them to him in Mexico.

Looking at Olga standing next to the camera Khara is told to say again that they wanted fifty million American dollars wired to an offshore account she would text him after he called her.

Olga told her "that should do it. If that doesn't get him crazed then nothing will. His machismo should do the rest for us. Now we wait." Olga took the video with her, and she sent it to her Mexican associates who would get it into Alejandro's hands.

As the women left the room Olga said to Khara the Mexican secret police will deliver the video to Alejandro, and also the money demands.

***

Khara went back upstairs, and as she walked into her apartment her phone rang. It is Al on her caller ID.

"Hey Khara, how do you like your new place? Settled in yet?"

"It's very nice, thanks. I unpacked before, but I need a big boy to pick up the rest of my stuff in Bayonne. Also I just now took care of a few things with Olga."

"Good, glad you are getting along with her. I'll be over in an hour or so. I want to shower and dress. Would you like some company?"

"Yes, of course. I missed you." Now that she understood he is the real boss of the operation, and not his uncle, she knew that she would need to now carefully play him. She ended the conversation with "I'll be dressed in something that you'll like."

"Great, see you soon."

With that settled Khara decided to shower and get ready for an early evening play time with Al. It is not too long before he arrived at the apartment building as he also lives in Brooklyn, and is allowed in the building. He is a known acquaintance of Olga and her Russian boss who is also her longtime lover.

When he rang Khara's doorbell she opened it and welcomed him into the living room. He embraced her, and after a passionate kiss, they retired to her bedroom.

Afterwards, they dressed, and Al suggested they go for an early dinner. He wanted to go to a new restaurant he invested in on Eighteenth Avenue in Brooklyn. An associate of Big Boys opened it with Al's blessing and backing.

"Why did you invest in a restaurant Al?"

"I liked the kid, and he went to school to be a chef."

"Did he ever work anywhere else as a chef before doing this?"

"Yer, he worked for my cousin Joey in Manhattan running the kitchen for him. Besides, it's a guaranteed home run. I know it's going to be a hit."

"How do you now that it's going to be successful?"

"It always is. I spread the word around that I'm behind this place and my associates will be lining up to go there. You'll see. Then after two years or so when it's a smashing success I sell it for a bundle to some sucker."

"Nice. I hope the food is good. I'm hungry. I can't wait to try it."

As Al drove up to Brighton Beach Avenue he made a right turn onto Ocean Parkway, and then went under the Belt Parkway. In the shadows, on the sidewalk under the overpass, Khara noticed a man with a shovel beating a woman. She is kneeling on the sidewalk in front of him with her arm raised to ward off the blows from the metal shovel.

"Al stop the car!" Khara bolted from the car and rushed towards the man with the shovel. Raising her detective's shield she wore around her neck she shouted as she ran to him, stopping almost with her face touching his. "Stop. Police. Put the shovel down and step away from her." He hesitated for a moment; looking at her in disbelief. Then he ignored her, raised the shovel high above his head to strike the woman again. Khara thought he is ready to lower it with all his strength on top of her head. She lunged towards him. Grabbing one of his arms she pushed him back while striking him in the nose with the opened palm of her other hand. Dazed he fell down and dropped the shovel. Placing one hand on the ground he tried to get up. She kicked him in the groin as he bolted back down holding himself in pain. Then Khara turned him over onto his stomach putting her knee on his back and pulled his arms behind him. Detaining him on the cement sidewalk she called out to the woman if she is okay.

Blood is running profusely from the side of her head as she stumbled to stand. "He beats me because I didn't make nuff money last night for him," she said to Khara. Then the woman fell back to the sidewalk sitting against the concrete walls of the overpass; dazed, blood now also dripping from her nose, and her eyes rolling back into her head.

"Al, call the police and an ambulance."

It is not too long before a squad car drove up, and Khara identified herself to the officers. She told them what happened, and that it is their arrest. She didn't want to be involved in any more paperwork, plus she is hungry and wanted to get to dinner.

She opened Al's car door and sat back inside.

"You do that a lot? Jumping out of cars to help someone?"

"I only do it when I need to. That pimp deserved a beat down."

"I wouldn't get between him and her. Why get involved. He's probably a maniac."

Khara looked at him with an air of confidence about her. "Pussy."

Al continued to the restaurant where they enjoyed a quiet dinner.

Afterwards, he dropped her off at her building, and then drove to Staten Island for work. Standing on the sidewalk in front of her apartment house Khara decided to go for a little excursion. She headed for Brighton Beach Avenue so she could walk under the elevated trains. She didn't know why, but she enjoyed the rumble of the steel wheels above her head as the subway traveled on the elevated tracks. She thought to herself to ask Eloise next time she saw her why she liked hearing the trains overhead. Must be some psychological thing from her past; she figured Eloise would know why.

Khara felt her personal cell phone vibrate in her jackets inner pocket. Looking at the caller ID she saw it is Don, and thought he must have some important information to tell her. It is too noisy to speak on the avenue so she walked into the first open store she went by. It is a kosher appetizing store with all kinds of delicacies. Walking to the back of the store where it is quieter she answered her phone call.

"Hi Don, Are you back in New York?"

"Yes, and I'd like to see you tonight. Are you available?"

"For you, I'm always available. Let me give you my new address. I am in a new place in Brooklyn with a doorman. When you pull up to the building you'll see a bright yellow curb in front of the apartment house. That's for valet parking. Use it because parking in this neighborhood sucks big time. Tell them you are visiting apartment 4H, and they'll park your car for you."

"Okay, thanks. I just flew in a little while ago. I'm at Kennedy Airport so give me an hour or so and I'll see you soon."

"Great, I look forward to seeing you."

On her way out of the store, she saw a seven layer chocolate cake, and a strange looking cake sitting next to it that she never saw before. She stopped and asked the counter clerk about it.

"It's a chocolate Bobka cake" he explained. "It's an Eastern European cake. Really good, try it."

"Okay, I'll take that and also the seven layer cake. I'm going on your advice, it better be good."

With her packages in tow, she walked back to her apartment and started to percolate some coffee for Don. She thought he might need some caffeinated coffee when he came in. Khara wanted him perky and fresh for the night time fun she envisioned.

***

Finally, Don arrived and rang her doorbell. She opened the door to greet him with a big smile and a hug. He reciprocated in kind.

"You always smell great Khara."

"Thank you. I've been waiting for you to get back for a long time now. Come in and let's get comfortable. I made some coffee for you, and I also bought some chocolate cake. Let's sit and talk first."

"Okay, sounds good. This place looks amazing. The furniture seems to be very expensive. How did you manage to get this so soon?"

"Insurance payment."

Khara ran her fingers through his hair and started to kiss his neck. She wanted to change the subject. As an FBI agent, she knew that he couldn't find out how she ended up in this fully furnished apartment. She didn't want him digging up information she didn't want him to know about. Khara felt he is too honest and would turn her in if he knew about her activities with Al.

As they sat and engaged in some light conversation about his flight, and where he stays when he is in Texas, the talk suddenly turned serious.

Placing his coffee cup down he told her that the Ecru Cartel is going all out trying to find her. His informants in Mexico told him that Alejandro is still seething about her killing his sister.

"I know I asked you this before many times, but did you have anything to do with the explosion and death of his brother Pablo?"

"Don, I swear to you, I didn't kill him. I was in Mexico when his house in Laredo exploded. It's impossible to be in two countries at the same time."

He reached across the table and placed his hand over hers. "I want you to know I am crazy about you. We have a lot of interests in common seeing that we are both in law enforcement. But I need you to trust me, and confide in me if you are involved in any way with these terrorists."

"Believe me, Don, if I am in trouble with them you will be the first one I call."

"Okay, don't forget that. I want to be in your life for a long time."

Khara smiled at him and placed her other hand over his. "I think you just like the sex, and that's why you want to be with me. No?"

"In all honesty, the sex is good, even great, and you are a very attractive woman. I like being with you. Is that wrong of me to say?"

She stood, leaned over the table, and kissed him. "Let's go inside and shower. I want to be with you tonight. I'll worry about tomorrow in the morning."

The next day when she awoke Khara tilted her body over toward Don in bed, and gently stroked his hair from his forehead to the back of his neck. She snuggled closer and started to lightly kiss him on his neck to wake him. Finally, he opened his eyes and smiled when he saw her. Turning towards her they embraced and kissed.

"Khara are you doing anything today?"

"No, I had no plans. What did you have in mind?"

"I thought maybe we could drive into the city, do some shopping at Bloomingdales, then go for dinner and see a Broadway show later. You know, make a day of it together."

"Don, I would love to do that. I have not been in the city in a long time. Let's go shower then we can go for breakfast. There's a nice luncheonette we can go to. I passed it yesterday when I was walking. It's only around the corner." They jumped out of bed at the same time and walked to the bathroom to shower.

Meanwhile, Olga emailed the video to the Mexican secret police that is to deliver it to Alejandro. They immediately called their contact and handed the movie to him on a disk so it could be viewed. That is guaranteed to start the plan that Al and Olga decided on. Now they have to wait for the cartel to make the first move.

After breakfast, Don drove to Manhattan and parked his car in a garage on a side street near Bloomingdales. They crossed the avenue walking to the department store hand in hand. It's been months since Khara heard the muted sounds of the massive crowds of people walking in the city. The smell of grime from the asphalt brought back memories of when she was stationed at the precinct in Manhattan. Strolling along with Don she took out a small sample sprayer of her favorite perfume and spritzed it on her neck trying to cover the odors of the city.

"You smell great Khara. What scent is that?"

"It's Chanel No.5, my favorite. Glad you like it."

When they strolled into Bloomingdales Don suggested he would like to buy a bottle of perfume for her. She squeezed his hand and said "I would love that. Thank you" Then kissed him on the cheek.

They walked through the women's clothing floors, and Khara started to pick out outfits that she really liked, but couldn't afford to purchase. Don didn't think twice about it, and he bought her two tops, a new leather jacket, two pairs of slacks, and three pairs of different colored jeans. Then he arranged for Bloomingdales to ship all the clothes to her building. This way they didn't need to carry packages with them the rest of the day.

It is now midafternoon, and they left the store to go get something to eat. Khara hailed a cab, and Don told the driver to take them to the Sunburst Diner for lunch. He ate there a few times before, but she never ate there. The bumper to bumper traffic is not too bad, and they arrived quicker than they thought they would.

It is packed with tourists but Khara pulled a waiter over to the side, told him she is a detective, and it is important that they are seated quickly; she is trailing someone. Khara then slipped the waiter twenty dollars, opened her jacket slightly to show her holstered gun, and then waited with Don silently. The waiter spoke to someone, and in a few minutes, they are seated.

The waitress walked over to the table and Don ordered the blue plate meatloaf with mashed potatoes and gravy. Khara wanted a cheeseburger with bacon and sautéed onions.

The food arrived, and while they are eating the crowds dissipated from the diner. They took their time, and when they are finished they each ordered coffee and a slice of pie. It is getting close to dinner time and the people are now leaving to go to a show.

Khara began to hyperventilate as they are passing the scene where the Ecru Cartel stopped the squad cars and shot her. She took a deep breath and continued walking gripping onto Don's arm firmly for support.

"Are you okay Khara? You're holding on to me very tightly."

"I think I'm having a TSD episode right now. My psychiatrist explained to me that this might happen if I were to go back to the scene of the shooting. This is the first time I have been back here."

"Come over here, and stand against the building with me. I want you to concentrate on my face and block out everything else."

He stood with her for a minute or so, and then she said she felt better, and they continued walking to the box office.

They went directly to the TKTS ticket booth and bought two tickets for a show that evening. As Don is taking out his charge card he received a text message from his office. It is about the Ecru Cartel. He read it but didn't say anything to Khara. He didn't want to spoil a nice day with her.

The Broadway show is very entertaining and took Khara's mind off the recent events in her life. She is relaxed sitting in the dark theater watching the play.

When it is over they walked back to Don's car via Eight Avenue instead of Broadway. This avoided another meltdown by Khara and ended a pleasant day together.

When the parking garage attendant brought the car to them they jumped in, and Don took off traveling downtown. He is heading for the Battery Tunnel to Brooklyn, while she is playing with the hair at the back of his head. Twirling it around her finger Khara told him what a great day she had with him. "And I'd like to end it with you in my bed again tonight."

They are driving out of the tunnel on the Brooklyn side when Don told her about the text message he received before they saw the play. "I didn't want to ruin the show for you Khara, but I received a text message sent to me from my office before we went into the theater."

"What did it say, Don?"

"Our sources in Mexico said that Alejandro and his crew are in the United States, and traveling to New York. The FBI lost them when they crossed from Texas into Louisiana. We know they are headed for New Orleans where they know a black market gun dealer that supplied them previously. We have his store bugged, and we know everything that goes on in there."

"Do you know if they arrived at the gun shop already?"

"They have not been in to see him yet. But we are staking it out. Once they leave New Orleans it should take them about a day to drive up here. We'll be waiting for them in New Orleans to stop them before they leave."

"Shit I hope your guys kill every one of those bastards. I'm tired of them already."

"I hope so too. Let's not think about it anymore tonight. There's not much we can do about it right now anyway. Look we're almost at your place."

"Don I can't wait to get in the shower with you, and put on the perfume you bought me today. I put it in my pocketbook."

"You smell beautiful already."

***

Later that night Don crawled out of bed, kissed Khara goodbye, and dressed. He had an early conference call that morning in the New York office, and he needed to go back to his place to change. "I'll call you later after my meeting. I think it will be about the cartel coming here."

"Yer let me know what's happening. I have to check in with my precinct captain tomorrow so I won't be able to see you for two days or so. Call me, don't forget."

"I won't, don't worry about that."

Khara fell back to sleep and awoke late in the morning. She had no meeting with her captain but wanted to have some space away from Don. Her thoughts are that he is stable, good looking and interested in her. Just what Eloise suggested she look for in a man. But at the same time, she liked her private time alone and also being able to play the field with different men. The thought of being tied down again did not appeal to her though he never mentioned a monogamous relationship. But she knew it is going to come up if she continued seeing him.

After soaking in a long shower she dressed and felt she needed to speak to Olga. Khara wanted to find out exactly what the plans are to kill Alejandro. Her nerves are starting to get jittery again. Plus she needed to call Al and see what is going on with him. She is very aware that he is paying for her apartment, and she wanted to spend some time with him too.

First, she called Olga, and they agreed to meet at noon to go over the plan. She told Khara that her significant other is on his way back from Cuba. He did discuss with her what he thought she should do if the Ecru Cartel arrived before he arrived back in New York. Now that the meeting to go over the plan with Olga is set she dialed Al.

"Good morning Al, up early today?"

"Very funny, Khara, you're a real comic. I just woke up and came into my kitchen to eat breakfast. "

"You know I'm just teasing you. Feel like some company this afternoon?"

"Can't meet you then, how about we meet tonight at the club?"

"Sure, I'd like that. See you tonight."

As Khara is hanging up she heard two women giggling in the background. That told her why he couldn't be with her that afternoon. She kind of knew that he played around knowing the business he is in. Anyway, he is paying for her apartment, and clothes, so why not go along with everything are her thoughts.

Going into the kitchen she made fresh coffee for herself and cut a slice of the chocolate Bobka that she bought the day before. The chocolate tasted even better this morning, she thought, as she peeled at the sides of the cake wrapper for the sticky chocolate cake that remained. Khara always drank her coffee black with two sugars. This morning as she sipped the coffee she started to think back to when she was married. For some reason, she remembered but did not understand her ex-husband used to get upset with her for not putting cream in her coffee. It always bugged him. He continued to harp at her over this until it unnerved her enough one morning, and she sent him to the hospital emergency room because of it.

Finishing her breakfast she realized it is almost time to meet with Olga in the penthouse. She put on her shoulder holster, her jacket, and went upstairs for the meeting.

"Hi Khara, come on in."

"Thanks, I am a bit uneasy about this meeting with Alejandro. I don't know how the exchange is going to happen."

"I understand. Let's sit down at my kitchen table. I bought a map of New York City, and I'll tell you generally how the exchange is going to take place."

"Great, I appreciate that."

"Okay, look on the map, and see Far Rockaway over there by the water. Once you go over the Flatbush Avenue bridge to the Rockaway's you have Reis Park. Now that summer is over the parking lot is deserted and open. He can't hide anyone there without our seeing him. That's where we are going to meet with the cartel for the exchange."

"And you think Alejandro is just going to give us fifty million dollars, and not try to kill us?"

"Oh, I'm sure he will think he can kill us. But look at the map. I want you tomorrow to drive on this route I highlighted for you. I will be bringing my laptop and check to see when he does the transfer. Once he wires the funds you will go along this route, and continue on Beach Channel Drive to the Kennedy Bat Sanctuary. There we will set up an ambush to kill whoever is still chasing us."

"Looking at this map you want me to drive under the elevated train on Rockaway Beach Boulevard to the bridge?"

"Yes, I'll be with you in your car. Your car does go fast, doesn't it?"

"It'll blow the pants off you if you don't hold on."

"Okay Khara, that's basically the plan. I'll have a few surprises for anyone who decides to chase us. We'll be fine when it's over, trust me, and they'll all be dead."

"Thanks, Olga, I appreciate your explaining it to me."

"Not a problem. Just remember to bring all your clips with you in the car. Oh, I almost forgot to tell you. This afternoon take your car to this address in Queens. They are going to do a few safety things to your car so we don't get killed in it.

"I'll leave in a few minutes. I have nothing planned for this afternoon anyway."

With that, they stood and together walked to the door for Khara to leave.

"Khara, really, don't worry. We're going to kill those bastards when they come here, you'll see."

With the Queens address on a slip of paper in her hand, she left the building and waited for the valet to bring her car around to the front of the awning. She took out her cell phone and entered the address in the maps app. It showed her where to go, and she tipped the valet when he drove up with her car.

The drive to Queens is slow with heavy traffic, and she eventually ended up in the shadows of the old Shea Stadium. There is a handful of rut-filled roads with small auto repair shops lining both sides of the street.

Slowly she maneuvered around the deep potholes until she arrived at the address Olga gave her. The steel gate is up, and she drove into the open garage door. She stopped and opened her door when this man in a torn tee shirt with grease all over him approached her. She saw his hair is sticking out in all directions; he is also unshaven, a half-smoked cigar dangling from his lips and looked like a cave man that time traveled to this century.

"Olga sent me."

She was standing on an oil and grease-stained concrete.

"Okay, I know what to do. Give me your keys, and you can sit in my office while I work on it."

"How long it is going to take? I want to be in Staten Island tonight."

"Bout a few hours or so. I need to take your trunk, fender panels, and all your doors off and apart. When I finish you'll be bulletproof. This shit I use is very rare, and hard to get, but it works."

"What is it?"

"We get it from Olga. Her boyfriend made some arrangement with a southern college research scientist to make it for him exclusively. He makes it in his basement at home. When it's finished one of Olga's men drives down there, picks it up, and brings it to us. It's extremely lightweight, and is a structured polymer composite. Nothing will penetrate it, nothing."

"What about my glass windows? What can you do for that?"

"No sweat sweetie. For the windows we use an acrylic sheet that's UL 3 rated. We form it to fit your back and side windows."

"What about my front window?"

"Sorry, but it's too curved for us to form fit it. You're on your own with the windshield. If someone is shooting at you better be in front of him, and not behind."

"I'll try to remember that. Any place around here I can get a cup of coffee?"

"Yer across the street is Hank's Hut. The coffee ain't great, but it won't kill you either. I only get a buttered roll there, and nothing else."

"Thanks, want me to bring a cup back to you?"

"No, I want to get my guys working' on this now. Give me about three hours and it'll be done."

Khara walked to Hank's Hut and sat at the counter. She noticed it is literally a small metal shack with a handful of tables and a few stools. She ordered a coffee and a buttered roll from the disheveled looking guy behind the counter. She assumed it is Hank as he is the only person working there at the moment.

"You want anything else besides the coffee and roll?"

"Nope, I'm good thanks."

He stood in front of her and leaned forward.

"My names Hank and this is my place. What's a good looking woman like you doing in this neighborhood?"

'I'm getting my car repaired. Is that okay?" as she pulled her jacket back to slightly open it. He saw her gun and detectives badge then backed up to walk away.

"Have a nice day Miss, and here's your check. Just leave the money on the counter. I have an order to get ready for pickup."

Khara sat there for two hours watching the television on his wall while he took care of a few other customers that wandered in. Finally, she is bored with the television and decided to walk back to the repair shop.

"You guys finished yet?" She yelled out to nobody in particular.

"Almost" is the answer coming from the back of the garage.

"Okay, just wanted to let you know I'm back."

"Have a seat in the office. And don't touch anything. I just cleaned it last month."

Khara walked to the small office on the side of the shop. She peered in and decided she'd rather stand outside than sit in there. About a half hour later the wild-looking man reappeared.

"My guys are just finishing up. When they bring your car to the front I want to go over a few important things with you."

Khara soon heard a familiar throttle sound as her car slowly drove up, and stopped in front of her.

"Here's your keys sweetie. Walk over here to the trunk. I want to show you what we did."

He opened the rear lid and she saw fabric attached all over the trunk and the lid also. "See those three gas cylinders bolted to the floor of your trunk? They are nitrous oxide tanks with tubes bringing the gas to the engine. We installed a few switches on the bottom of your dashboard. Flip the switch and hold on. You're going to fuck'n' fly when this gas hits your engine."

"Wow. I can't wait to try it."

"You better be on a straight line when you do. You'll lose control if you're on a curve. Here's your key. Be careful."

"Okay, I'll remember that. Thanks."

Khara opened the driver's door, adjusted the seat back to her comfort, and slowly drove out of the garage trying to avoid the potholes. Being she is already in Queens she decided to scope out Far Rockaway.

She drove south on Route 678 to the Belt Parkway, then swung over to the Cross Bay Boulevard to Far Rockaway. Although the route that she is taking is in reverse of how she would be actually driving it, this would still give her a feel of the streets and the curves on the road.

Driving under the elevated trains she noticed the I-beam pillars supporting the tracks above. They are surrounded by very thick concrete. One false twitch of the steering wheel and she could easily slam into them due to the street is narrow and only one lane in each direction.

When she reached Reis Park she drove into the empty parking lots looking to see where the exits and entrances are. Taking her time she drove around all the lots, and finally left; satisfied with the open layout.

Khara looked at her watch and realized she needed to go home to change. Al is expecting her at the club later that night. The drive back over the Flatbush Avenue Bridge to Brooklyn is quick, and she is back in Brighton before she knew it.

A hot shower is refreshing, and she used her coconut body wash as usual. After drying off she spritzed Chanel No.5 on her inner thighs and neck. Now she felt ready to get dressed. It is after dinner time when she left her apartment and asked the valet downstairs to get her car.

The trip to Staten Island is almost uneventful. The traffic is heavy and slow. When she made the turn to the back highway the cars thinned out, and she saw a stretch of open road ahead of her. She flipped one of the nitrous oxide switches and smashed the gas pedal to the floor. She is driving at fifty miles an hour when the rear tires screeched, burnt rubber as if the car started from a stationary position, shot up and sped forward with blazing speed. Holding on with a firm grip she is able to steer, and then she took her foot off the gas pedal to slow the M3 down. It's been a while since she experienced an adrenalin rush like she just had.

"That is amazing," she said to herself.

When the exit for the club came up she turned off the highway and pulled into the lot stopping at valet parking. Big Boy stood at the top of the stairs and smiled at her when she approached.

"Hey Khara, how you doing?"

"I'm okay Biggie, you?"

"Fine, Al is inside by the bar."

"Okay, thanks."

He opened the door for her, and she went directly to the bar where she saw him speaking to a male customer.

When he saw her approach Al excused himself with the customer, turned to give her a hug, and then kissed Khara on the cheek. "Boy, you smell good. What are you wearing?"

"It's Chanel No.5. Like it?"

Putting his hands on her hips he pulled her in close to him. "Like it? I could just eat you up. I missed you" he whispered in her ear.

"Listen, Al, I want to speak to you. I need you to do something for me when I meet the cartel."

"Anything you need. Let me know, and I'll take care of it."

"Can we sit over there and talk?"

"Yer, come on, let's sit down."

He took her by the arm and escorted her to an empty table at the rear of the bar. She moved her chair closer to his, her back to the wall, and bent over to whisper in his ear.

"When I meet them I'm going to be in the second parking lot at Reis Park after you go through the closed toll booths. About two hundred feet directly ahead of me will be a grassy island with a curb that separates the lots. Tonight, before I meet them, I need you to bring two skateboards and a four by eight plywood sheet one inch thick."

"You're going skateboarding with those assholes?"

"No, I need you to place the plywood against the curb like a kid would do if he used it to skate over it. Then I want you to place one skateboard on the concrete to the right of the board, and one on the grass to the left of the board. It needs to look like kids left everything there."

"Okay, that's easy enough to do. I'll tell Big Boy and his crew buy the stuff tonight so everything will be ready for when you call me."

"Good. Now Al, tell me how I can show you my appreciation."

"Listen, it's early in the night. How about we eat dinner in my restaurant at the club? Then we can go someplace cozy. How does that sound?"

"I can't wait."

They walked over to the young maître d' and are seated in a rear booth. After a light dinner of burgers and fries, they decided to leave the club.

Al escorted her outside, and after the valet brought his Cadillac he drove to the hotel they usually went to in Staten Island. Khara took her own car and followed him there.

Walking up to the desk clerk instead of Al Khara this time asked for a room on the third floor, away from the elevator.

On the way to the room, Al is puzzled as to why she asked for a room instead of him.

"I like to switch hotel rooms. I never use the same room twice in case someone notices a pattern, and they bug the room. When I talk I like privacy."

"Now I understand. Are you going to stand here with me in front of the room, or are you going to use the key?

"Don't be in a hurry Al. I have nowhere to go tonight."

"I'm glad to hear that."

After entering the room Al took off his jacket and shirt and placed it on the club chair by the drapes. Khara took her .38 out of her jacket pocket and placed it on the top of the dresser. Then she took off her jacket, her shoulder holster, removed the throwing knife from her boot, and finally her blouse.

"Any more weapons on you before we shower?"

"Cute Al. Don't be a wise ass. Come on and shower in here with me."

After they showered and dried off, Khara asked him a question after she slipped into bed with him.

"Whatever happened to that picture Big Boy's guy took of the presidential candidate from Texas with the underage girl?"

"Funny you should ask about that. My uncle is reading the newspaper that the man is a front-runner in the polls so he decided to let him know we possess that picture."

"How did he do that? Mail it to him?"

"No, and don't be so sarcastic. He hired one of his more mature looking hookers to go to his hotel last week when he was having a fundraiser in Manhattan. It was held at that big hotel near Fifty-Seventh Street. There were a lot of fancy people attending with big bucks in their bank accounts."

"He sent a hooker to talk to him? That's a very upscale place. Your uncle thought she would look like she belonged there?"

"Yes, she was dressed appropriately for the fundraiser. He also sent her with a twenty thousand dollar bank check made out to the campaign. We did that to ensure she is admitted to the dinner."

"So you guys thought that by waving that check in the air she would be able to get in? Are you crazy? And you gave her a legitimate bank check too? Don't you know he has Secret Service protection?"

"I know, she got in, and yes she waved the bank check in the air to do it. When she was stopped at the door she asked to see the assistant campaign manager; that she had a large donation to make. When he saw the large check in her hand she was immediately let in, and ushered into a private meeting with the candidate."

"That's unbelievable. What did he say when she gave him the check?"

"He didn't say a word. We gave her a real bank check that we are able to loan from a top-five national bank. Don't ask about that. But it could never be cashed because they keep records on those things. Secondly, she switched the real check with a copy just before she met with the candidate. On the face of the copy is everything that should be there. We printed on the back of the check a picture of the candidate with that young girl in the car in Laredo with a phone number printed on it that said to call the number."

"Did he call?"

"Of course he did. As a matter of fact, he called during the reception at the hotel. We told him not to worry. If he won we would be contacting him again with the code word 'young angel'. If there is something we needed he would have to take care of it for us. Otherwise, we hold on to the picture for future use. You never know about the future."

"Okay Al, it's interesting. Now let's go to bed."

Chapter 19 -

The next morning Khara is in bed with Al when the burner phone rang. She sat up in bed and reached over to her jacket to answer it.

"Hello, who is this?"

A man with a British accent answered her. "I am calling you from the Bahamas. My financial management firm represents Mr. Gonzales, and we manage his international finances. I was told to call you this morning for wiring instructions and also obtain a location to meet for an exchange. Do you have the information I need?"

"Yes. I am going to text you the wiring numbers, and the location for your client to meet me. I will have a laptop at the exchange to ensure the transfer is made, or else."

"I understand everything you are saying. The money will be wired immediately when my client instructs me to do so."

"Thank you. And tell that asshole I will be there at six o'clock tomorrow morening. He is not to be there before, or I won't meet with him."

Khara closed the phone and cuddled nextt to Al who awoke when he heard her talking.

"I'm sorry Al. Did I wake you?"

"Was that Alejandro?"

"No, it was his money manager. The meeting is on for tomorrow morning. You must have Big Boy set the stuff up about two in the morning. It needs to be there or I won't stay. It's important."

"Don't worry. I may go with him to make sure everything is placed right. Come lay back in bed with me."

"Can't Al, I have to meet with Olga to get things rolling. She told me there are things she wants to put in my car before we go."

"I understand. Did I mention before that she was an assassin with the Russian Secret Police before she came here?"

"Yes, you did."

"And she is also an excellent shot. Alejandro doesn't know what he is dealing with between the two of you."

Sarcastically she told him "thanks, Al. I appreciate your vote of confidence."

"Don't be offended. You know I dig you. Come on over and lay down next to me. I want to hug you."

"Another time, I have to go. I'll try to see you tomorrow when everything is settled."

Khara dressed and left the hotel to drive back to Brooklyn. In the car, she called Olga to let her know that tomorrow is the day.

"Thanks for calling me Khara. I want to let my men know to get in position late tonight. We will have some surprises for Alejandro when he chases us. I'll see you later to go over a few things."

"I'll be back in the apartment in thirty minutes or so. See you then."

While driving over the Verrazano Bridge she called Don.

"Hi Khara, What's going on with you?

"Nothing much going on. I'm waiting to hear from you about the Cartel. Hey, did you ever find out about that gun dealer in New Orleans that they are supposed to be going to buy from?"

"Yes. I was going to call you this morning. They did stop there yesterday. Our men and ATF were waiting for them. There was a big firefight when they arrived at the dealer's shop. The gun shop was blown up, we killed about ten of his men, and wounded another fifteen. He must have crossed the border with all his gunmen. They counted about nine cars that were able to get away. Our intelligence sources feel they went back into the city to obtain new vehicles so they couldn't be tracked and followed. "

"That sucks big time. They'll probably be up here in two days. I'm driving right now, and need to go. Let me know if you hear anything else. Miss you."

"I miss you too Khara. But before you hang up I was again thinking of putting a security detail with you for protection."

"No, don't do that. I'll be fine. Plus they don't know where I live, and I'm not back at work yet. Miss you, bye."

Khara knew they would be in New York by tomorrow morning, and she also didn't want to have the FBI screw things up by having a detail protecting her.

Coming off the exit ramp she glanced at the open bay, and a cruise ship is about to enter New York Harbor going under the bridge. Opening her windows she inhaled the salt air, and the smell of the sea invigorated her.

In a little while, she is at the apartment house and dropping her car off for the valet to park it. But he told her to drive around the back through the narrow alley to the rear of the building. "Olga wants to put some things in your car."

'Thanks, I'll pull around now."

Khara drove through a very tight passage that a larger car would not be able to get through. She noticed one of Olga's men standing next to a small wooden ladder-back chair.

She stopped next to him and popped her trunk open when he asked her. Then he carefully placed the chair in it, and told her to wait. "There are some other things Olga needs to take along tomorrow. I'll be right back." Then he disappeared walking through a steel basement door. When he reappeared he is carrying two black small canvas bags that are bulging at the seams.

"Olga wants these placed in the back seat of your car."

"What's in the bags?"

"A bunch of American made grenades are in each. They are set with a five and ten-second fuse; thought you should know that."

He opened one bag and took out a grenade and handed it to Khara. "Here take this one. You never know when it can come in handy."

"Thanks. I'll treasure it" placing it in her left jacket pocket.

Then he went back into the basement and reappeared shortly with a large amount of black nylon rope and silver duct tape. He placed the items in the trunk alongside the chair and closed the lid.

"Olga wants you to keep your car parked here tonight. We'll watch it. She doesn't want anyone to steal it. Keep your keys; no one is driving this car until tomorrow."

"Okay, thanks."

Khara walked around to the front of the building and went upstairs to change and relax. She made a cup of caffeinated coffee for herself and brought it into the living room to sip while she watched television. There is a lot of time to kill so she decided to clean and oil her guns including the MP7.

Carefully she made sure all her clips are fully loaded and ready to be used. Then she polished her boots, ironed her blouse, and pressed her slacks before hanging them up in her closet. She knew her nerves are on edge because of the coming night, and she tried to take her mind off the meeting.

Going for a late midday walk seemed the thing to do for her to burn off some energy so she dressed and went downstairs to walk on the avenue. The wind is gently blowing in from the sea, and again the salt air permeated the neighborhood. Passing by a kosher delicatessen she went in, and immediately Khara smelled the aroma of the hot deli meats in the air. Her mouth started to salivate. She thought maybe lunch or an early dinner is called for.

Standing next to the glass showcase she waited for the counterman to take her order. He saw her and walked to the side of the counter opposite from where she is standing.

"What'll yer have Miss?"

"I'd like a hot corn beef on rye with mustard please, and a potato knish also."

"Okay, for here or to go. And do you want a half or a full sour pickle with that?"

"For here please, and I'll have a full sour pickle."

"Oh, I need a soda too. Do you have Dr. Browns Black Cherry soda?"

"Does Israel have Jews? How many cans do you want?"

"Just one thanks." She ignored his sarcastic comment as a Brooklyn thing.

The counterman opened the steamer and with a long fork took out a massive piece of corn beef. He placed it on the cutting table then carefully trimmed the fat from between the layers of meat. He used the rotating slicer to pile the corned beef onto the fresh rye bread. He swabbed mustard on the top piece of bread, cut the sandwich, and took the hot knish out of the microwave oven.

"Okay, take a seat by any table in the back and we'll bring everything to you."

Khara saw an empty table by the rear wall and sat down facing the front of the store. The other tables are mostly filled with elderly men and women having their lunch.

She noticed that two older men are sitting together at a table in front of her, and to the side. When the waitress, who appeared to Khara to be in her nineties, brought them their sandwiches one of the men took out his false teeth and placed it on the table. He looked up at the waitress and asked her for a kiss. She laughed, told him she liked much younger men, and then she went back to the front counter to get Khara's food.

When she came back with the plates she placed it on the table for Khara.

"Let me know if there's anything else you'd like to order."

"Okay, thank you."

"I never saw you here before; new to the area?" the waitress inquired.

"Yes, I just moved in a few days ago. It seems like a nice place to live."

"I know it is. I've been in Brighton most of my life."

The waitress turned to the two men in at the next table in front of Khara.

"Hey guys, look at this beautiful girl. She's new here. So put your teeth back in your mouth when you talk to her."

The elderly man picked up his dentures and placed them back in his mouth. Turning around to face Khara he looked directly at her.

"You're a good looking woman. I can teach you a few things. Wanna date?"

Khara took a bite of her sandwich, chewing and savoring each morsel in her mouth, and then she looked at the elderly man. "Naw, I don't want to give you a heart attack."

"You're probably right. Forget the offer." He turned back to his friend, took out his dentures, and ate his food quietly.

Khara smiled. She is enjoying this place. In the back of her mind, she made a mental note that she'd like to bring Al here or maybe Don.

The delicatessen had a television on, and the Mets are playing. They have signed a new second baseman, and he is on the field today, by the name of Mark Levy. He is drafted right out of a Brooklyn High School, and they thought he would eventually be a Hall of Famer. She ate slowly and watched the game for a while. To her, this is the calm before the storm.

Finished eating she paid the check and walked back to her building to meet with Olga. She wanted to review the final plans. Khara is curious if some changes are being made in how things are going to happen at the exchange with Alejandro.

The concierge informed Olga that Khara is back in her apartment, so she came downstairs to meet with her.

"Hi Khara, all set for tomorrow morning?"

"I'm ready to do it now."

"Good, I hate to wait also. I wanted to let you know that I will have me men parked along the sides of Rockaway Beach Boulevard under the train tracks. I only use retired Russian GRU Spetsnaz soldiers. In your country the name they use is special ops, I think. They will be prepared with RPG's and will fire at cartel cars as they pass by. I want them to take out the last one driving by so the front cars won't stop and not follow us. I want Alejandro to be concentrating on catching us."

"Sounds like a plan. What happens if some of them are still chasing us when we get to the Kennedy Sanctuary?"

"I'll station men there also. Alejandro is going to die tomorrow morning. There is no question about it. Now try to rest. It's going to be an active morning very soon. I'll meet you by your car at 4 am."

"Okay, see you then."

Khara closed her door after Olga left, and settled in watching television to pass the time. In her mind, she is playing out different scenarios of what could happen tomorrow morning. Relaxed she stretched out on her sofa and dozed off.

About nine in the evening she woke up and felt refreshed. Walking into her bedroom she changed into the clothes that she is going to wear for the exchange. After putting on her boots she inserted the throwing knife into the top of her right boot, put her shoulder holster on, and made a cup of regular coffee. She wanted the caffeine to get her up and running.

She felt confident things would go well, but she again felt a need to call Eloise. Picking up the phone to call her she hesitated. Khara didn't know if her phone calls are being recorded or not. She realized that if they are then Don would probably know what is going down in a few hours. Or maybe he didn't know. Not sure she decided not to call anybody. She put her jacket on, slipped her .38 in her pocket, and fully armed started to take a walk on Brighton Beach Avenue under the elevated trains.

It is a brisk evening, the wind is coming in off the ocean, and the shops are starting to close up for the night. Only the fancy restaurants and Russian nightclubs are still open with people entering. Walking by them she started to think of what Eloise said to her about finding a guy she could stay with for the long term. But marriage is not something she really wanted to do again. She liked the diversity of sleeping with different men when the mood struck her.

Ocean Parkway is almost ahead of her so she decided to turn back and go home. The walk killed some time and calmed her nerves somewhat.

As she entered her lobby the doormen already were familiar with her and wished her a good evening.

She took the elevator upstairs. Once inside her apartment, she packed her MP7 in the backpack and sat down to watch the evening news.

When the late show went off the air Olga sent one of her men to tell Khara to come down to the basement with him.

As they entered the room where Pablo is being kept Khara saw he is wearing only a tee shirt, and summer shorts exposing his partial leg. His hands are tied together behind his back with plastic cable ties and duct tape. Three men lifted him up and started to carry him out to the car in the backyard. One man supported his good leg while the other two each grabbed him by an arm. Pablo seemed very weak to her.

Olga told her that "he's not eating. He's on some kind of hunger strike. It doesn't matter because he won't be around long anyway. I'm going to finish him, and his fuck'n brother off tonight. Let's go now."

They brought him up the rear stairs then placed him in the back seat of the M3. After strapping him in with the seat belts Olga sat behind Khara in the back next to him where she could keep an eye on Pablo.

Pablo turned to Olga and looked directly at her, then to Khara. "You bitches are goin to die tonight. My brother is gonna slit your throats like the pigs you are."

Olga asked one of her men to get the duct tape from the trunk. She tore off a strip and placed it over Pablo's mouth. "I'm not going to listen to your shit all night."

Khara watched as they closed the trunk. Then she started the engine. Slowly she maneuvered through the narrow alley to the street. Shifting into second gear she headed for the Belt Parkway East to Flatbush Avenue.

Olga wanted to get there early and make sure her men are in position along the route Khara is going to drive.

As she turned onto the bridge driving to Far Rockaway Khara noticed that there is a full moon out tonight. She knew the visibility is an asset to her in that the Cartel cars would be easier to see, and it is also easier for them to see her car. But controlling the moon is something she has no control over.

Turning onto Rockaway Beach Boulevard she followed the road as Olga is checking to see that her men are parked where she specifically told them to be. There could not be any screw ups tonight. Although all of her crew is retired Russian special forces she still wanted to double check everything.

Finally about three in the morning Khara drove back to the Jacob Reis Park parking lot. She went through the unattended gates, stopped in the back of the second parking lot, and in the middle of the lot facing the first lot to the east. Directly in front of her, about one hundred and fifty feet away is the plywood she made sure to tell Al to leave. It looked like some kids left their skateboards to return another day to play on a makeshift slide.

Khara popped the trunk. Olga lifted the lid and took out the small wooden chair. She set it up next to the car. Then she reached in, took the black nylon rope out, and tied a tight loop onto one end of it. Bending to reach the bottom of the chair, she placed the loop through a back lower spindle on the lowest part of the chair and threads the other straight end through the loop. Pulling on the rope she made sure it is secured to the chair. Walking slowly away Olga stretched the rope out until all fifty feet of it is straight. Then walked back to the M3 and put one end of it through the open window in the back seat where she is sitting. The black rope blended into the dark pavement. It is totally unnoticeable.

Both of them went around to where Pablo is sitting. Olga grabbed his collar and yanked him closer to the edge of the seat, causing him to choke. Then both women lifted him out of the car and sat him on the chair. Olga wanted to make sure the tape is still secure on his mouth so she wrapped it three more times around his head. Pushing him to sit back into the chair Olga then took the roll of duct tape and began circling him, and tightly taped his arms to his upper body. She only did one circle to tape him to the chair. That is to keep him sitting upright for the moment. Only his one remaining leg is free to move.

"Olga, why didn't you tape his good leg to the chair also?"

"In about two hours Khara you'll find out why. Let's finish this, and get back in the car. It's getting too chilly out here right now. It's beginning to remind me of when I had been stationed in Novosibirsk Siberia."

Once Olga felt he is secure in the chair they returned to sit in the car and turn the heat on. It is a chilly morning on the Rockaway Peninsular. They are only a few blocks in from the Bay on the west, and the Atlantic Ocean is on the east. Pablo is left sitting in the parking lot wearing only a tee shirt and cutoff summer shorts.

To pass the time the satellite radio is turned on, and tuned to an oldies station. An hour flew by when they saw many headlights drive through the entry gates, and stop in the first parking lot. The cars lined up next to one another facing Khara's car in the second parking lot. Janis Joplin is playing on the radio "Me and Bobby McGee" when they saw one car pull slightly out of the pack, and stop. It put on its bright lights and is able to see Pablo sitting in the chair next to the black BMW M3.

Olga started her laptop then hopped out of the car, and stood in front of Pablo blocking the view from the cartel's cars. Pablo opened his eyes and looked at Olga. She pulled the pin from a grenade and placed it between Pablo's thighs pushing it up against his genitals, with the spring lever held in place by his thighs. "If you as much as twitch this is going to go off and blow you to pieces, understand Pablo?"

Pablo shook his head affirmatively. Then she took out her knife and cut the tape that is keeping him secured in the chair. He is now free to fall if he dared. His one good leg is balancing him as he sat upright. If he moved his free leg the grenade would go off killing him.

Olga took her time walking back to the car so as not to arouse suspicion as to what she just did. As she sat back in the car she took the end of the black rope in her fingers, and wrapped it around her hand three times, and held it tightly in her grasp.

The burner phone that Khara was given rang. It is Alejandro calling. She put it on speaker so Olga could also hear him.

"I want my brother now. Or you don't get any money."

Olga heard him and replied.

"I don't give a shit about your brother. You have thirty seconds to wire the money or I'm going to shoot his other knee."

"Vete a la mierda!"

"Olga, he just told us 'fuck you' in Spanish."

"Don't move the car yet Khara. Wait for them to make the first move."

The Rolling Stones came on the radio singing "19th Nervous Breakdown". Khara turned the music up, the beat percolated the adrenalin in her system, and she is now psyched for action.

The Cartel's cars split into two groups driving to either side of the grassy island that had an opening which is separating the two parking lots. The entryway on both sides is now blocked as they entered individually into the second parking lot. They lined up in a row on each side of Khara's car in the second lot. The only escape is the plywood ramp in front of where Khara arranged to stop.

After all the cars are on both sides of the lot Olga yelled out to Khara. "Now, gun it."

Khara shifted into first while popping the clutch with screeching tires leaving a trail of unseen smoke behind in the dark. She drove straight towards the plywood ramp shifting into second as the final cartel cars entered the parking lot and headed directly to where Pablo is sitting. The Cartel is shooting at the M3 while they are passing it on each side. None of the bullets penetrated the interior of the M3.

Olga is holding the rope until she felt it jerk tightly in her hand. The fifty feet of rope is extended, its full length stretched out straight, as the M3 pulled away. The chair Pablo is sitting in is yanked out from under him flipping him backward smashing his head and body onto the hard concrete parking lot floor. His one good leg swung upwards into the night air releasing the grenade. The cartel's first and second cars are speeding towards Pablo and stopped a few feet in front of him when the grenade between his thighs exploded in the air. Shrapnel and body parts flew through the mist from the sea. The occupants in the front of the two vehicles near the explosion are probably killed. Shrapnel from the grenade seared through the rear of the cars and must have done heavy damage to any cartel gunmen sitting back there. Pablo no longer exists in this world.

As the M3 sped towards the ramp Olga pulled the pins on two more grenades, and simply tossed them out of her window. "Nineteenth Nervous Breakdown" by the Stones is still blasting from Khara's radio as she is about to take off from the ramp escaping into the next parking lot. The other Cartel cars in the second lot began to leave it chasing Khara while shooting out of their side windows at her.

Hearing their bullets pinging into the car they were stopped by the protective fabric Olga had arranged to be inserted all around the M3.

The third and fourth cars in the second lot stopped to see if they could help their buddies when the two grenades went off two seconds apart. The fifth and sixth cars immediately behind Khara are consecutively blown up as they ran over the grenades in the darkened lot. American grenades are able to send shrapnel out almost 200 meters once they explode.

The M3 flew over the ramp and landed with a hard thud. Khara turned to the right and headed for the entry gates with the seventh and eight cartel cars jumping the ramp after her. The rest of the Cartel's cars turned and gave chase through the side entry to the first parking lot. She is out of Reis Park already when they finally are able to turn around and follow her on the city streets.

The Stones are still singing "Nineteenth Nervous Breakdown" with the volume turned way up as Khara swung out of the entry gates onto Rockaway Beach Boulevard. There are four Cartel cars trampling down on their gas pedals speeding after her. As she left Reis Park she needed to make a looping turn to head back towards the overhead train tracks. By doing this the cartel gunmen are able to make broadside shots at her car. Khara heard the bullets ping through the black highly polished sheet metal, but didn't enter the car. The Cartel's cars are now behind her trying to catch up.

Shifting into third she is on a straight path blowing past stop signs and red lights. It is still dark out and she could see if any headlights are coming in front of her. Olga pulled the pins on another two grenades and gently flipped them out her window. They bounced backward, under the first of the four remaining cars in pursuit, and exploded as the closest car drove over them.

The car immediately behind it rammed through the carnage and continued the chase. There are now three cars left following behind Olga and Khara.

Ahead Khara could see the elevated trains, and the road went directly under the tracks. She flipped the first nitrous oxide switch. The front of the M3 lifted up and took off burning rubber at 65 miles an hour. The street narrowed and is a tight one lane in each direction with thick concrete castings surrounding the supporting I-beams. Khara took her foot off the gas and coasted towards the overhead tracks a bit slower.

As she continued under the tracks she is trying to keep her car steady on the road due to the fine mist from the morning breeze making it a slippery surface. One of Olga's men is behind an I-beam and waited until she slipped past him. After the third cartel car drove past he walked out onto the street, aimed, and shot his RPG at it. The last car in the chase exploded sending metal and body parts in all directions. The remains of the car slammed into a pillar then burst into flames totally blocking the middle of the road.

Olga turned her head to look at her and saw a gunman standing in the largely opened sky-roof of the car just behind her. She noticed he is trying to aim a large fifty caliber machine gun at them. "You better get out of here fast Khara. I don't know if the protective fabric stuff can keep out a fifty caliber bullet."

Slamming on the brakes she slowed the M3, and then downshifted while trying to turn behind an I-beam while continuing to drive on the side where cars would normally park. But the road surface is moist and her rear end slipped out and skidded into an I-beam by the passenger side trunk panel. Khara is rocked into her driver's side door, but continued to step on the gas, speeding forward and turning onto the parking lane of the street.

Bullets whizzed by bouncing off the I-beams behind them. About two blocks up there is a parked car, and when Khara saw it she knew she had to get back in the main lane under the tracks. Meanwhile in her rearview mirror is the car with the gunman sticking out of the sky-roof. He is now on the same parking lane side as she is and began shooting at her.

Olga again tossed two grenades out the window while Khara spun the steering wheel, and headed back onto the main street. An I-beam blocked her from seeing a passenger car coming along, and it clipped the left rear of her car spinning it in circles across the street and into another I-beam crunching the right side door panels of her car.

Olga and Khara are bounced around, but their seat belts kept them anchored in the car. Khara threw the M3 into reverse and turned her wheel to back out of the I-beam. Then she downshifted it into first and stomped on the pedal. The Rolling Stones are now on another verse of the "9th Nervous Breakdown" as it blared out of all the speakers. Being an adrenaline junkie she is now at her peak.

The two grenades Olga tossed out her window dropped to the pavement and went off in the street, but the two Cartel cars also pulled back onto the main street when they saw Khara do it. They are not stopped by the explosions or shrapnel.

The first of the remaining two cartel cars saw the M3 smash into the I-beam and sped towards the scene expecting to finish the chase by killing them.

Khara is able to extricate her car from the supporting I-beam and banged on the gas pedal while flipped the last nitrous oxide switch. The M3 reeled ahead pushing Olga back into her seat. Khara is holding on and trying to steer a smashed car with a bent body frame that is now taking off to the moon. The M3 is now driving forwards but is slightly sideways and slanted due to frame damage. Her eyes opened wide, and a smile came to her face. This is a real charge to her.

Within seconds she is closing in on Beach Channel Drive, and heading for the bridge. She backed off on the gas due to the sharp turns at Bay Ninth Street to get onto Cross Bay Boulevard.

The first remaining Cartel car is still in hot pursuit. The second one passed another of Olga's men with an RPG. As the second car passed him he walked out from behind the I-beam, stood in the middle of the street, and took aim. He never saw the car coming from behind him. It slammed into his body sending him flying into the air and hitting an I-beam. He instinctively pulled the trigger and off it went hitting an oncoming car that is not involved in the chase. The charge set off the gasoline tank in the car and a fireball reached almost to the tracks overhead.

The Cartel car continued the chase and followed the wobbly M3.

As the cartel cars are about to leave the boulevard and cross the bridge a flatbed tow truck that is waiting and parked on the side street drove out, and slammed with immense force into the midsection of the last cartel car in the chase. They are Olga's men and are a last resort in the chase if needed. The truck pushed the car and pinned it against an I-beam. Jumping out of the truck Olga's men ran towards the pinned car shooting at the dazed occupants in the Cartel's car with automatic weapons fire. Then they restarted their truck and followed the chase at a distance to the Kennedy Bay Sanctuary.

Khara sped over the bridge noticing in her rearview mirror there is one car left chasing her; she thought. Alejandro had all his men pursuing her while he stayed far back, and watched the action from afar. As the chase progressed he stayed behind a safe distance. Driving around the carnage on the streets he didn't want to show himself yet. If his men couldn't kill her but are able to corner her, he wanted to personally blow her brains out.

She saw the Sanctuary on her left side, crossed the highway, and turned into the parking lot. The M3 is now smoking from under the hood. The I-beam hits must have loosened something because gasoline is also leaking from her gas tank onto the pavement.

"Khara gets out of the car" Olga yelled at her.

"Head for the side of the building by the bushes while I set off a grenade in the car, I'll meet you there."

Olga opened her door, stepped out, and pulled the pins on two grenades while tossing them into the back seat.

Both of them ran to the side of the Kennedy Bay Sanctuary building and laid flat, in a natural depression, on the ground.

The grenades went off and ignited the gas tank causing a large ball of flames shooting into the air. The cartel car is now on the bridge and saw the explosion. When they reached the turn to the Sanctuary Center they drove into the parking lot and stayed at the other end watching the fire.

A short time later Alejandro drove into the lot with three gunmen in his car. He ordered two of his men to go closer and see if they could see any bodies still sitting in the flaming vehicle.

As they approached the flames Khara stood up and walked out from the side of the building with her MP7. She shot the two men multiple times. As they fell beside the burning car Alejandro and his remaining men ducked behind their car at the other end of the parking lot for cover. Then they returned fire as she backed up, and used the building as a shield.

While Khara acted as a diversion, and everyone is shooting at each other, Olga ran around the back of the building. She came out the other side directly behind Alejandro. On the way she picked up two of her special ops men that she stationed there previously to wait for her. Now she and her men rushed out from behind Alejandro shooting at him and his men. Caught in a crossfire his gunmen are riddled with bullets and dropped to the cold ground.

Only Alejandro is left. He turned and raised his arm to shoot back at Olga. Carefully taking aim Olga stood still, aimed, and shot him in the shoulder area smashing bones and tearing ligaments. Those are Olga's orders from her lover. He didn't want him killed if possible. He is worth more alive than dead. The information he has in his head is invaluable. Alejandro fell to the ground bleeding heavily. Khara ran out from behind the building and heard him cursing in Spanish at Olga.

As she approached him he looked up at her. He said in Spanish "you are the devil come alive" and spit at her.

"Gracias" Khara replied as she stomped on his genitals. "You son of a bitch made life difficult for me. Fuck you, and your whole fuck'n dead family."

In the distance, she heard police and fire trucks with their sirens blaring. She assumed they are going to the burning cars on the Boulevard.

Olga opened her phone and called for her flatbed truck to come over now. They are driving slowly waiting for her call, and only seconds down the road.

The flatbed truck arrived, loaded Khara's M3 onto the back, and drove off taking with it the only evidence that Khara is involved in this shooting.

"Hey Olga, what's with my car?"

"No worries. We are going to crush it in a baler in Brooklyn, near Pennsylvania Avenue. Al said he's going to buy you a new one after this if something happened to it."

"That son of a bitch must have been pretty sure I was going to survive this."

"Khara, Al told me he had no doubt you would."

Olga then ordered her men to grab Alejandro, and bring him around back where she stashed a small stolen pickup truck and is waiting for them. They tossed Alejandro like a sack of potatoes onto the truck bed and started to drive down a long and narrow trail to the water.

Behind the Kennedy Bay Sanctuary Building is a path to the bay with a sloped landing area. Boats can let people off, or pick people up from there.

As the truck approached the site Khara could see Big Boy standing on a cabin cruiser waiting for them. She waded into the water then climbed onto the boat with an outstretched arm from him lifting her onboard.

"Hey Khara, welcome aboard."

"Hey yourself Biggie, get me the hell out of here."

Two men tossed Alejandro onto the boat. Olga and Al wanted him alive. The information on how he ran his organization, his sources and suppliers is most important to them.

Big Boy brought along a friend who is a New York City EMT. He started to stem Alejandro's bleeding below deck while the boat headed for a pier in Staten Island.

The End

The second book of the trilogy is
"Khara Bennet - Vengeance"
followed by…
"Dead Girls Don't Die"

www.ingramcontent.com/pod-product-compliance
Lightning Source LLC
Chambersburg PA
CBHW070105280626
47159CB00016B/1324